THE ~~BOMBER~~

Andy Fletcher

STA BOOKS

Published by STA BOOKS 2014

www.spencerthomasassociates.com

ISBN 978-0-9933957-0-3

All characters represented in this novel
are entirely fictional

Dedicated to 'Little Irish'

THE BUMPER

Brighton Pier Autumn 1996

It was a Saturday afternoon late in September; a bitter southeasterly hurled salt spray and rain at the pier. It had done all morning, shutting the candy floss stall and driving all but the hardiest of day-trippers inland. The place was almost deserted; a retreating tourist hurrying past might be forgiven for concluding that there was nothing unusual about the two men sitting quietly beneath that dripping shelter. Several feet of bench separating them, they both stared silently over the angry waves.

At first glance they're just strangers, without any kind of story to tell. The shorter of the two, Tony Hurley, is about 35. He's dressed in an expensive suit but it's crumpled and there's a beaten sadness to him. The other man, Ted Fisher, is about twenty years older, dressed in a cheap though neatly pressed suit and a raincoat. He turns to Tony, almost speaks, then refocuses his attention somewhere back over the thundering seas. Theirs is a massive story and though they'd never dream of sharing it with anyone else, at least Fisher might be able to make amends; perhaps even gain a degree of absolution by filling in a few of the blanks for his old adversary. Fisher knows the part he's played in this "fucking tragedy" and more besides. He thinks he's figured most of it out, so does Tony but neither man can know the whole truth; who can? His eyes fix on a gull high above. "Perhaps you know the rest," he whispers but his words are drowned by the wind.

Tony Hurley and ex-DI Ted Fisher

Sitting next to Fisher on Brighton Pier is the start of another day in a year, which has been almost too painful to bear. The sea thundering into the iron framework beneath the decking is as grey as the clouds above. I try to keep my hands from shaking, wondering if it's really down to the whisky? God knows I've been drinking too much for too long. I'm about to share everything I know with a retired policeman. I learned the rules a long time ago and until now I've never broken them. So it may be that I'm shaking because of the enormity of it all. At least, being September, there aren't too many people passing this bench and the wind carries our voices out over the empty sea. I seriously concentrate trying to still my hands then give up. Maybe it's just the cold. Fisher tells me he quit the police on account of what happened to Rebecca and me but, with that mop of grey hair, he looks old enough to have retired without needing any special reason. I never liked this man but I did think he was honest.

I give him a look and say, "I suppose you ended up with the money?"

He shakes his head. His eyes give nothing away; I've lost the knack of being able to tell a lie from the truth. Got to put that down to the booze. I really was sharp once but now? Well I don't care much either way. What good's money when you've lost the only person that you ever truly cared for? I suppose I should be grateful that at least I'm still alive.

"Never thought I'd ever be talking to you like this."

The gulls scream down as I continue. "Where should we start?"

He ducks away from the wind to light a cigarette then turns back to face me. I still can't weigh him up, so I stop trying.

"Why don't we start at the beginning Tony?"

Three Months Earlier
The Bumper – Tony Hurley

Dawn light spilling in through the half open hotel curtains plays red through Tony's closed eyelids as he begins to come to. The first thing to hit him is the sweet fragrance of last night's whisky, mixed with expensive perfume. His hand ventures out exploring the bed and comes into contact with warm smooth female flesh. He wonders what she's like. The white sheets momentarily blind his opening eyes. She's facing the other way and seems to be asleep, her straight blond hair fanned out on the pillow next to him. Carefully he raises the sheet to take a look and smiles. She's naked and beautiful. Perfect.

Tony Hurley was a most deceptive man. Warmth and friendliness seemed to radiate from those large brown eyes. The honest smile, combined with his small stature, would put anyone at ease. No sane person would trust their life to a complete stranger, but the ability to form fast friendships was one of Tony's greatest attributes. He never remained a stranger for very long and, while you mightn't trust him with your life, you may just let him get a little too close to your money. If you were dumb enough to do that, then you'd be well and truly 'bumped'; he often said. "All it takes is a second and I'm gone". He was a con man, though not the cultured 'Raffles' kind. He was a Dublin born Liverpool Irishman, home grown, natural, one in a million and gifted. What he lacked in education was more than made up for by plain cleverness, slippery as a fox.

If he'd ever taken time to learn the game of chess, he might have became a great master but, having watched one or two games, he quickly decided that is was 'un-cheatable-at', so he left it out. Instead he studied the finer arts of card play, the double shuffle, how to deal from the bottom of a pack; never failing to give good enough hands to the other players. He'd practiced these skills to perfection by the age of eighteen but, by the age of twenty-six, he'd finished with such simple tricks and pulled only real scams. Rip-offs, sometimes employing strategy so complex they'd baffle Albert Einstein, others so blatantly perilous that only a fool would dare try them. Without knowing a square root from a tangent he was a self-taught mathematician. He could formulate the sharing of loot between four accomplices so that it looked perfectly even but invariably, he would end up with twice as much as anyone else. Any criminal who had ever grafted with him was terrified of the 'Chinese-chop'. They would go to any length to keep the cash out of his hands but he would usually end up in control. He'd share the money in such an inscrutable way that even he lost track of what the real figures might've been.

Such creative accountancy often caused fury in the hearts of very dangerous people. As soon as they counted their spoils, they would vow to kill him, torture him or just break his legs. But when they caught up to him, he'd flash those eyes and cower. He would beg, plead and say that they were right to hate him. He would admit that he was no good, apologise for spending their money, promise to pay it back and, above all, swear on a thousand bibles that it would never happen again. Then, for some unfathomable reason, his potential murderers would soften and give him a walkover, often laden with guilt for thinking so badly of their little friend. Tony was priceless, blessed by the gods, but even he believed that it couldn't last forever.

He resists the urge to stroke that perfect skin, not wanting to wake her. Instead he remains perfectly still on his side, drinking it all in. Her arched spine barely embosses the surface of her skin and disappears further down, replaced by two dimples as the flesh thickens and her hips widen into a perfect peach. He draws a slow deep breath through his nostrils and savours the perfume. It must have been a wonderful night, if only he could remember.

Tony was always busy scoring points in some secret contest. He would nick your cigarette lighter, your pen, your car, or he would sell you a car and later steal it back to return it to the hire company. He would go through your pockets, rifle your till, cash your cheques, seduce your daughter or screw your wife but, with all of the points scored in these numerous deceptions, he actually missed the point. The point being that the biggest victim of this endless trickery was himself because, for all the planning, scheming and running away with the prize, he always ended up broke.

As if cursed by some joker he'd failed to remove from the pack, he was a philanthropist. Regardless of the surgical callousness with which he separated you from your money, he was disabled by his own generosity. Almost as soon as he had parted you from your cash, he would be falling for some hard luck story. A smile from a whore, a bum with his hand out and he was back, headed downward, the usual direction. Soon he'd be looking for someone else to knock. It might've helped, had he been able to stay sober, but he needed booze to take the edge off it all and give him courage to front the angry victims. Sleeping with prostitutes never made him feel cheap. It hadn't even crossed his mind that he might be using them. Business girls were on his side of the law, like different branches of the same firm. If you told him that they only saw him as a punter, he could never believe you.

Tony was different, he didn't just think it, he knew it; had done ever since the age of fourteen when his probation officer called him 'amoral'. He met plenty of other kids in youth custody who'd stolen cars but he didn't know any that were amoral. The fact that he hadn't even looked up the definition made no difference. Anyone could be moral or immoral; he was very definitely one of a kind. A long time had passed since that court appearance. Six months since he'd been released from his most recent pitfall, he'd been lucky recently, not so much as a single pull.

The sun is higher now and the room is much brighter, though there's still pinkness to the light. He feels that familiar sense of impending doom descending over him as bits of the previous night start creeping back. He's in the Thistle House Brighton and half remembers a scene at the reception desk. He hates it when he can't quite recall how much of a fool he's made of himself. He sits up on the side of the bed to an instant thumping head. The sheet slips away from the woman as she stirs and turns on to her back. She stretches with her eyes closed, blond hair clashing sexily against the olive tone of her skin, her exquisitely slender body lying right next to him. She's almost completely flat chested apart from those odd marshmallow nipples. Those nipples made even more wonderful by the pink dawn. He gazes at her, the perfect navel and again those wonderful, special breasts that must've excited him so greatly the night before. He's barely able to resist touching them. Her wide hips and those long smooth legs, but no, no he mustn't get at it again; not yet. Now he sees her face and remembers that she pushed him away, refusing to kiss him or to be called Mrs Smith. He pictures the receptionist's smug grin. No, shame is one thing but such a massive sense of impending doom must be generated by something far greater than post alcoholic paranoia.

It crashes back into his damaged brain like a tidal wave. He's suddenly wide-awake as the realisation hits him. "The money! The cash!" He springs to his feet, drags his suit jacket from the bedside table and checks that the briefcase is underneath. He grabs the handle; it's still full. A hundred and fifty thousand pounds is quite a lump, even if it is in fifties. Sighing, he lowers it back on to the bedside table and turns. Even if she has started to snore, she's allowed; she's probably worked very hard.

Tony often told working girls he was a porn movie director. His usual line, saying that he could make them famous in Europe and America, always managed to draw the best performance out of them. There had been times when he tried promising them a cash bonus at the outset but that never failed to cheapen the whole thing. He rather enjoyed doubling or trebling their fee at the end, simply as a sign of his gratitude, at which point they would usually fall in love with him.

There she lays that beautiful young working girl he can't quite remember recruiting in London the previous evening. He wonders for a moment if she really is a prostitute or has he actually managed to pull her, but quickly lets go of that one. The idea of bedding such a beauty while shit-faced on Jameson's, is just too ridiculous to consider. Yes, she probably is a prostitute and has every right to snore. It was almost certainly a very physical and intense screen test, it must've taken hours.

He gets up from the bed and pulls the hotel dressing gown on, realising that the embroidered monogram matches his own initials, T. H. Brighton. He's delighted, not even full daylight and he's been handed a free dressing gown, complete with a monogram commemorating his Brighton visit. Tony Hurley, Brighton. It's a good omen; his luck must be in. Quite naturally he believes in luck, he's depended on it so greatly for most of his life. "A little gift before breakfast," he thinks as he hangs it on the back of the bathroom door and steps into the shower. The jets of lukewarm water begin to have the desired effect and start soothing his sore head. His mouth stinks of whisky. It seems he's always in one hotel room or another phoning down for a toothbrush but he'll leave it until later before calling room service. He'll just have to suffer the stale taste and hopes she won't notice. He needs one more foray into this luscious lady, one delightfully hung over lust-laden fuck before cleaning his teeth. No, she probably won't notice his whisky breath by the way she's snoring; she probably drank just as much as him.

The shower is loudly rejuvenating, steadying him and bringing a degree of sanity back into his aching head. He lets the jets of water spray into his mouth and her snoring quiets. She must be awake. He imagines her lying in bed waiting, doubtlessly barely able to contain herself in anticipation of their early morning lovemaking. She's almost certainly fallen in love with him and will find it embarrassing to have to ask him for her cash. He rubs his body with a hotel towel and studies his own reflection in the bathroom mirror. No she won't have to ask for the cash, as soon as he's finished teaching her the true meaning of sexual ecstasy, he'll pay her twice the going rate then the same again just for luck. 'Bob Hoskins', that's what his friend Kenny calls him, the cheeky bastard, or 'Little legs'. Not the best looking man in the world, OK, but he can't blame that girl for falling in love with him. Apart from a slight pot belly, he's still in great condition. He'll soon drop that extra weight when he gets swimming in the Caribbean every day.

The ticket's in the briefcase. Gatwick – Antigua – Grenada, then a short boat trip to Carriacou, where he's arranged to meet up with his old Rastafarian prison friend Moses. He considers for a moment stealing the towel, same monogram as the bathrobe, but it's wet. It may just fit into the girl's handbag, though doing so would shatter her illusion. A porn director of international fame might nick a bathrobe but he'd hardly steal a towel. He considers for a moment simply telling her the whole truth and offering to take her with him, because he's fallen so deeply in love with her; then laughs as he tries to remember her name. He's amused also by the fact that he's almost willing, telling her the truth; amused, because the truth for him is always a hard thing to put his finger on. Except on those occasions when he says, "Sorry I've spent your money." He gives his mouth a final rinse with tap water and realises that while he hasn't got a full erection, the anticipated sex has added a certain weight and meatiness, he decides to return naked and almost proud.

He pushes the bathroom door aside and strides in; the bed is empty. He rubs his eyes and focusses again. He almost calls her name but remembers he's forgotten it. This has got to be a joke. He looks behind the curtains, then back to the bed. He lifts the quilt in case she's somehow managed to melt into the folds, then runs to the door and opens it, looking along the empty corridor. The penny suddenly drops. The realisation that his beautiful woman really has gone hits him like an iron fist.

Slamming the door shut, he flies across to where the briefcase had been, but it's disappeared. She's taken it with her. He looks for his trousers but they've gone too. He throws the door wide open oblivious to his own nakedness and screams at the top of his voice, "You fuckin' slag!" Then he steps back and slams it shut.

A depressed calm subdues him as he settles on edge of the bed, back bent, rocking, cradling his head in his hands. "All right, you can come out now," but there follows only silence against the muffled sound of early morning gulls laughing at him through the double-glazing. She really has gone.

He isn't so hurt by the loss of the money, though God knows it could bring about the end of his life; trousers can easily be replaced, even Armani. Somehow he's hurt, offended and almost mortally wounded by her loss. He had trusted her, believed in her and he had thought that she really did care for him, even more than that, he actually believed that she might've loved him, because he loved her as he always loved them. But what was her name? He lifts his feet from the floor and rolls up on to his side alone. Alone, so terribly alone; loveless and fuckless, just when he needs it most of all, just when he's filled with hung over lust. Despite his deep feeling of rejection and absolute dread over losing the money, he's still drunk enough to believe he can send it all away by drifting into the fitful and sweaty nightmare of post alcoholic sleep.

The Creeper - Rebecca Moseley

Rebecca Moseley was no prostitute; she was on the creep, a professional hotel thief. She'd been at it for about eight years, during which time she had almost earned enough money to pay off the mortgage on her small Brighton flat.

When she met the little Irishman in that Soho bar she became interested in him, not because of the 'film director' line, but because he said he was going to book into a Brighton hotel for the night. She wasn't in need of a lift home; she'd already earned quite well that evening, having visited two Park Lane hotels, and could more than afford a taxi. The hardest part for any creeper is to get into the hotel unnoticed and the Thistle House Brighton was a particularly good one, that's why she suggested it. The guests found those old-fashioned American doorknob locks so confusing that it was usually just a matter of trying half a dozen before she'd find one unlocked, and there were a lot of doorknobs to try. Her last foray into the Thistle House had netted her £7,000 cash and £12,000 in assorted jewellery.

She pushes the service room door and smiles as it opens. Inside are a few trolleys loaded with towels, sheets and the usual housekeeping stuff. She lays the heavy briefcase on a trolley, drops the Irishman's trousers on the floor and kicks them into a corner. Then she tries the briefcase but it's locked. Seeing a large pair of housekeeper's scissors hanging from a string, she cuts them free and takes an individual sized KitKat from one of the trolleys. Munching away at the sweet tasting chocolate, she considers forcing the case open. It's far too heavy to be full of cash; perhaps it's cocaine or something? He did say he was off to Grenada; no that'd mean he was taking his drugs in the wrong direction wouldn't it? Whatever the case may or may not contain, she decides against forcing it; far too suspicious walking out of the main door clutching a briefcase under her arm because the lock's been broken. She opens another KitKat and sits wondering how she ended up getting undressed.

She'd almost had sex with a complete stranger. What could she possibly have found so attractive about the man? Hardly a gorgeous hunk, he was almost bald, too short and looked to be about forty, but something must have attracted her. If there had been any sex with him, it would've been her first time in years. Maybe it was his eyes, more likely it was just the champagne. Thank God that the little Irishman had been too drunk to perform. She'd gone off the idea of sex, moments before he got in next to her and had become so repulsed that she'd been close to hitting him over the head with that Jameson bottle though, fortunately for him, its contents did the trick and his eyes closed of their own accord.

In her years of successful hotel theft, she had learned to use the back stairs. In the early days, she dressed up and frequented hotel bars with groups of prostitutes but each time, she would slip away without attracting a client to walk along the corridors trying doors. She always moved from floor to floor silently on the back stairs. Hotel security watches the lift indicator to get a clue as to what's happening in their building. It's a dead giveaway when the lift stops a few times, without returning to the ground floor. The back stairs were always the best bet for Rebecca but she was coming to the end of her career. It was 1996, advances in technology had begun their gallop and even the most dedicated of professionals were being caught.

For a moment, she considers calling it a day and just walking straight out of the hotel, taking with her whatever may or may not be in the briefcase, but quickly decides against that. That little Irishman spent hours telling her all about his criminal past and his times in prison. He certainly wouldn't be setting any alarm bells off; not with a track record like that, and he definitely wouldn't be coming after her without his trousers. It'd be a crying shame to have taken the trouble to get into the hotel and just walk out at dawn, without trying a single door. Dawn's the perfect time for her, when people are in their deepest sleep. She pulls on a pair of thin black cotton gloves matching her neat business suit. To anyone observing, she looks more like a legal secretary than a thief, especially carrying that briefcase. She exits the service store and smiles at the security camera, figuring that, just because a camera is turned on, doesn't necessarily mean that anyone's watching. A few doorknobs are tried before one turns; she pushes the door open. The curtains are closed tight, so she allows a moment for her eyes to adjust, before venturing inside. Her heart begins thumping so fast that it's hard to keep her breathing quiet. A pair of crocodile skin cowboy boots are parked neatly next to the bed. A large middle-aged American is on his back, snoring in a very rattling pig-like way. A wallet and watch are on the bedside table;

she silently scoops and slips them into her already open handbag, avoiding looking at his face, having always believed that doing so can cause a victim to wake. Then she glides to the jacket hanging close to the door and lowers the briefcase to the floor before searching the pockets. Nothing; so expensively tailored but nothing in the pockets. She retrieves the briefcase and slips out, quietly closing the door behind her.

Brighton Pier Autumn 96

Horizontal rain begins to blow at us and Fisher suggests we shelter in the café.

"You hungry?" he asks.

I shake my head and sit near the window watching him walk to the counter as I take my hip flask out. The whisky causes me to shudder clear through to the bone. I often say I'll put it down one day but I always was good at lying, especially to myself. The windows are opaque with condensation. Using my finger, I etch a round cartoon face on the glass. The corners of its mouth turned downward in sadness, crosses for eyes. Fisher comes back with two teas and pushes one in my direction. I stir it waiting for him to speak. This man sitting in front of me is no longer an enemy. There's a vulnerability about him I've never seen before. Eventually I prompt him.

"So?"

He wipes his spectacles before speaking. "As I was beginning to tell you when the rain started. There were things at work here that even I didn't know about. If I had known, I certainly would never have remained on the

Force. But you know I can understand your reluctance to believe me, especially after what happened to Rebecca."

The condensation starts running through the sad face on the glass. Teardrops stream from its eyes down to the window frame. I'm almost choked, swallowing trying hard to control my emotions. I'm not really expecting to discover anything I don't already know by hearing what Fisher's got to say but just the act of listening somehow seems to numb the pain, so I just sit, silent and attentive.

"In the early eighties, the term 'super-grass' was invented and frequently used by the media. It was a powerful tool to add to our arsenal in the fight against organised crime. Offering informants complete impunity was an easily acceptable deal worked out between the Crown Prosecution Service and the police. After all, it was for the good of all decent law abiding citizens. However, creating new identities for our informants required the raising of national insurance numbers, medical records, passports and school records, all without leaving any kind of track. These goals were simply unachievable without a degree of expert input from MI5. Try not to misunderstand what I'm saying here; there were no official policies about MI5 working with the police. Not in the early days at least, so all meetings and discussions were held very much on the quiet."

"MI5 suggested that some of the more active super-grasses were perhaps too valuable to be squandered on a single operation. Far better to use them as double agents, so the idea of the inside man was cranked up. They were invaluable to us and, rather than being slipped the odd fifty quid beneath a pub table, were paid directly into the bank accounts MI5 helped set up. It was a dangerous job. Some of them disappeared; others worked year after year always mysteriously managing to 'escape' arrest. Some were allowed to carry firearms for their own protection and some of them were bound to abuse their untouchable status. You must remember, we are not talking about police officers going bad, we're talking about full time criminals recruited on the strength of their credibility and involvement in the criminal world. To say that some of these operatives went off the rails would be to make a massive understatement. I'm certain Rutter was one such agent, operative, infiltrator, 'little helper' or whatever you want to call them and I believe that my old boss, Detective Chief Superintendent Commerford was his controller."

Rutter

Brian Phillips was on the up and up. Since starting work as a bouncer in that Ashford nightclub, his prospects improved daily. What a stroke of luck when Jimmy Rutter walked through the door. Jimmy Rutter, the short, quietly-spoken fifty-year old. The South Londoner with connections. Getting to know him meant that Brian would be now able to buy ecstasy pills for a fraction of the going rate. He couldn't help but end up making money. They were en route to a meet in the countryside just a few miles outside Bexhill.

It's 7 a.m. and Phillips feels good behind the wheel of Rutter's new Audi. He might even buy one of these for himself in a few weeks. Rutter sits in the passenger seat watching him exercising by flexing a thigh muscle, as he depresses the brake pedal over and over, waiting for the lights to change. He resents this steroid head's youth as well as his size but doesn't feel the need to do anything about it, not yet. Phillips is from another generation, a different school and a softer one.

The lights change and the car moves off. A little way along the road, Rutter leans across to needle Phillips by usurping his driving skill and operating the indicator. Phillips takes a left turn; Rutter's interference offends him. It spills out.

"You wanna drive?"

There's amusement in Rutter's eyes as he turns on the radio, Classic FM.

"I would if I wanted!"

They cut off the road on to a farm track; Rutter continues needling.

"Take it easy, it's a new car."

Phillips slows down. He knows it's just a side effect of the steroids but he really hates anyone telling him what to do. With great difficulty, he manages to control his temper but he can't keep it in, not all of it. He glances sideways at Rutter before speaking.

"I'll bet you were a hard man in your time."

Rutter doesn't bother rising to it. He's fifty, a long time since he climbed up the front of his first giant and discovered that most of the big ones are just wind and piss. He stretches over the seat into the back and lifts the box of Ees on to his lap. Phillips pulls up next to a red Range Rover, the only other vehicle on that otherwise deserted track. The two suited thirty-year olds inside smile nervously; between them they've raised twenty-eight thousand pounds for the deal.

When Rutter walks towards the Range Rover, there's nothing about his manner that might suggest what's about to unfold. The size of the deal, a poxy twenty-eight grand, indicates to him that Brian Phillips and the two in the car are just wannabes. He slides into a back seat next to Phillips speaking as he closes the door.

"Got the cash?"

The driver lifts a briefcase over the seat. Rutter opens it, looks inside then closes it, smiling.

"What about the Ees?" the driver asks nervously.

This is so easy, Rutter almost grins as he slips the pistol from underneath the box of ecstasy. Hardly moving the gun, he shoots Phillips in the jaw. The two in the front freeze for a second, then try to duck, shield themselves and get out all at the same time. He shoots them through their seat backs first then raises the gun to give them both one in the head. Next to him, Phillips' jaw has been smashed by the .38 calibre bullet. He's shocked and frozen, choking on his own blood and splintered jawbone. There's an insane calmness to Rutter as he addresses the young victim. "You're right you know, I did used to be quite a hard man in my time."

He shoots again, this time the bullet enters Phillips' eye and exits the back of his skull. Rutter quickly ejects then replaces the empty clip and collects every spent shell. A flock of birds take to the morning sky as he steps out of the Range Rover. Inside the blood-spattered vehicle, a chunk of Brian Phillips's brain finishes sliding down the rear windscreen and lands on the rear parcel shelf. Pools of blood and piss are beginning to form in the front floor pans.

He goes back to the Audi, places the briefcase and Ees in the boot, then takes out two five-gallon plastic drums, one full of warm water the other full of petrol. The track is still deserted as he strips and washes the blood from his hair, face and body. He quickly changes into full set of new clothes, bags the bloodied ones and carries them with the petrol over to the Range Rover.

The fire doesn't take hold properly until the Range Rover is shrinking in Rutter's rear view mirror. Satisfied that all the evidence will be consumed in the inferno that's now beginning to send a pall of black smoke high into the sky, he's quite calm when turning out on to the main road. No big deal, it's over. He always shakes a little a moment before such excitement but never afterwards. His mobile phone rings, the caller display lets him know Commerford is on the other end. He ignores it, not wishing to reveal a position so close to a murder. Commerford knows nothing about Phillips or the others. This has been no more than an interlude, a little sideline that Rutter has planted, cultivated and harvested all by himself.

Be Careful What You Wish For

The Thistle House in Brighton never lingered when it came to acquiring the latest security technology. The board of directors had dedicated a large office to house the expensive CCTV monitors. There were ten screens, each displaying eight separate images. Robert Brindle was alone in the room. His nightshifts were supposed to be spent watching the screens but he was an avid reader and hardly ever looked up from his book. He was an ex-policeman with a nose for trouble and not much of a believer in electronic surveillance. If something untoward was afoot in his hotel, he'd know all about it. His instincts alone would tell him. At the start of every shift he would quiz the night porter and the receptionist about any 'walk ins', the term used for guests without prior bookings. Last night there was just one couple and they seemed to be quiet respectable types, even if they were a little drunk.

The sound of the dawn gulls screaming outside the hotel indicates that it will soon be the end of another uneventful shift. Just a couple of hours to go and he'll be home in bed. Bored with the reading, he closes his book and notices movement on one of his screens. "You're up early," he thinks as he operates the controls and zooms in on the image of a young, smartly dressed woman walking down the stairs from the third floor. A fitness freak? No, too slow. Why doesn't she use the lift? Now he's mildly suspicious; he glances up at the picture of a woman on the wall above the screen "Jesus Christ. Rebecca fucking Moseley!" He catches her on the next screen and zooms the camera for a closer look at the face. He reaffirms it with another look at that wanted poster created from security camera printout.

"UK Hotel Security Association's Most Wanted. Rebecca Moseley. Watch out for this woman? Convicted seven times for thefts from UK and European hotels, believed to be still active and responsible for numerous offences."

His coffee goes over as he rushes out of the office to apprehend her in the foyer; she's carrying a briefcase. God only knows what she might have inside it, definitely a lot more than just hotel towels.

Rebecca casually rounds the corner from the stairwell into the marble foyer to find Brindle standing in front of her, his arms outstretched in an attempt to block her way. Completely unphased by the fifty-five year old's six feet or his sixteen stones, she stops for a moment and smiles confidently. "Yes?"

He's suddenly no longer a hundred per cent certain it's her. If he gets this wrong and she turns out to be a genuine guest, he could lose his job.

"Could you let me have your room number please, madam?"

"Not really, I can't remember it but it's on the fifth floor, one of the end rooms, why? What's this all about?"

Brindle lowers his arms.

"There's been some trouble in the hotel so I hope you won't mind coming over to reception while I check your details against the register?"

Rebecca reads the uncertainty in his eyes. "What did you say your name was?"

"I didn't madam, but it's Brindle, head of hotel security. Robert Brindle."

She feels she's got the upper hand and gives him a patronizing smile. "Well Robert, I don't mind helping you in the least but I'm just a little pushed for time at the moment. Perhaps I should call in to see you at lunchtime."

She begins to walk around him. His hand lands on her shoulder. She glares at him, as she breaks free.

"How dare you."

"Sorry madam."

It's now or never for Rebecca; she decides to front it out and just walk away. Not too fast, the perfect speed. She's almost at the main door when he calls after her. "Rebecca! Rebecca Moseley!"

Brindle's trained eye recognises something. Something barely discernable; an infinitely small change in her pace or body language; a change so subtle that even he doesn't know what it is but, at that moment, all doubt disappears. This definitely is Rebecca Moseley. He breaks into a run.

"Stop Moseley!" This time his hand grabs her elbow like a vice. She wrenches it free.

"Come on Moseley, give it up, you're nicked!"

Now she's fighting for her life. She drops the bag and briefcase, grabs the hand that crushed her elbow and draws it to her mouth. Ignoring the iron tasting blood as it spurts out, her teeth dig in as hard as a log splitter. This is the first time in Brindle's entire life he's ever hit a woman. However hard, it's a badly aimed blow that glances off the top of her head. The punch only serves to harden her resolve and the teeth sink deeper. Brindle's pain is so extreme it causes nausea and he falls to his knees. He becomes extremely dizzy and tears come to his eyes. She releases the finger, spits out the blood, recovers her bags and runs out of the hotel. Robert Brindle doesn't give chase. He's still on his knees watching in disbelief as blood spurts from his almost amputated index finger. The night porter comes running towards him from the direction of the kitchen.

"Jesus Brindle, what's happened?"

Now the pain has subsided a little. Brindle starts to recover, his hands are shaking as he wraps a handkerchief around the injury attempting to stem the flow of blood.

"Phone Brighton police station now!"

"It's a bloody ambulance you want Brindle!"

"Now I said!"

The night porter dials and Brindle gets to his feet almost sobbing, he takes the phone to speak to one of his ex-colleagues.

Rebecca walked into Brighton Station still out of breath. Having been identified, it was pointless running along the prom for home. Just a matter of time before the police would turn up with a warrant. First she had to get rid of her night's wages. There'd probably be an assault charge to answer, maybe even a wounding but the man was very large, very powerful and he did punch her. It was definitely in her favour that there hadn't been any witnesses. Her defence would only need to prove that the punch came before the bite.

It's still early and the station is almost deserted when she walks into the ladies room. Safely behind the cubicle door, she removes the blond wig, revealing her natural short, dark hair. Then she hoists the briefcase on to her knees; a good flat surface on which to sort out her takings. She's already posted the previous evening's Park Lane prize, just the cowboy's stuff and whatever's in that briefcase to see to. She takes a large A3 sized padded envelope from her handbag, already addressed with enough stamps attached to more than cover the cost of posting whatever such a large envelope might possibly be made to contain.

She fishes the watch out of her handbag and smiles, "Nice, a Rolex". Then she empties the wallet, three plastic cards, only a couple of hundred in English currency but about twenty, one hundred dollar bills. She's smiling, "Nice, very nice"; in it goes. The hotel scissors are good and strong, string trails from the handle as she digs the blades into the case and uses them to force locks. She's still smiling but when that lid flies up, her expression changes. She hardly notices the airline ticket ski off the pile of cash and land on the marble floor. This is suddenly more serious than it's ever been.

She thinks back to the little Irishman telling her about his criminal pursuits. She tries to estimate the value of a case this big filled with fifties, she guesses fifty thousand, but it's more than twice that. Why isn't she filled with joy when she's always dreamed of such a find? Time's a great healer but what kind of person might be able to get over losing such a large amount of cash? Definitely no crook; she tries to picture the Irishman's face but can't, she can only hope that his memory is equally as faded. She takes her other two A3 Jiffy bags out of her handbag wondering if it'll all fit, she's filled with dread. There's bound to be a serious comeback for stealing this much.

Brighton Pier Autumn 96 - Tony

Fisher's placing a great deal of trust in me by sharing that stuff about Rutter. He seems to feel genuine guilt over the way things turned out; I suppose that's only to be expected, since he was unable to do anything about it. You know, trust must be infectious, because now I really am losing my inhibitions and starting to run off at the mouth. I mean, I'm actually telling him stuff he couldn't possibly know, things I wouldn't usually tell anyone; personal stuff. He's already well aware I've been in prison a few times; in fact it was his efforts that landed me there more than once. So I suppose the real beginning is to say that I always worked it so I did my time up in Liverpool's Walton jail. Even though I lived in Dublin 'til I was eight, I was brought up in Liverpool and I know a lot of people there.

I thought five years was quite heavy for a half a dozen deceptions but, as my brief pointed out, thirteen previous for similar stuff does add up to quite a track record. Never used to have a problem with doing time, a sentence here and there, eighteen months, two years, so what? When I was on the out I partied full time and prison was just a way of paying the bill. Like confessing to a Holy Father so you can go out with a clean slate and do it all over again.

To tell the truth, I was gutted when I trotted down those steps from the dock. That five-year sentence came as big shock. It meant I'd be getting close to forty when I got out, with nothing behind me other than memories of the times when I nearly stole enough. Then, when I lost the appeal against severity of sentence, Judge Wallace put the cap on it by calling me a "persistent and foolhardy petty criminal." I felt like a real idiot and it certainly lost me a lot of face when the Liverpool Echo decided to publish his snide remark.

Times had changed, there wasn't so much cash lying around. All the big money was in drugs. Me? Well all right I did try to adapt, I sold my fair share of beeswax blocks disguised as kilos of rocky. I even bumped a big shot Italian with five kilos of baking powder. Left him standing on a crowded platform waving at him through the train window, the dumb fucker. They never take it with any degree of grace, drug dealers, angry bastards the lot of them; they'd pay to have you killed if they weren't such completely tightfisted bread heads. I always did like a drink me; liked it so much it fucked me up. So, even though I'll smoke an odd joint or snort one of your lines, I never did take to it, not properly or the potential fortune that could be made out of it. Fear of becoming addicted I suppose. Instead I chose to look down on smack dealers from my elevated position as full time thief and bumper, making statements like "You'll get no luck selling that shit" and "What goes around comes around".

I'd been at it since I was fourteen, feasting on other people's greed, fucking them over, leaving them waiting for goods that would never arrive as I drove in the opposite direction with their cash, but what did I have to show for it? Judge Wallace was dead right. I had become a petty criminal. I was a complete failure, I'd started to lose my hair and I'd had enough of prison. The way I saw it, there were just a couple of choices open to me. First, to go straight, maybe get a job in MacDonald's or learn to stack shelves for some fucking supermarket. The other was to invest some time in the McGregor's drug empire; just long enough to leave them waiting for their goods to arrive.

I'd known Joey McGregor since I was fourteen. I shared a cell with Billy McGregor for the last year of his sentence. They both trusted me but to tell the truth and I didn't care much for either of them. They were a pair of morons, fuckin' bullies, dangerous and bordering on backward. It was an easy enough decision to make but what about the comeback? Everyone knows their reputation; if they caught up with me, I'd die. If I disappeared they'd take it out on my family. Well of course that's true, but then again, I didn't think the McGregors had much of a name in the Caribbean and I'd been free from the clutter of relatives since I was fourteen when my Ma died. Oh yeah, and I'll tell you something else, there's nothing like a five year sentence to make you feel like travel.

It was Moses Freeman sold me on the idea of The Spice Islands. He was a bit like me in a way; an outsider.

Didn't care if he walked around the exercise yard with the blacks or the whites. Me? Well being Irish, I know all about prejudice. He was a Rastafarian and that's where he was born, Carriacou, one of the Spice Islands. He said I'd be like a millionaire there; maybe we could even buy a boat.

Billy McGregor picked me up from Walton in his black 7 Series BMW. Before even pulling away from the nick car park, he had the Charlie out. A ridiculous image, this scar-faced, skull-shaved, ugly steroid-head studying his own reflection before pouring neat a pile of Charlie on to the mirror of an antique lady's compact. I often wondered who'd given him those scars, he didn't have them when we were fourteen, but I was never foolish enough to ask. He had an ego bigger than New York and, like I said, he was an angry bastard.

"Pure Columbian flake," he grins, flipping his lock-back knife open to chop a few lines. A screw walking past us on his way into the prison unnerves me.

"Fuckin' Hell Billy! Are you sure?"

"Fuck him. He wouldn't dare pull me."

He vacuums a couple of lines though a rolled fifty and hands it to me. The car glides under the car park hoop out on to the street as I do my line. Billy sneezes white snotty spots all over the windscreen.

"Jesus my bugle's fucked," he says, causing me to burst into hysterical laughter as the understatement is magnified by the coke hitting my brain. He's had a flat nose ever since his uncle tried to train him as a boxer but gave up on account of his murderous temper.

"I'm going private to get it fixed."

I close the compact and place it on the centre console. Quite naturally I unroll the fifty and pocket it. It must be mine, I've just got out. All the humour disappears from his face as he holds his hand out.

"Don't take the piss Tony."

I hand it back. Grudgingly.

"Fuck me Billy. I just got out."

He pulls over and stops to emphasise what he's saying.

"If you want something you ask. Don't try and fuckin' mug me off."

"Leave it out Billy."

"Just don't ever take the piss out of me or Joey, that's all". He throws a bank wrap of twenties on to my knees and pulls back into the traffic talking as he goes.

"You don't need charity."

"Well what do you call this then?"

"Advance on your wages."

"So I'm on the firm?"

"Looks like."

That's just how easy it was, straight out of Walton and into their firm with an executive position. A higher level than anyone else that wasn't a McGregor could ever reach. After a day of partying, I got to work stacking shelves for them, moving their stock around. Being a kamikaze wasn't such a bad job. Once a month I'd drive down to south London and meet the Turk. The McGregors weren't exactly full of trust, but all things come to those who wait, and I knew I only needed to be patient. They'd follow in their car; sit off while I did the biz, then follow me all the way back to Liverpool. The meet was always in the same place, a storeroom behind a wholesale off-licence. I thought it was kind of stupid to always use the same location but that's the way they'd been doing it for years; it was a crazy situation.

Things got even worse when the Turk started that big VAT fiddle on the spirits. There were suddenly queues of lorries and vans loading and unloading through the back door. I was seriously worried but the McGregors wouldn't listen. As luck would have it, it never did come on top. Three or four months passed before a little trust began to develop. They'd sometimes send me off alone with a hundred grand or so to collect their stuff. I really was stacking shelves, each hundred grand brought them back four or five hundred and I was on a grand a week. From their point of view I was the ideal courier and a total mug. Not only was I cheap, but I hadn't come out of the drug world and therefore had no desire to pilfer any of their stock or steal their contacts.

One day I asked Billy for a raise and he just laughed. I intended to wait a little longer to see if their monthly order grew bigger but Billy's reaction pissed me off so badly, I was ready to turn him over there and then. Though, as luck would have it, he came along with me to do the business that month, so I had no choice other than to wait a little longer. Suddenly Fat Tommy from Birkenhead was busted, complete with his whole crew and the McGregors business doubled overnight. Billy decided to let me have another monkey a week. I only just managed keep a straight face when he told me, I mean this fucker was so tightfisted he made me rob him. I didn't have a choice.

So, there I am down in Peckham, sitting in a run down travel shop looking at a faded picture of palm trees with a case completely full of fifties on my knees. The way

I saw it, I had about an hour before the genius brothers got the idea anything was wrong. They'd phone the Turk and figure I'd been busted on the way. Billy would jump into his car and come looking, while Joe would make inquires through his bent drug squad inspector. When he drew a blank, he'd race down to join Billy in the hunt. I figured, at the very least, I'd have a five hour start and where would they begin to look in London, with its millions of people? They'd do better to stay at home and buy a lottery ticket along with the rest of the mugs.

I was a generation ahead of the girl behind the desk. She had a crisp, clean, Swedish look and I was finding it hard not to fantasise watching her fill out the paperwork.

"So, 11 a.m. from Gatwick to Antigua, you'll need to check in an hour and a half before take off. The plane stops for an hour at Antigua and then you go on to Grenada. Wish I was coming with you"

"Yeah."

I'm dying to invite her along but don't wish to make a fool of myself.

I'm still smiling at the idea as I get into the car and drive down to Soho for a drink. I remember going into that bar but I don't remember meeting Rebecca. I remember bits and pieces like... but, well, too much to drink I suppose. Must've been all right though because I managed to drive to Brighton safely and that M23's a dangerous bloody road, isn't it? Anyway, modern technology bewilders me, I mean I'm only just getting to feel comfortable with answerphones; that stuff gallops ahead at such a speed it's easy to get left behind. The day I saw Billy playing with his Game Boy, I laughed, couldn't help it, he looked like a little excited kid. Then there was the other time I walked in on him. He was looking at a smutty website. Dozens of photos of ugly middle aged couples screwing; he justified what he was up to, by telling me he was learning how to use the internet for research. I didn't ask exactly what kind of research he was talking about; I knew he was a hopeless wanker, having shared a cell with him and been kept awake by his ever-creaking bed. Yeah, Billy certainly was miles ahead of me with his understanding of modern technology. Even so, I never would've imagined that either of those two dumb fuckers would use it to give them an edge, but there it was, pulsing away under my dashboard, sending signals to a satellite and I didn't even have a clue. Maybe they weren't so dumb after all. They'd had a tracker fitted to the wiring of my Merc.

Do Not Disturb

Tony's Mercedes looks more abandoned than parked, straggling double yellow lines with a front wheel resting on the pavement; it's about 10 a.m, the driver's window is partially open and a parking ticket's blowing in the seafront breeze. A traffic warden climbs out of the tow truck that's been sent to remove the car. He collects the ticket from the windscreen and writes the tow away details on his clipboard while the truck driver operates the hydraulic crane, positioning the lifting arms over the vehicle. The warden tries the driver's door; it's unlocked so, as a matter of course, he calls the truck driver over as a witness before he fully opens it. They're initially shocked by the stink of alcohol that hits them, then disgusted to see such a mess in a luxury vehicle. An empty bottle and several crushed beer cans are bedded on the layer of empty crisp packets, takeaway food packaging and sweet wrappers. They're distracted by a police van passing them as it slows down to stop outside the hotel's main entrance.

Brindle is grateful that his ex-colleague was kind enough to wait while he got his finger stitched back together, then give him a lift back to work but the local anesthetic's beginning to wear off and his finger hurts like hell. He's further discomforted by the bruised thigh and still annoyed by the way they administered the anti tetanus jab with what felt like a 'bloody blunt horse needle'.

The constable driver smiles as he addresses him. "Tell you what Sarge', why don't I just drive you home instead? You must be able to pull a few sickies with a finger like that."

Brindle winces as he gets out, holds the door open and leans back into the van.

"It's not Sarge' any more Smithy. I'm in the real world now; no results means, no job. Anyway, thanks for looking after me and be careful when you lift that little bitch, she's a fucking savage."

He closes the police van door and walks into the hotel, determined to get to the bottom of whatever she's been up to.

From their vantage point inside the BMW parked at the other side of the promenade, the McGregor brothers watched Tony's Mercedes being lifted on to the council truck. Joe McGregor always liked wearing suits and as far as he was concerned, his smartness wasn't just restricted to dress sense, he considered himself to be the brains of their family business.

He's far less convinced that Tony's dared to knock them than Billy, whose knuckles go white each time he makes a fist and flexes his muscles staring at the hotel entrance. As soon as he catches sight of that little piss taker, he's going to fly out of the car and kick the shit out of him. It's definitely a large sum of money to lose but it's much more than that to him, he's taking it personally. Joe shares his thoughts with Billy, in an attempt to cap the anger and regain control of the situation.

"Look Billy, ask yourself what's really going on here. We've seen them take his car away haven't we?"

"Yeah."

"OK, and we've seen the plod drop a detective off haven't we?"

"Yeah."

"We're both agreed that where he parked his motor tells us that he's either been in that hotel or that he's still in there right?"

"Yeah."

"Alright, good, we both know he's a slippery little bastard; if he was in the middle of fuckin' us over, that car'd be gone and so would he. He definitely wouldn't do anything to attract police attention, not with a hundred and fifty thousand fuckin' quid in used notes on him. No, I believe it's something else, there's more to this than meets the eye, there's something else going on here. Maybe he's been robbed or something."

"Yeah? Well what the fuck was he doing down here in the first place? And why the fuck didn't he turn up at the Turk's yesterday?"

"I don't know, all I know is, something's fuckin' occurred and we're not going to get to the bottom of it sitting here."

He opens the door; Billy starts to open his.

"No. Stay there and, if he comes out while I'm inside, just follow him until you find somewhere quiet. Don't lose your temper and bring it on top. Right?"

"Yeah, right."

Billy closes his door.

The six foot four American, Hal Dixon, will not be moved from the reception desk. Regardless of Brindles pleas to be allowed to deal with the complaint discreetly by taking it into the manager's office, the man's a Texan and in true Alamo style he simply refuses to budge. Two guests checking out, hear everything he has to say about the hotel. No amount of apologies from Brindle or the hotel manager, are going to be enough to quell this man's anger. He's been robbed and he's determined to let as many people as possible know about it.

"You call this a hotel? What kind of place are you running here? I stay for one night, I end up losing more'n three thousand bucks and you tell me it's not your responsibility. Well, what I'd like to know is, just whose responsibility you think it is?"

Joe McGregor waits, quietly listening as the two guests in front of him settle their accounts. Brindle starts to become angered and says a little too much. "There isn't a hotel in the world Sir, that can be expected to accept responsibility for its guests not locking their doors. But don't worry, the police have been informed and they'll be along shortly to take your statement. They've already got the name of the woman they believe to be responsible.

She's a local woman and, with any luck, she'll be arrested today."

"Is she a hooker? What kind of people do you let into this place?"

Brindle takes the security association wanted poster out of his pocket, unfolds it and hands it to him.

"No Sir, unfortunately not, if she was, she never would have been allowed past the door. Rebecca Moseley. She's a professional thief." The hotel manager decides to end an embarrassing scene with half an offer to settle the matter.

"I can't promise anything, Mr Dixon but, under the circumstances, I think the hotel might well be able to find a way to make good your losses. Though I'm not able to discuss such matters out here, Sir. So if you would be so kind as to follow me into my office we'll..., well, we'll see what we can do."

Joe McGregor finally reaches the front of the queue. The receptionist, a bright well presented young woman, smiles at him. To her he looks just like any other potential guest.

"Yes Sir, can I help you?"

"Yeah, Tony Hurley, give him a call and tell him I've arrived will you?"

He's somewhat let down by his own coarse Liverpool accent but the way he's dressed more than makes up for it. Perhaps he's in a band or something.

"Do you know his room number Sir?"

"No but I think he arrived last night, phoned me up and asked me to meet him here this morning."

She reads last night's guest list on her monitor, then the previous night's. "No Sir, sorry no Mr Hurley's checked in the night before either."

"Are you sure? Little fella about five six, smart suit, going bald."

"Yes Sir, I'm sorry, no one at all of that description."

Walking out of the hotel, Joe McGregor takes a pen from his pocket and writes the name 'Rebecca Moseley' on his hand. It might mean something; it might not.

Noon

Tony is snatched from unconsciousness by the loud and extremely annoying banging on his room door. He ignores it for a while but it doesn't go away so, head throbbing, he sits up in bed. His mouth still tastes like shit.

"Yeah! What do you want?"

"Hotel security Sir, we need to speak to you."

"Well I don't need to speak to you, come back in a couple of hours."

Tony is instantly repulsed by the idea of talking to any kind of policeman. He resents police so badly that he doesn't even like bus conductors on account of their similar uniforms. Hotel security? As far as he's concerned, they're just a watered down version of the same kind of shit person.

"I'm sorry, Sir, but we do need speak to you right now. There's been an incident and we really must talk."

Brindle's persistence infuriates him. He shouts so loudly, his head is in danger of exploding. "Well you can't, so fuck off and come back when I'm awake."

When the knocking ceases, Tony lays down again,

imagining he's being allowed to slip back into the sanctuary of that dream world but the door quickly flies open, shattering his illusion. His eyes focus on Robert Brindle next to the bed, fumbling with the passkey, while grinning at PC Smith who's standing next to him. Seeing a real policeman, Tony's anger becomes tempered with a degree of caution. He sits up complaining.

"Wonderful hotel this; the notice says 'Please don't disturb' doesn't it? Or does it really say, 'Feel free to walk in and take the piss'?

"I sympathise with you but you must realise, there has been a crime committed. A great deal of money was stolen from one of the guests, and I do think you'll be needing these won't you? I mean they are yours aren't they Sir?" Brindle dangles Tony's trousers in his face.

Stripped of alcoholic insulation, he's almost completely sober and the previous night's events flood back into his head. If dread can be measured as a ripple, then this is a tsunami. He gets up, takes a miniature whisky out of the mini bar and shudders when he knocks it back.

Brindle continues, "The register says you booked in with a woman, er 'Mister Smith'. Do you know where she might be right now?" There's an unmistakably cynical tone to the way he pronounces 'Mister Smith'.

Tony opens another miniature and knocks it back.

"Oh come on, you must know that that's not anyone's real bloody name."

The police constable raises his hand, silencing Brindle.

"You are aware that it's a criminal offence to use a false name in order to obtain credit aren't you Sir?"

"Yeah right, and I'd be the first person to book into a

hotel as 'Mister Smith' wouldn't I? Give me a break."

He eyes Tony with no small degree of suspicion as he takes his pen and notepad out.

"So what's is your real name?"

"Hurley, Tony Hurley."

"Any identity?"

Tony reaches down and lifts his jacket from the floor; he takes his passport out of the inside pocket and hands it over, wishing he'd been lucky enough to leave his airline ticket in the same place. The constable flicks thought the passport.

"Right then Mr Hurley, was the briefcase she took yours?"

"Yeah."

"Anything important in it?"

"Yeah bits and pieces, you know, bit of cash and stuff. Look, you don't mind if I take a shower and get dressed before I make a statement do you? I mean it's a bit embarrassing sitting here like this."

Brindle and the constable have no problem with Tony's request. They leave the room thinking he's quite ordinary, just another one of Moseley's unfortunate victims. His hands are shaking almost out of control as he splashes cold water on to his face, but the shaking is only partly due to whisky. Regret over the way things have turned out comes nowhere near to describing the way he feels now.

The McGregor's alarm bells must certainly be ringing but there's no way they can possibly know where he is. Even so, some sixth sense compels him to balance on the edge of the bath and look over the frosted glass down on to the prom. He's just in time to see Billy McGregor's BMW making a u-turn. He doesn't realise they're leaving, having given up; he thinks they've just arrived. That massive feeling of dread instantly turns into one of pure terror. His first instinct is to escape through the hotel's back door on to the Lanes. A quick check reveals that the car keys and phone are still in his pocket, along with some loose change. A minute is all it takes to get dressed but in that time his mind races like a computer, automatically crunching tales of woe, excuses, reasons, stories. He'll have to come up with an outstanding piece of fiction to convince the McGregors but even mainframe computers sometimes run into unsolvable problems. He finds no solution, no way of explaining the disappearance of their hundred and fifty thousand. No there's no option, no choice other than to cut and run.

Brindle and the constable come back into the room, this time they don't bother knocking. The constable has used his radio to check Tony's previous and he's holding a pair of handcuffs.

"Anthony Hurley, I'm arresting you on suspicion of theft. You don't have to say anything..."

Tony protests. "Arresting me? It's me that's been robbed. I'm the only victim here; she robbed me."

The constable isn't even slightly convinced. "Victim? With your form? I don't think so. You probably arrived as a team. More likely a lover's tiff and she's sneaked off with the loot. Come on turn around while I put these on."

Tony's protests fall on deaf ears and he finds himself being led past the front desk with his hands cuffed tightly behind his back. The young receptionist looks in his direction and smiles nervously.

Tony smiles back at her. "Don't worry love I'm

innocent I'll see you later"

Brindle can't resist chipping in. "When will that be Hurley? About three years?"

It's a bright summer's day and the prom is crowded with day-trippers, Constable Smith controls the urge to smile at the faces but he's filled with pride guiding his prisoner towards the police van. Tony looks down at the pavement, it seems quite shameful being paraded this way but that's not why his head's down. He's expecting Billy McGregor to burst through of the crowd and punch him. A punch to the top of the head will be far less painful than one in the nose. Sitting safely in the back of the police van, he looks up for the first time. The black BMW has gone, no matter how temporarily, he's gained a reprieve. He takes a deep breath of the clean sea air.

Rutter

Rutter's flat above an estate agent's office next to Clapham Common is thirty miles from the murder scene. Safely inside behind its locked door with all the evidence scrubbed from his skin, he sits reading the Sun newspaper. It's an article about the Home Secretary pledging to use MI5 in the government's fight against organised crime. The report amuses him, though not without causing a slight niggle. He almost gets his head around the idea that, when MI5 are officially on the job, they might dispense with his services but he doesn't even begin to consider what might be the fate of a redundant 'little helper', especially one who's been allowed to get away with murder.

He sees himself as one of life's true achievers, having frequently ended up with large sums of money, but such successes were never due to brilliant ideas or careful planning. He owes his achievements to the fact that he's a predator, plain and simple. If he wants what you have, he just takes it. If you resist, he'll hurt you but if he sees you as any kind of threat, he'll kill you. It's an unbeatable formula. It's paid for this flat, a smallholding in North Wales, a house in Birmingham and it's never failed to keep him well supplied with cocaine.

He bends down to the coffee table and snorts another line, then aims the remote at his TV. No mention of the murders on the lunchtime news, they can't have found the Range Rover yet. He tries another channel, then the radio; nothing, not so much as a whisper.

He feels lucky to have this place in London, this sanctuary. His mobile phone goes off, giving him a start. He answers it. DCS Commerford, his handler and only police contact, quizzes him about Brian Phillips and the other murder victims. Commerford isn't even slightly suspicious when Rutter denies ever having heard of them, there's no reason to disbelieve him. In fact today is the first time Commerford himself had ever heard of those strictly small-time criminals. He's simply phoning around, fishing for any kind of lead that might help his friends in the South East Regional Crime Squad. When he draws a blank, he decides to end the call. He never did much enjoy dealing with Rutter. He almost gives in to the urge to let Rutter know that he'll be getting a new handler but not quite. Rutter'll discover that soon enough. When the call ends, Rutter rests his phone on the arm of his chair, puts his feet on the coffee table and goes back to reading The Sun. His wrinkled and freckled face breaks into a coke driven smile, oblivious to the storm that waits just over his horizon.

Brighton Police Station

Like most UK police cells, the custody suite in Brighton police station is too hot in the summer because they fail to turn the heating down and too cold in the winter because they never turn it up. Tony sits on the bunk sweating, with his shirtsleeves rolled up and his jacket folded neatly on the plastic mattress. He's certain that the maladjustment of the heating system is quite deliberate. Three hours of nothingness, wasted looking at graffiti when he could be putting distance between himself and the McGregors; seems to be the biggest crime anyone could ever commit. How come the police had the right to squander what might be the last three hours of his life? But they did and so and it was his fault for letting them.

He's given up trying to picture her face; it's gone, just like the cash. He doesn't even hate her; he almost admires her. If it had been the other way around, he definitely would have taken her money. Yes, it must be his fault, no doubt about it; he accepts the blame completely. He can only pray that Billy McGregor might find a way to accept his excuse with grace and show him a little mercy. But what excuse? What on earth can he come up with to explain being in Brighton with their cash in the first place? The squeaking of rubber shoes on the polished corridor floor outside draws his attention to the cell door. He's almost certainly about to be released but he doesn't want to add to any policeman's feeling of power by looking too eager, so he resists the urge to get up straight away. A key clatters in the lock and the metal door opens loudly. The custody sergeant steps inside. "Come on Hurley, DI Fisher wants a word with you."

Tony gets up slowly, he was already feeling low enough, but the mention of Fisher sends his spirit into free fall. The last time he thought he was about to be released but was interviewed by Fisher, he ended up in prison for three years.

DI Fisher is sitting alone at a table going through Rebecca's file and CCTV footage. He turns the video player off when he hears them coming, then closes Rebecca's file and gestures to a seat at the other side of the table as Tony walks in.

"Sit down 'Mr Smith'. Must be what, four years?"

Tony goes straight on the defensive.

"No crime to use an alias once in a while."

Fisher is slightly amused.

"Kind of defeats the object though, don't you think, using one like Smith?"

"That's because there was no 'object', other than to show a little discretion on behalf of a woman I thought was a lady. You know, I don't even remember checking into the place. Maybe she came up with the name."

Fisher was hoping for a little more than this. All of his humour disappears.

"Never did say a lot did you Hurley? And what you do say usually adds up to sweet fuck all. Let's get this straight. What you're telling me, is that you woke up this morning wondering where the fuck she'd gone."

"It was a good night. What do you want me to tell you? Met her in a bar; don't know where she is now."

Fisher presses the 'play' button and the TV screen comes to life. Tony seldom loses his composure being interviewed by Fisher or any other policeman but it isn't easy disguising his emotions when he sees Rebecca's image on that security video. Fisher hits the 'freeze' button, holding the image of her smiling straight into the camera. She looks as though butter wouldn't melt in her mouth. He feels like screaming but somehow manages to hold it in.

"Is this her?"

"Maybe, it could be."

"No one'd ever accuse you of being loose lipped would they Hurley? Look, you haven't been cautioned have you? No tape running is there?

"So?"

"So we're just having a friendly little chat, could be having it anywhere couldn't we?"

"If you say so."

Fisher lifts Tony's briefcase on to the table. The locks are still closed and hanging from the lid when he opens it.

Tony never expected to see any of the cash; he was in no doubt that Fisher would have been more interested in discovering where he came by such an amount of money. However, he did hope that he might see his airline ticket. He tries to hide his disappointment but it's impossible. He looks like a kid who thought he was opening a PlayStation but ended up with a game of Monopoly.

"Recognise this don't you? Turned up this morning in Brighton Station with a couple of empty wallets. It is yours isn't it?"

"Looks like."

Tony isn't able to disguise the way he feels; Fisher gets straight on to it. He can't resist rubbing it in a little but there's an unmistakable tone of resentment in his voice when he mentions her name.

"Done you up good and proper hasn't she? Rebecca Moseley. Still there's no one easier to con than a con man is there? You just don't see it coming. Difficult to swallow is it? 'Tony the Bumper' had over by a creeper. Well, at least you can console yourself with the knowledge that she's quite the little professional herself. I wonder what you really had in that case."

"Nothing to worry about, just bits'n pieces. Pretty though isn't she? Sounds as though you're quite fond of her."

Fisher gets up from the table. "Fond of her? I'm in fucking love with her. Had her in this morning, charged her with wounding but my governor made me throw her out on police bail, down to another potential harassment suit. I'd go and lift her right now if you'd give me a little just cause, instead of your usual bullshit. Come on Hurley, what did she steal?"

When Tony doesn't even bother replying, Fisher walks out of the interview room disgusted. As soon as the door closes, Tony drags Rebecca's file closer, spins it the right way up and opens it. 'Rebecca Moseley, DOB 20/03/75. Active. Current known address: Flat 5, 17 Marine Square Brighton'. Now at least he's got something to go on. He fully accepts that she probably isn't going to give him the money back but she might just let him have enough to get away.

Brighton Pier - Autumn 96

Fisher takes his cigarettes out.

"I could almost feel you watching me through a two-way mirror when I read that address. I was right, wasn't I Fisher, you know, thinking it was no accident when you walked out of the room and left me with her record?"

A waitress approaches as he begins to light up,

"Sorry but this is a no smoking area Sir."

The rain's stopped now, so we get up and go out. Fisher lights his cigarette and stands leaning on the railings, looking out to sea for a moment before he replies. "I'd rather you called me Ted now Tony, what I mean is, we do know each other quite well, don't we? And, yes, yes you're quite right, it was deliberate. I could usually remain objective but she was such a little bloody wind up."

He stands there absolutely loaded with guilt; almost begging for absolution as though what happened was his fault and that being forgiven by me is the only thing that can set things straight.

"Thought I was right, putting it down to a bit of needle on your part. OK so she was clever enough to make a fool of you as well. She certainly got the better of me. Look Ted, none of what happened was your fault right!" He comes over and sits next to me in the shelter.

"Yes, if you say so Tony. If you say so."

I never thought I could end up actually empathising with a policeman, seeing things his way, but I do and I decide to try and make it easier for him, cheer him up a little by telling him how it unfolded for us.

"So, I spent about an hour walking the streets around the hotel, wondering where I might've left the Merc'. I mean, I was that drunk when I arrived, I couldn't remember a thing. I had no idea where I might've parked it, other than it must've been within staggering distance or

I never would've managed to reach the hotel. After a good hour of looking, the car was still nowhere to be found, so I was forced to eat humble pie; you know Ted, that's the only thing on the menu, when you've got no cash."

He doesn't react, not so much as a smile, so I continue.

"Alright, then I walk back into the hotel, feeling about as welcome as a heavy smoker in a fucking dynamite factory. Anyway, Brindle takes great pleasure in loudly telling me that the hotel will sue me if I don't pay the bill. He's even more delighted letting me know me the car's been towed away, as he throws me out. So I phone Levi Marriott, the pikey car dealer who rents the McGregors and me our vehicles; he might whinge as though he's mortally wounded but he does agree to temporarily fund me up by paying the fine in order to spring his car. By then it's night, quite late but he says he'll phone and do the biz with his plastic in the morning. He promises me he'll say nothing to the McGregors and, even though I can't find it in me to really believe him, I get on with my next problem; having hardly any cash. I try phoning Kenny Robinson, my best friend. You know him, lives in North Wales. It takes a few minutes for his daughter to tell me he's off in Spain looking for a villa. So I decide to call his son Wayne; he's like a nephew to me but my mobile phone dies completely. The battery's flat."

"A quick count of the change she was kind enough to leave me, adds up to twenty-one pounds fifty. I mean, you don't need to be a genius to work out the fact that twenty quid isn't going to get you anywhere to stay but, that definitely was Billy McGregor I saw in the afternoon and I really needed to get off the main roads. Every time a car slowed, my heart nearly stopped. So, even though I really felt like leaving it until the morning, I decided I'd try and find a way though the back streets to Rebecca's flat. I was just going to front it out and tumble in on her. There was no other option until I turned up Rock Gardens and saw The George Hamilton V Hotel. The sign read, '£20 a night' and another in the window told me there were vacancies."

"Trust me Ted, twenty quid a night suddenly seemed expensive when I walked into the stink of that room, broken shower, peeling wallpaper and a stained mattress with a few moth eaten blankets on it. Still, I was off the street until the morning and it did have a gas fire, so I lit it and took the phone battery out to give it a warm. Wayne was my best bet, if I could just get him to come down and liaise with the McGregors, I mean at least calm Billy and make him agree to talk first, I might just be in with a chance of survival."

The Real Trouble Starts When
Wayne Goes To Work

Benzyl methyl ketone, or BMK, is an essential ingredient in the production of amphetamine sulphate, amphetamine and methamphetamine; in other words speed or whiz. Without the creation or acquisition of this complex chemical, the drug simply cannot be manufactured. It's such a controlled substance that even legal businesses with genuine reasons for using BMK, need to obtain a license issued by chemical industry regulators, before they can order it. Then, when they do make a purchase, they can expect unannounced visits from The National Crime Squad's Illicit Laboratories Unit. Every one of the chemicals used in the manufacture of BMK is licensed and regulated in the same way, so there isn't much chance of a criminal gang actually creating it, then going on to manufacture the final product, without getting caught.

Demand for amphetamine paste far outstrips supply and immense wealth can be generated by anyone able to make it. The McGregors had long been aware of the potential fortune that was waiting to be made. They had managed to find and recruit a pharmaceutical chemistry student, who happened to be a heroin addict. They'd even acquired the pressure vessels and extra chemicals used to cook the BMK into speed but they didn't intend drawing attention to themselves or leaving tracks by starting any businesses, just to obtain a licence. Their idea was to get around the whole system simply by hiring a team of blaggers to steal it for them.

It's almost midnight and there's no moon. Following signs for the ICI Rocksavage Works, Wayne Robinson drives the seven-ton box van down the slip road off the expressway. His mask is rolled into a hat and in front of him there's a panoramic view of the southern end of the River Mersey. The distant lights of Ellesmere Port are glittering yellow on the river and glowing against the night clouds. The view changes as he rounds the corner on to the Rocksavage service road. Mile upon mile of silver pipework, walkways, valves and vessels, illuminated by thousands of electric light bulbs, gives the massive chemical plant a beautiful, surreal, almost science fiction look.

He mounts the grass verge, killing the lights as he goes, then stops next to the fence; he applies the handbrake but leaves the engine running, then turns to his forty-year-old accomplice, Pettit. "You sure you know what to do?"

Pettit nods with a blend of edginess and excitement in anticipation of the massive crime they're about to commit. He's got plenty of respect for Wayne. The kid might be ten years his junior but he's certainly the top man on this firm. The passenger door is hard up against the fence. Wayne rolls his window down and gets out. Then, using the resulting opening as a footing, he climbs up on to the cab. Pettit slides behind the wheel and accidentally revs the engine a little as his foot feels for the accelerator. Wayne's heart begins to thump. A few feet from the other side of the fence and he'll be out of sight but right now, he's on offer. He moves quickly back from the cab roof, opening a trap door on top of the truck's box.

Billy Jones emerges from the opening and Wayne helps him pull the aluminum ladder he just scaled, up through the opening. Working together, they awkwardly lower the ladder over the razor wire, landing it on the other side of the twenty-foot security fence, attaching it to the top stringers by two hooks. They glance at each other's faces in silence before simultaneously rolling their hats down into masks.

Wayne steps from the top of the box on to the ladder. Jones follows. Pettit isn't cold but he's trembling as he pulls the truck away from the fence back on to the road. As soon as Wayne and Jones are on the ground, they lift the ladder up, freeing its hooks then, both walking backwards, silently lower it and hide it behind the nearest giant chemical vessel. They keep down, weaving their way through the tangled mass of steaming pipework in the direction of the main gate. Wayne suddenly grabs Jones's shoulder. They both stop. There it is, dead ahead, the security lodge. Wayne raises his binoculars and focuses through the distant window on to the security guard; he smiles 'clear' through his ski mask. The door is open, the guard's alone and he's watching a portable television; this should be very easy.

Completely unexpectedly, Wayne's mobile phone rings out an excerpt from the 1812 Overture. He unzips the overall, furious with himself for forgetting to turn it off, snatches it out and opens it. He can really do without this shit. "Yeah!"

He hears Tony's voice. "It's me, I've..."

Wayne interrupts. "Not now for fuck's sake." He turns the phone off, offering a one-word explanation to Jones. "Tony!"

They move in on the lodge.

John Burgess, the fifty-year-old security guard, sits watching *Planet Rock,* wishing he could go back in time and regain his youth. He no longer enjoys this job; he hasn't since the area controller had him re-located from the Runcorn branch of Asda. They couldn't prove he'd been dipping into the cigarette stock, he hadn't even taken enough to make a difference but they did have an idea, so they moved him anyway. Rocksavage is the most boring site he's ever worked, nothing ever happens, it stinks of rotten eggs and there's nothing worth stealing.

Suddenly an arm clamps around his throat dragging, smashing him and his chair backwards on to the floor. Wayne gives him a short hard jab in the nose. It bursts. He kneels on the security guard's chest and grabs his jaw.

"Give me the fuckin' gate keys."

Burgess is terrified. "There's no money here. What do...?"

Wayne interrupts with another jab. Blood spots fly everywhere. "I didn't ask for a guided tour did I? Keys, now!"

"Next to the telly."

Jones rushes past them, snatches the keys up and races out of the lodge. Wayne takes out a roll of duct tape and unwinds a length.

"Take it easy mate, I'm bleeding."

"Want me to put a tourniquet around your fuckin' throat?"

The security guard is having difficulty breathing, due to the air being expelled from his lungs by Wayne's knee. The duct tape refuses to stick at first, the guard's head being so wet with blood. Wayne wipes it with his overall sleeve to get a start. Then mummifies the guard's head, covering the eyes but leaving a small slit over his nose. Burgess blacks out. Wayne gets off his chest, kneels down and listens to his heart; it's all right, he's still breathing.

Jones's hands are shaking as he fumbles the key into the brass lock. Pettit is parked completely on show in the streetlights in front of the gates outside, waiting to be let in. Struggling to control the adrenaline racing through his body, it's hard to keep his legs from shaking and very difficult to control the clutch. He breathes a sigh of relief when Jones rolls the gates back and he drives through, stopping just inside, waiting for him to close them again. Jones hoists himself into the passenger seat and the truck moves deeper into the plant, finally stopping at the dispatch area. He jumps down and shines his torch on pallets with four 45-gallon drums stacked on each. He's about half way along a row of about a hundred pallets, when his torch illuminates three that are loaded with black drums, each of which has a white cross chalked on it. Things start to move quickly. Pettit's screwdriver flashes, brightly earthing out on the forklift starter motor. He tries again, this time it doesn't touch earth; he makes the right connection on the solenoid and the forklift fires up.

"These are the ones." Jones whispers so loudly he almost shouts and, within a few seconds, Pettit's driving the forks into the pallet to lift it. Jones rushes ahead of Pettit to the rear of the truck. He releases the hasp allowing the roller shutter to fly up. The suspension creaks as Pettit lowers the first pallet in and withdraws the forks. The forks come in again pushing on the pallet blocks, driving it home. Two more pallets and they're finished. Jones swings on the rope and the shutter crashes down. He closes the hasp and slips a padlock in without locking it. Pettit jumps up into the driver's seat and the truck is already on the move when Jones climbs in.

Wayne is standing perfectly still in the doorway, counting the seconds, listening to his own breath. He looks behind, checking his work; the security guard couldn't move even if he were conscious, being bound to the chair and laying on his side. Suddenly, hearing the truck, Wayne runs for the gate. Jones throws him the key. He lets the truck out, locks the gate behind them, then piles in, pushing Pettit out of the driver's seat and moves off towards the Runcorn Bridge.

As the seconds pass by inside the truck and the distance from the robbery increases, the mood becomes lighter. They're no longer wearing ski masks. Wayne's neat blond hair and boyish fair skin flashes yellow as they pass beneath the amber lights on the expressway. He trains regularly and keeps himself in good condition; he'd have no problem passing for twenty-five even though he's thirty. He looks down at Pettit's bald head which is also flashing yellow with the lights. It's difficult to keep the smile off his face now they're all high on adrenalin. Pettit and Jones are lying on the cab floor unable to stop laughing. To anyone they pass, it looks just like an average truck, lone driver at the wheel, even if that driver is struggling to keep a straight face.

Soon they're half way across the bridge with the scanner on, the police aren't making any significant broadcasts, it hisses away in the background with details of a pub brawl as Wayne flicks through stations on the truck radio. Pettit stops laughing.

"Have you fuckin' farted Jonesey?"

"No"

"You've shit yourself then."

"Fuck off Pettit, I was only a kid when that happened. Always find a way of bringin' it up though don't you?"

"Well it stinks down here."

"You wanna check your own underpants, you looked pretty shitty to me on that forklift."

Wayne turns the volume up. "Shut up you two, the news is on."

He turns the volume even higher. It's an average day's UK news. A stepfather who's been found guilty of murdering a three-year-old child, gets six years. The broadcast continues, "The speech made yesterday by the Home Secretary, in which he pledged to use the full resources of MI5 to assist the police in their war against the Britain's organised drug gangs, came in for heavy criticism last night. Several civil liberties groups, including Amnesty International...

Wayne turns the radio off. "Same old shite." Perhaps he should have left it on.

Brighton Pier Autumn 96 - Tony

I continue telling Fisher what happened next. When I gave Wayne another call before leaving the luxurious George Hamilton V Hotel, I was left in no doubt that something was wrong. He went totally weird on me again, telling me not to mention the name 'McGregor' over his phone and quickly ended the conversation. He was up to something and he really didn't want to talk about it. Well, it was none of my business so I didn't ask, instead I told him to find a public phone and get back to me as soon as he'd got a spare minute. I must admit though, Wayne talking to me that way really hurt. I mean, I thought the world of that kid, even if I was intending to give him a bit of a using by putting him between me and Billy McGregor. In fact I was so sad and offended, I decided I'd try to manage without his help altogether. I began walking across town with the sunlight warming the back of my head. That two-mile trek to the car compound was really sobering. It was the first occasion in years I'd run out of whisky at the same time as cash but, if I was going to get through this, I wouldn't just need luck, I'd need my wits about me too; so perhaps a little unavoidable sobriety was a blessing in disguise. Sure enough, Marriott was good to his word. A quick flash of my identity was all it took and I was mobile again, driving along the prom towards Rebecca's flat, with the fuel light flashing and one pound fifty in my pocket.

Marine Square is one of Brighton's smaller seafront squares. It's not exactly a square, being three sided with the front opening on to the prom. It didn't take long to estimate that, being so small, everyone who lived there probably knew each other so, fearful of having my registration number phoned in to the police by some bored curtain twitcher, I decided to park on the prom and walk in.

There I was, in front of number 17. The five-story white stone terrace looked to be well maintained, as did the other houses. Paranoia almost got the better of me climbing those steps to her front door. I couldn't help but feel conspicuous standing there in my crumpled suit. Suddenly startled by the loudness of the doorbell, I considered just walking away; I mean what the fuck was I going to do if she answered the door? I always tried to be studious and learn as many new tricks as possible whenever I was in prison but I never managed to enrol on the 'how to terrorise small, defenseless women' course.

Flat 5, is in a four-story building with a cellar, so hers must be on the top floor. The curtains haven't moved and there's no sound of footsteps coming down the stairs. She must be out. If getting the car back was my first break of the day, the second comes when she doesn't answer the door. This presents me with the golden opportunity of exploring her flat. Perhaps she's been decent enough to leave my cash under the bed.

I've never been much of a burglar, at least not of houses, but I've always been quite an optimist. So I moved out of the square, counting the number of front doors from hers to the corner, and began losing the paranoia as I walked away from those dozens of watching windows. The discovery that her flat only backs on to an estate agent, a pizza place and an ironmonger's, might've have begun to generate a positive feeling but, seeing the dirty uncurtained windows above them, was truly uplifting. The upstairs of every shop was either unoccupied or being used as a storeroom. Broad daylight or not, I'd have to be very unlucky to get seen. I continued my inventory of the rear; it was the seventh yard gate but it was locked, I only had to wait a few minutes for the street to empty then I moved.

Going over the top, I got my first view of the rear in its entirety. It seemed quite high and much taller than the front because there was no cellar, just a yard. First step, quietly unbolt the yard gate; it's one thing walking into an unlocked yard and quite another to climb over a wall that's meant to keep you out. Having always been terrified of heights and never much of a climber, it was a relief to see the newly painted fire escape with not a single speck of rust. The solidly built and reassuring steel structure was firmly fastened to the brickwork; it had safety railings alongside each flight of steps and taller ones around the platforms. Thank God for recent building regulations. Fifteen years earlier and I might've been forced to rely on the loose looking cast-iron drainpipe, in which case, I would definitely have given up. My biggest risk now, is actually being seen by any of the other tenants as my ascent takes me past their windows. Even that wouldn't be the end, when it's easy enough to say you're a surveyor from the local council, checking the fire escape. Or what about a little honesty?

"Sorry, I know I shouldn't be up here but I think Rebecca's doorbell is out of action, I'm only trying to catch her attention without disturbing the whole building."

Fortunately for me, the only movement in any of the

flats comes from a middle-aged woman sitting with her back to me, watching a television with her black cat sitting on her window ledge, staring at me through the glass.

'Never look down', that's the advice if you suffer with vertigo. Whoever came up with that little gem must've been either a mountain climber or a skydiver. If you're genuinely scared of heights, fear compels you to do it and you just can't resist the urge. Safety railings or not, the sight of the cobbled yard sixty feet below sends me weak at the knees and giddy. Suddenly sweating, with trembling hands, I raise the open transom window, freeing it from its hook, and reach down through the opening to lift the latch on the larger window. Seconds later I'm in, sitting on the empty draining board silently listening to the sounds of the old house. Several creaks filter up from the floor below, an antique clock ticks somewhere in another room, otherwise it's quiet.

You'd expect to be negotiating a minefield of dishes and cups on a draining board, or at least avoiding a bowl full of washing up in the sink that's the usual hazard when you climb through someone's kitchen window, but the stainless steel sink was clean and empty. There was an over scrubbed kind of sterility about this kitchen, it smelled of bleach rather than food; she must've just cleaned up. Slipping out of my shoes to avoid unnecessary noise on the bare varnished floorboards, I looked around the kitchen/dining room. On the table, a single place mat and coaster, in the fridge a pack of organic yogurt and nothing else. I had an idea she might have hidden my money beneath the rubbish in her pedal bin but the only thing in that spotless receptacle, was an equally sterile white plastic liner.

Creeping along the carpeted hallway, the ticking grows louder. That massive wall clock with its fading roman numerals is completely out of place, hanging in the hall of such a small flat. It's the kind of clock you'd find in an old village schoolroom. The plain oak case which houses it, holds no secrets and gives up nothing more exciting than the key to its own movement.

The door creaks as I push it aside to discover that the bedroom's just as sterile as the kitchen; a single size, antique brass bed, with nothing underneath it, not even dust. The neatly turned down white, ironed cotton sheets are cold to the touch and of course the pillowcases contain nothing other than pillows. I thought I was getting warm opening the bedside cabinet but they weren't bundles of fifties, just elastic bound collections of hand written letters, all signed *'Gran'*. I sat on the bed to read one, before pocketing it for the address; perhaps the obsessively clean orderliness of this place indicates that she mightn't even live here. If Fisher's line about her being "quite a little professional" is true, then maybe she keeps this flat purely for the police's benefit, kind of a buffer zone, and she may not turn up here very often. I console myself with the fact that, at least now I know where her grandmother lives, she won't shake me off as easily as Inspector Fisher.

Determined to let go of such negative thoughts, I continue scouring the flat. In the wardrobe, there's a row of plain, expensive designer suits and blouses, all of which have empty pockets. In a the pine chest of drawers next to it, dozens of blouses, tee shirts and sets of underwear, all ironed, folded and stacked so neatly, they could almost be presented for a military inspection. "No one lives like this," I think, still attempting to erase the buffer zone conclusion from my mind before it takes root. It's almost criminal to disturb such a meticulous display of ironing and folding but it is my cash and I've got to find it, if it's here.

Holding one of her tee shirts in my hand, I experience again the sweet fragrance of her perfume and, as I do, a perfect image forms in my mind. Those large innocent brown eyes clashing so sexily with that bleached blond hair. Touching my face against the softness of her tee shirt causes Rebecca's image to disappear, as the perfume drowns beneath the chemical smell of fabric softener. Touching my lapel, I realise that the fragrance is coming from my own suit, the very fibres of which must have been indelibly marked by her perfume. We must've been very close for that to occur but still, I can't remember any more than a few frozen frames, a few snapshots of the evening. I know she's not stupid, I mean, she did end up with my cash didn't she? But if only she would've been smart enough to know that, all she needed to do was say the word, she only had to ask, and we could have just shared it. We'd be half way to Grenada by now. I'd have told her all about the McGregor brothers and we'd be sipping our champagne, laughing at them. Instead, she's dropped me into a quicksand of the deepest shit anyone ever landed in. Billy McGregor is not just a dangerous man, he's a dangerous moron and will be incapable of understanding, let alone accepting, a rationally thought out excuse. Even so, I can't hate her for it. There was no way she could've known what kind of an earthquake she'd visited on my little world.

Inside the bathroom there's a single electric toothbrush, one tube of toothpaste and a roll of floss. I didn't need to be particularly gifted to work out that she lived on her own. The side panel of her white bath is secured to the framework with mirror screws, the chrome heads of which are unmarked and tight, so it can't be behind there. After an unrewarding investigation of the back of her washing machine, I rested on the side of the bath. Searching that place was a daunting prospect, it was going to take me forever; with carpets covering the wooden floor of every room except the kitchen it could be absolutely anywhere. I'd just have to lift them one by one, in the hunt for loose floorboards.

The sound of footsteps coming up the stairs caused me to freeze; I was certain it must be Rebecca. I definitely needed to compose myself but what was I going to do if she screamed? Heart thumping and mind racing, I stood straightening my suit and tie, determined to look as normal as possible. Perhaps I should go into the kitchen, yes that's it; let her find me in there, standing with my back to her then slowly turn to face her and deal with her arrival in a very matter of fact way. That'll gain me the upper hand and hopefully won't involve too much in the way of loud voices. She'll definitely be shocked to see me and, as long as I remain calm and aloof, to her it'll seem all the more sinister. The footsteps stop outside the door and a woman's voice calls from outside. "Rebecca! Rebecca!" Then a loud clattering from the letterbox as the mail is pushed through.

Two large brown envelopes; one was postmarked London, the other Birmingham. I didn't stand on ceremony or waste any time before opening them; thank God for the cash inside, however small the amount. That fifteen hundred out of the London envelope and the couple of thousand out of the other might've come nowhere near replacing the McGregor's money but at least it provided me with funds enough to escape.

By now, I'd almost convinced myself that yesterday's sighting of Billy McGregor's BMW was probably just a case of mistaken identity; there must be dozens of cars the same as his and at least one or two of them being driven by similar looking square headed giants. No, there was definitely no way they could've figured I was down in Brighton. If Marriott had said anything, they'd have pounced on me at the car compound. The idea of losing a pound and finding a penny might conjure up the image of a sad person but when that penny can buy you a ticket away from the end of the world, it's the luckiest one you'll ever find.

Filled with a true sense of relief, I pocketed my cash, then sat looking at the bunch of credit cards that had arrived with it. In an ideal world, I'd sell them up in Liverpool or Manchester but that would be more than pushing my luck. The brothers may be dimwits but they do fuel hundreds of crack and smack heads, from now on Liverpool would definitely be out of the question.

I decided that, if I failed to recover the money, I'd present myself at Gatwick airport, buy another ticket to Grenada and pay Moses a visit. A new ticket might be expensive and only leave me with a couple of grand but Moses' home on the island of Carriacou, is just a couple of miles from Union Island and, according to him, Union Island is more or less the centre of the universe as far as cocaine distribution is concerned. He hardly ever stopped going on about the place; telling me that, even though there are dozens of Columbians who must never be fucked with, there are also boatloads of dumb Americans dying to get their greedy little hands on a few kilos of pure Columbian flake. What was it he used to say? Oh yes, "A man like you could make a fortune on Union Island". So that was my plan, if I didn't manage to get the cash out of her, I'd just wipe my face and go.

Sitting there waiting for her to arrive, I decide that, as soon as she walks through the door, I'll let her know all about the McGregors. She'll have to realise what an awful mistake she's made, then when it's sunk in and she understands the danger, I'll offer her the gift of a lifetime, split the cash straight down the middle. Half's better than nothing; seems fair to me. I nicked it off them she nicked it off me, fifty-fifty with no hard feelings. I'm even willing to offer her a means of escape, why not?

My mouth and throat are so completely dry it's becoming uncomfortable and there's nothing proper to drink, not so much as a can of beer, so I drop a tea bag into her mug and fill the kettle. In the cupboard, just a can of powdered skimmed milk and no sugar. The water is just starting to boil when I hear footsteps coming up the stairs, then a key going into the door. This time I'm cool, I'm deadly serious about getting the cash back and I'm going to make it as sinister as possible. Keeping my back to her for a moment too long, I stand watching her reaction reflected in the kitchen window. She looks so different without the wig, almost boyish, but boys don't have such beautiful eyes. She remains very still, vulnerable, obviously shocked. I speak slowly turning to face her.

"Where's the sugar? You do use it don't you?"

She's still looking silently around the room; I suppose working out if I'm on my own. Her eyes fix on the credit cards and torn envelopes.

I continue, "Well?"

"Well what?" she asks with a noticeable tremor in her voice.

It's working; she's really scared. Perhaps I should've run my own terrorisation course in prison. Desired effect or not, it definitely doesn't feel good to be doing this.

"The sugar?"

"It's in the blue container. How the...?"

"How did I find you?" I interrupt seeing the sugar. "Ah got it. You know, one serious enemy will alter your life much more than a hundred good friends, especially when he's a policeman."

Her mouth drops open.

"Fisher?"

"That's the man."

She's suddenly furious but it could be an act.

"Got some fucking nerve hasn't he? Steals the cash off me then sends you to pay me back, puts you on my case. You're an idiot Tony. Best thing you can do is get out of here, before my boyfriend gets home."

I take a sip of the tasteless tea and it isn't easy, but I manage to give her my most slimy and sinister grin.

"I've been all over this place. No men in your life. Only mention of a man's in that letter from your Gran. You know the one I mean. She was kind of wondering if you're a lesbian but couldn't quite find the words to ask?"

Suddenly fury gets the better of her. She comes at me with fists flying. I grab her wrists and hold her still.

"Get out!" she screams.

I let go and she backs off still furious but still scared.

"Get out or you'll what? Phone the police? I don't think so. No you're not going to do that. Even if that screaming brings one of your neighbours you're going to tell them there's nothing wrong."

Lifting the credit cards by the edges, the way a policeman might when holding a piece of evidence, I drop them into one of the envelopes and pocket it.

"I'll bet you didn't even bother wiping these did you?"

It looks as though she's finished with the screaming so I continue to quietly present her with the outstanding account.

"There was three and a half grand in cash. Let's see, that leaves a hundred and forty-six thousand five hundred you owe me. Where's my fucking money, Miss Moseley?"

She looks genuinely surprised by the amount but, then again, she was quite believable the other night wasn't she?

"How much?"

"Come on, you must've counted it before you posted it."

She replied, "I told you. Fisher took it."

I've known you for a long time Ted and would never have imagined calling you a friend. When you were on the job we used to hate each other didn't we? Maybe I was a fool for thinking it could be just needle on your part, using me to get back at a woman you couldn't nick. But it suddenly occurred to me that this could be just your way of rubbing it in. It all added up. So, there I am standing, looking at this very beautiful young woman and starting to believe her, when the doorbell rings.

"One of your neighbours?" I ask, but it's written all over her face that she's not expecting anyone.

She goes to open the door and I get a kind of premonition that fills me with dread but fail to act on it. Instead I fight the urge to escape back down that fire escape. I just stand there frozen to the spot like a bewildered rabbit caught in someone's headlights. Suddenly, my own sinister act pales into insignificance as Joseph McGregor explodes into the room, dragging Rebecca by the throat. He swings her almost full circle before letting her go, sending her flying across the room. Her head hits the wall with a sickening thud. His foot draws back to kick her and, before I know what's happening, I find myself diving on his back, my arm closing around his neck, but I only manage to hold on for a moment. Billy's fist jabs my kidneys, then the middle of my back; the second punch expels all the air from my lungs and I'm down on the floor struggling to breathe.

Joseph hisses, "Always a gentleman weren't you Hurley" then he kicks me in the face.

Before I can get up, Billy stamps on my fingers and continues the conversation where his brother left off.

"Where's our fuckin' money Hurley?"

"Gone"

They each grab an arm and hoist me into a chair. Billy slaps me first, bursting my nose; blood splatters all over the front of his shirt. Joseph's fingers close around my windpipe as Billy unwinds a dirty piece of rag from around his razor sharp butcher's knife.

"Where's our fuckin' money?"

Rebecca, still on the floor, answers before I can. I would've given anything if she could've just kept her mouth shut but she couldn't.

"Leave him! I stole it off him. Then the police stole it off me. It's gone now."

They don't move for a moment then Joe releases my throat, as their attention goes to Rebecca. Billy smiles and begins speaking calmly though his crooked and tobacco stained teeth, but the smile's only on his mouth, his eyes are stone cold and without pity.

"We'll have to do them both."

No doubt they're serious. They've killed before. She doesn't deserve this. Suddenly I'm out of my chair, trembling in front of them.

"For fuck sake Billy. Give us a break; if you top us, you'll never get the money back. Tell him Joey, tell him I'll get the money back."

Billy presses the ugly butcher's knife against my chest, not quite applying enough pressure to push it home. For a moment it feels as though it's about to burst through my clothes and sink into my lungs. I'm trembling as he reduces the pressure slightly before speaking.

"You really think that's what this is all about? Think you can talk your way out it? Remember when I told you never try to fuck us over? Never try and mug us off?"

Now I'm begging for my life.

"Jesus Christ Billy, never. You know me better than that".

They look at each other for a moment then Joe regards me with what seems to be genuine empathy and continues.

"What happens when you buy a ticket for the Spice Islands? Well I'll tell you, that place is cocaine central; there's nothing there for a white man, its fuckin' bonga bonga land; no tourist industry nothing, the only whites there are collecting Charlie. Had no idea that the airline would automatically forward your details to the national drug squad did you? Yeah, well the drug squad'd never heard of you, your name didn't even ring a bell; not until I got through to our bent copper this morning."

Billy interrupts, punctuating every sentence with a little more pressure on the knife, almost a stab.

"Had it all planned all along didn't you, you Irish prick? Every time you walked around the exercise yard with that black bastard, you must've been laughing at us. Fuckin' Moses, what kind of a name's that?"

Eager to avoid antagonizing him further, I lower my head and avoid eye contact, much as you might avoid looking into the eyes of a wild animal. I never expected to die like this but there's no way of escaping and begging is a waste of time, still I try.

"Billy, I'm sorry, please don't do this, please."

Joey's phone starts ringing and gains me an extra moment.

Kenny Robinson

Set on a hill overlooking the River Dee, Kenny and Janice Robinson's three-acre smallholding is about five miles from the nearest town. Being surrounded by a maze of narrow leafy lanes makes it a difficult place for a stranger to locate. In fact, the tiny farm is so isolated that first-time visitors are always met and guided in from the main road. The cosy seventeenth-century cottage has been a warm family home and, over the course of the last thirty years, the Robinsons have watched their children grow into adults and leave the nest. Those thirty years passed so quickly that Kenny hardly ever gave it a thought, unless one of his old friends from Liverpool was on the phone calling him Taffy. It used to annoy him when they first started insinuating that he had actually become Welsh because, in the early days, he hated the Welsh people so badly.

Being from Liverpool, he quickly experienced the true meaning of prejudice. Older kids regularly beat up his boys in school, just for being English. Pubs would fall silent if he had the audacity to walk in and the customers of those that didn't fall silent, would resort to taking Welsh and pretend they couldn't understand English.

Kenny never rushed to defend his three boys, believing that if they were to make their way in the world, they'd better learn to fend for themselves. Instead, he taught them how to box, then he taught them how to fight dirty. He taught them so well that the bullying changed direction and, one by one, they began to be excluded from school. As for the unfriendly reception in pubs, occasionally over the years, he'd responded in kind and been involved in several brawls but no one ever got the better of him. Even at the age of sixty-five, if he lost the fight, he would consider it to be just the first round and would always go back for seconds.

It was unusual to be falling out of bed at ten o clock, but his flight from Portugal had been delayed and he hadn't got home until 5 a.m. He'd probably still be asleep now, if the smell of that fresh bread baking hadn't drifted into the bedroom and stimulated his appetite. A smile comes to his face as he's getting dressed; Jan must've been up for hours. He ducks beneath the low beam of the doorway into the living room and spends a few moments in front of his CCTV monitor, the camera of which is focussed on the deserted lane. The oak beams and walls of the plainly decorated room are loaded with antiques and memorabilia, collected during his career. Brass plaques taken from the front of safes, a few police helmets, several truncheons, sets of handcuffs and the ceramic pig dressed in a constable's uniform, along with his own tall, straight build, might suggest that he's a retired policeman, but nothing could be further from the truth.

Kenny's entire adult life has been devoted to serious crime. It's been a long journey since those early beginnings on Liverpool's Lime Street Station when, under the guidance of his father, he stole luggage from wealthy Americans coming to meet the Transatlantic liners. Since then, he's stolen lorry loads of every high value cargo imaginable, from tinned salmon to cigarettes. In the sixties, there had been all those wage snatches and in the seventies, dozens of security vans. These days he's retired, leaving the family business to Wayne, the sharpest, toughest and eldest of his sons.

He walks into the kitchen, pours himself a cup of tea from the pot and eyes Jan without talking to her. Then he goes out into the yard carrying his tea with him. There's been no argument with Jan but, ignoring her once in a while, keeps her on her toes. With his three hefty Rhodesian Ridgebacks looking for a feed and sniffing at his heels, he makes his way past the barn and sits on the old tree stump to take his tea in the morning air. From this, his favourite position, he can just make out Liverpool's distant skyline. One of the Ridgebacks, excited by seeing him swallow a mouthful of tea, begins to drool and shakes its head covering his arm in saliva. He springs to his feet to chase them, "Go on get out of it!" and the pack runs back towards the kitchen.

Settling back on to the tree stump he wonders why those dogs seem to smell more like horses, then his intense blue eyes concentrate back on the Liverpool skyline. He seldom interferes in Wayne's business ventures, never even offers advice, but this time it's different. This time the kid's stolen too much and, somewhere out there, beneath that hazy horizon, he's sitting on 300 gallons of BMK waiting for them to come up with the cash. The worst way three hundred gallons of that stuff must be worth a couple of million quid. Of all the people he could have chosen to deal with, he's mixed up with the bloody McGregors. Pair of morons, drug dealing bastards; no good can come of it. Wayne should have stuck to stealing cash. Kenny's unable to stop himself flipping his phone open and making the call. Wayne answers after just one ring.

"Yeah?"

"It's me son, have you done that bit of business?"

"No I'm waiting for them to call."

"Are you fuckin' stupid or something? Call them, unless you want me to."

"They said they'd be in touch at half ten, they're only five minutes late."

Kenny finds it difficult to keep a lid on it.

"You're bloody scared of them aren't you?"

"No."

"Look lad, get them phoned now. Tell them I'm on the firm!"

"But..."

"Just do it and do it now. Have you heard anything from the little fella?"

"Tony! Yeah phoned me yesterday but I couldn't speak. Yeah you're right Dad, they are taking the piss, I'll get on to it right away."

Kenny closes his phone and goes back to drinking his cool tea. He smiles at Suzie, the largest and most affectionate Ridgeback, as she saunters back from the kitchen and leans on him, until she pollutes the air with a loud and vile fart. Even before he springs to his feet, the highly intelligent bitch knows she's shamed herself, gives him a guilty look and canters away out of range of his tea.

"Go on get out of it you stinking bastard."

As Kenny throws his tea at Suzie, he has literally no idea that he has saved Tony's life. If Wayne calls the McGregors before Billy pushes the blade home he will, even if unwittingly, at least cause them to grant Tony a stay of execution.

Wayne Robinson

If you ever found yourself in the position where you needed to hide twelve 45-gallon drums of incredibly valuable liquid from every policeman and serious criminal in the UK, where would you begin? Wayne always made his own decisions and, while he often disregarded Kenny's fatherly advice, he always valued the stories of old times, like the time when Kenny and four others dressed in pinstripes to rob a city centre bank. "If you don't want to be noticed, if you don't want to be found, then blend in. A needle of hay in a haystack is only difficult to find because of the other needles."

He's alone, sitting in his cousin's riverside drum recycling yard next to the river Mersey. Low water now and he should smell the exposed kelp and bubbling mud of the bare riverbed but, being so close to the fire that his face is almost burning, he can only smell the smoke. He pokes an old piece of steel reinforcing bar into the few remaining embers of last night's evidence. Nothing left, no overalls, cans, boots or gloves, all just ashes. He glances across the wet muddy yard towards the mountainous pile of 45-gallon drums in every colour imaginable. That priceless BMK left Rocksavage Works in brand new, dark blue ICI drums.

As they unloaded those drums on to old pallets, Billy Jones beat them randomly with a lump hammer; not enough to puncture, just enough to scuff away their newness. As he did, Pettit used a selection of spray cans to camouflage the dark blue. Wayne's eyes focus on the three pallets planted somewhere in the middle of two thousand misaligned others, barely certain he's looking at the right four. They should be safe enough here for a while, even so, he knows his father's right, the McGregors do need a kick up the arse. It was supposed to be cash on delivery and he'd been able to deliver their goods since last night. He opens the contacts on his phone and presses Joey's number.

Tony

Joey's face almost breaks into a smile when he answers Wayne's call. He raises his hand to halt Billy and the pressure of the blade disappears from my chest. Joey's mobile is almost as loud as a hands free set. We all hear both sides of the conversation.

"That you?"

"Yeah it's me, you got our stuff?"

I instantly recognise Wayne's voice and begin to feel as though there might be some way of postponing our funeral. Joey gets on to it straight away, must have shown on my face. He raises a finger to his lips and menaces me into silence before I can speak.

"And some, we've had a right little tickle", replies Wayne then continues,

"Yeah we agreed fifty grand on the barrel, right?" Joey's face reddens at his own indiscretion.

"Just hang on a minute, Billy and me are on a bit of business down south and we're not alone. I'll just take you into the bedroom."

He closes the door behind him but we can still hear most of the muffled conversation, especially when Joey's voice suddenly gets louder.

"Twelve fucking barrels!"

"That a problem?"

"No, not a problem to us. Just the price goes down a little."

"The deal was fifty K a barrel."

"True, but half a million cash is a decent night's wages for your little firm, Wayne and a 100K reduction for the parcel seems fair enough for getting shot in one hit."

"OK."

Wayne had been working out a way into the Rocksavage plant for months, so it was easy for me to fill in the blanks. He certainly didn't take after his father. I mean how dumb was that? Letting them know he had twelve barrels of the most impossible to nick liquid in the world. To any enterprising home chemist, that stuff must be worth at least £2,000 a pint. A little chloroform, a few easily found chemicals and a fractional distillation, turns

£2,000 into £200,000 and he's just let the lot go; £8,640,000 pounds worth for £500,000. While I'm not even slightly interested in any kind of drug, I can see the simple mathematics.

Wayne continues, "So when will we do it?"

"Tomorrow night OK?"

"Have to be won't it. Seen anything of The Bumper?"

"Yeah, he's down in Brighton somewhere."

"Thought he was on your firm? Anyway if you run into him, tell him to give my dad a call."

My heart starts to slow down. Almost impossible to keep from smiling; while these two dimwits might be short of a few million brain cells, even Mad Billy wouldn't do anything likely to screw up their once in a lifetime deal, and this is about where my simple mathematics runs out, I'd need a calculator.

I remember thinking, "If a pint makes two hundred thousand pounds worth of whiz, how much would you get out of twelve forty-five gallon drums? Quick answer? A lot."

The bedroom door opens and Joey steps out; the calm mood of the room reverts instantly to Armageddon. The back of my head crashes into the wall and Billy's fingers resume crushing my windpipe, but I can still just about croak "You don't have to do this Billy, I can get your money back. Tell him Joe. Trust me. A dozen bumps with that Merc."

The blade almost punctures my chest as Billy hisses, emphasizing each word with a jab.

"Trust you? We already did. Remember? You fucked us over. Now you're gonna pay."

Joe grabs his shoulder. "Leave it Bill, we'll let him get our money back."

"It's not about the money. It's the fuckin' principle."

"Yeah well, you and me are going to be busy for the next few weeks, aren't we. No problem giving him a walkover for a month."

Billy's grip relaxes and I can breathe again. As my lungs fill, I watch his facial expression change as his mind wrestles with two thoughts at once.

"What's going to stop him doing it again?"

Joe is a total bread head and I suppose the imminent arrival of several millions of pounds worth of BMK trivialises their loss of £150,000.

"Didn't have a pretty little woman before did he? He won't do it again Billy. No, we'll defer it for now. A month, that's what you got, Hurley, four weeks. If you come up with the cash, we'll wipe our faces. If you don't, you can watch me kill her before Billy tops you."

Billy looks disappointed, sliding the knife into the back of his waistband. Joe is already out of the door and on his way down the stairs. Billy's eyes are filled with hatred.

"And you can watch me chop her face up before he does it."

He walks out leaving the door open. I get down on the floor next to Rebecca and put my arm around her loaded with regret and fear.

"Why couldn't you have just picked on someone else to rob?"

She sobs a little, I help her to her feet; she limps into the bathroom and bolts the door behind her. By this time I'm almost convinced she's lost the money but I give it one more try and shout through the bathroom door.

"If you've got it, you know we really should give it back."

"How many times do you need telling? That bastard took it off me."

"Yeah well, even if that's true, it doesn't change anything. It was me delivering it for them, you're stealing it off me. No doubt about it. It's us got to pay them back."

Anyone with just an average amount of grey matter would take the next plane out of Gatwick and never come back. If it wasn't for her thieving little fingers I'd be gone, living my life in peace and prosperity but, for some reason, maybe the way she spoke out, putting herself into the frame by trying to save me, I find myself bonding to her. A partnership, not exactly forged in heaven but a partnership nevertheless. Besides which, she is so very beautiful and though I can remember lusting after her beautiful naked body, I can't remember actually screwing her, which is very unusual because no matter how drunk I get, I never forget actually doing the deed.

Keeping such a promise as I've made to the brothers will certainly land me back in prison. It was the car job that sent me there last time. In those days things were easier, punters knew less, counterfeit logbooks were almost unheard of. The easiest thing in the world was to ring the paperwork and run adverts up and down the country, 'Prestige company director's car at a bargain price'.

No one caught on to what was happening, simply because it was the first time anyone had ever done it properly. I'd rent a new Merc, visit a car showroom and take the number off one of the cars for sale. Then make a set of plates and a logbook to match. I always used the engine and chassis number from the hire car so, even if the punter was smart enough to lift the bonnet and check the serial numbers against the paperwork, everything matched. I ran adverts and sold the car all over the UK but kept a spare set of keys and nicked it back a day later.

Local police dealt with hundreds of stolen cars and didn't have an overview of the national picture. It took the insurance companies about six months to figure out what I was at but they still had no idea of who I was. I believe I was just plain unlucky getting caught in the act, selling that Merc to an ex-police inspector. I still wonder what that ex-cop prick had been up to, having twenty-four grand under his bed to spend on a used car. Even in those virgin times, it took six months of working every day for me to build the tank up to £150,000. A hundred and fifty grand in three weeks was more than a tall order. It was plain impossible, and I knew it. I'd need to sell the car five times a week. That's just about impossible.

"Well at least we're both still breathing," I think, washing the blood from my face. My nose has stopped bleeding, there's a shoe graze on my forehead but it doesn't look as though my eyes are going to blacken. I mean, you wouldn't buy a prestige car from a Liverpool Irishman with a pair of black eyes would you. As soon as the first newly bought Mercedes disappears and the punter tells the police he's bought it from a little Irishman, it'll probably be pasted all over 'Crimewatch', name and all. No, it'll be better if Rebecca fronts every sale. I'll just recover them. I finish drying my face on her tea towel. She comes out of the bathroom.

"Sorry about the blood on this."

She sits opposite me across the table.

"Not as sorry as I am for getting you into this mess."

"For getting us into this mess; what did you do with my plane ticket?"

"Threw it away sorry."

I pick up her mobile phone and turn it on.

"Never mind. Is this down to you?"

"No it's just a pay as you go."

I take her grandmother's letter out of my pocket.

"OK to write on the back of this?"

She nods, I take the pen out of my inside pocket, pull the top off and it falls apart. She starts laughing then I join in. She passes me another pen to use, still laughing. I'm impressed by the way she's recovered so quickly. As I write out the advert, it occurs to me that she must've had quite a hard life to be so resilient.

'Mercedes 500sl. Company director's car
Less than a year old. Fully loaded
Downturn in trade forces sale,
hence giveaway price - £15,000'

The advert's ready to publish as far south as Brighton and as far north as Glasgow but first I need to call Kenny Robinson up in North Wales. She doesn't mind me using her phone. It rings a few times before Kenny picks it up.

"Yeah."

"Hi Ken, it's me."

"Jesus Christ, you're in the shit, it's all over Liverpool."

"I know. Can you still get the paperwork?"

"How many sets?"

"At least twenty."

"Fuckin' hell Tony, you really think you're going to get away with that many?"

"Like you said. I'm in the shit."

"Look Tony, come back to me with the details for the first few and I'll get working. Oh yeah, our Wayne sends his apologies for hanging up last night. He was on a bit of business."

It seems odd that Rebecca looks so excited by what she's about to get into.

"You'll have to front them you know. It's not going to be easy. You've got a lot to learn in a short time."

Now she looks even more turned on by the prospect.

"I could do with learning a few new tricks."

"Good, so pack enough clothes to last a couple of weeks."

I get the feeling that I'm going to be enjoying the near future. Who knows? We might just end up in the Spice Islands together.

Brighton Pier - Autumn 96 - Fisher

So, about the time you and Rebecca were travelling up to North Wales for your logbooks, I drove my boss Tom Commerford to London. He didn't tell me much, other than to say that he was meeting a snout he'd had for too long and needed to let go of. However, he did say that it was part of the new government policy to use MI5 in the prosecution of serious criminals. He also let me know that there was a potential lead to the gang who had stolen the BMK up in Runcorn but he never mentioned Rutter's name. No, it was chance that Rutter walked past me while I was parked outside waiting.

The Major - Patterson

Major Patterson had been a career soldier and had served all over the world. He had risen through the ranks to the height of Major by the age of thirty-five but a 'volatile temperament' as it said in his record, had halted any further promotion. He was an impeccably presented Scot but a Scot without a trace of regional accent. He leaves the MI6 building, crosses Vauxhall Bridge Road and walks smartly towards New Covent Garden Fruit Market. Back erect, there is no mistaking his military roots as he almost marches across the road next to Nine Elms Cold Storage. It's a dry morning but he still carries his umbrella. It's part of his uniform. From a distance he could pass for an ordinary London businessman but the powerful gait and ruddy, far too healthy complexion is a dead giveaway. The perfect cut of his Savile Row jacket discloses nothing, the .38 Browning automatic in his shoulder holster would be undetectable to anyone other than a radiologist. Down through the concrete tunnel into the fruit market, he walks beneath a sign that reads 'Covent Garden, London's larder'. That sign always gives him a secret chuckle, as do many things in civvy-street. He is quite disconnected from the normal world, having spent all of his adult life with the army for a family. Even now, working for MI5, he is still being cared for by his mother, his country. If anyone insults or threatens her, he will definitely deal with them.

He has been seconded from MI6 and landed with the unenviable task of estimating the value or threat of those supergrasses still employed by the various UK police forces. This is part of a much wider operation against organised crime and drug dealing. It promises to be a tacky sort of business, dealing with untrained non-military people, all of whom have prison backgrounds. As far as he is concerned, they'd best all be incarcerated for life or simply removed, his preference leaning towards the latter but, as his commander said, it is at least fair to give each SG a personal appraisal before taking any action. It may well be that some of those black and tans have reformed, or at least will be of further value to his department.

His overall brief is straightforward; 'To track down the top twenty UK drug importers/producers and neutralise them by whatever means suits the situation', quite an open charter. There is a force of fifteen men beneath him, each highly trained in the use of weapons and subterfuge, all of whom have proved themselves and will follow orders without question.

One of the early morning fruit wholesalers bids him "good morning" as he passes but he doesn't even raise his head in recognition. Instead, he opens the yellow steel door, reassured by the way no-one in London is ever offended by being ignored. He begins climbing the concrete stairs that lead to the vacant office suite above Greenhill Mushroom Wholesalers. The office smells musty, having been closed up for several months. He closes the door then goes through a second one and locks it behind him.

Flicking though his pocket notebook, he refreshes himself with the business at hand.

"Ah yes, Detective Superintendent Commerford with the SG James Rutter. Yes Rutter seems to be completely out of control but might be able to make inroads into the Robinson gang. Yes, quite important to contain that little lot."

He decides to remain behind the locked door and observe Commerford's meeting through the surveillance cameras. All such meetings from now on will be filmed as a matter of procedure, therefore he doesn't really need to be in the same building but he does much prefer the hands on approach, can get a much better feeling for the SG listening at close quarters. Dennis, Greenhill's top salesman, watches Commerford go through the yellow door then, a few moments later, Rutter. The sign on the door reads 'London and Midland Fruit Wholesalers'. Dennis has been in the fruit business since he left school thirty years ago and knows that no such firm exists. Intrigued or not, he goes back to calculating his pro rata return on the closed cups.

Hearing the office door slam shut, Patterson silently moves his chair closer to the inner door. The equipment will begin to record automatically as it picks up their conversation but he much prefers to hear it first hand. Superintendent Commerford has an idea that someone will be listening from the inner office, having been told to stay away from the door but Rutter is completely oblivious to the fact that the Major is just a few feet away from him.

"So Jimmy, what do you think of the news?"

"What fuckin' news?"

"The Home Secretary pledging to use MI5 in the prosecution of serious criminals."

"Yeah, fuckin' wankers; just like the police, present company excepted. What can they do Tommy? You're better off with the likes of me. They never expect it from their own."

"I've told you never to call me Tommy, haven't I?"

"Yeah, yeah; get off your fuckin' high horse Superintendent Commerford; you're just as dirty as me."

"I suppose I must be."

He pauses momentarily, wondering who might be behind the door listening to this lot; then he continues, "So Jimmy, what kind of relationship have you got with the Robinsons?"

"I've been thinking since you called me. Not that good really, I know them and they know me but if I turned up on their doorstep, I doubt if they'd invite me in. Might be an idea if I met up with Johnny Pettit, he's more friendly and a drinker. I believe he's still living in Liverpool. Perhaps you could get someone from the NW Regional Crime Squad to find out where he's drinking and I could accidentally bump into him. He's definitely on their firm."

"OK Jimmy I'll get on to it as you're on your way up to Liverpool."

"Right then, that it?"

"It is for now Jim."

Superintendent Commerford is sorely tempted to kick in the door in order to see who might be behind it. An exchange of intelligence would be a good thing but he knows that's impossible. Anonymity is crucial to MI5. On his way back down the concrete stairs he wonders, as he always does, why on earth he had to be the one to end up as Rutter's controller. At least now it may be coming to an end.

The Workaholic

There we are, driving north from Brighton. Even though I had decided to put the car job behind me, I've been pressed back to work and I'm at it with a vengeance. There's hardly a mechanical noise as, like a magic carpet, the silver Mercedes floats over miles and miles of tarmac. I used to avoid selling cars in Liverpool, not just because I was too well known, but also because I needed to keep a bolthole free from angry punters and ambitious coppers. This time it's different, Rebecca will be doing the business, besides, given the impossible program ahead of us, excluding whole areas from our attention can't be an option.

Sitting watching her eat at that Midlands motorway services, embarrasses her. I'm teasing her, mimicking her mannerisms and she reddens. I love the cute way she shields her mouth with the back of her hand as she begs me to stop.

"You want to drive for a while?" I say finishing my coffee.

"Can I?" she asks with all the excitement of a mischievous girl.

"Of course, I need a break, I'm tired"

While that's partly true and I am quite tired, it's not the whole reason. She is so incredibly beautiful I want to spend some time just looking at her, and that's a dangerous pastime when you are doing eighty-five along the M6. I half recline my seat and settle on my side, lusting after her smooth olive-skinned legs as that beautiful, tiny bare foot operates the accelerator; gazing along the smooth cream fabric of her skirt to the white silk blouse which shows a hint of those perfect breasts.

"Stop it," she says, reading my mind.

"Stop what?"

"You know exactly what. All we're doing is working together, that's as far as this partnership goes."

"But..."

"But nothing, Tony. In the hotel you were just another victim, too drunk to do anything, that's why I singled you out."

"You know, I really thought we had something going on."

"Well we don't and if you push the issue, I'll leave you to get out of your own shit."

I'm absolutely gutted. She is so beautiful, besides which, what will my friends think if any of this gets out.

"Just one thing though and it's very important to me."

"What's that?"

"When you meet my friends, especially Kenny, don't let them know that we aren't a couple and that you robbed me. They just wouldn't understand."

We spend an hour at a Stoke on Trent Mercedes dealership, gathering vehicle details from their two silver SLs, then on to St Helens where we gather details for two more. Those four identities are just the beginning; still, at least we've made a start. One more dealership in Liverpool city centre provides us with three more identities. It's all good; the first seven ready to go. Two days before the national advert appears in the Auto Trader, so I decide to impress her by booking us into the Adelphi and introducing her to a couple of my friends.

It was early evening, just losing the light when we pulled up at The Adelphi steps. This is a truly historic building, in its day one of the most luxurious hotels in Europe with solid marble walls in most of the bedrooms. I handed the Merc keys to the doorman and we followed the porter to reception.

"What do you think?" I asked, walking into the wide towering marble entrance hall.

"Looks like a giant public toilet."

"Wonderful," I thought, though I didn't say anything, "two hundred pounds a night to sleep in a fucking toilet."

My spirits drop another notch when I try to book us into a double room and she insists on a twin. I mean, did you ever try to screw on twin beds? Even if you push them together and lay the mattresses across both beds, all it takes is a few heated moments, the beds separate and you end up tumbling down the resulting crevasse. No matter what kind of an optimist I might be, the evening isn't exactly filled with the promise of romance.

Following the porter into our room, I catch her smiling for the first time since she declared that our relationship would be purely business. I tip the porter a tenner, order a bottle of champagne and he leaves.

"You like the room then?"

"I do" she replies opening one of the black Japanese lacquer cabinets.

"This is beautiful, do you think it's real? Looks so good against the pink marble."

"I'm sure it's real, this is a special old hotel. When they built and furnished it, they only used the very best. In fact, one of my friends stayed here for a while, bought a passkey from one of the porters and had it away with the antiques from half a dozen vacant rooms."

"Did he get away with it?"

"He did the first few times. He got caught in the end, greed you see, kept coming back for more; used to lower them out of a second floor window on a rope. You're not the only one who can steal from hotels."

"No but I'm good at it Tony, been doing it for a long time and I've only been caught twice."

Her look becomes more serious and somewhat proud as she starts sharing with me her adventures as a 'creeper'. The first bottle's finished so I call room service and order another.

A 'creeper' is someone who is not a guest but enters a hotel to sneak around the landings trying doors with the prime purpose of petty theft, some of which is not so petty. It's easier for a female to gain entrance, since all hotels have bars open to the public, most of which welcome beautiful women, as long as they at least appear to be respectable. Sometimes she'd drift in with groups of prostitutes and simply slip away. As I pour another glass of champagne, she gives me some tips gained out of her ten years' experience.

"The most important thing is that you never use the lift. Always use the back stairs; the security men sit all night watching the lift indicators and it's a dead giveaway if it keeps stopping on odd floors without coming to the ground floor."

I'm intrigued listening to her exploits, especially by the way she creeps past sleeping guests to rifle their pockets and search their luggage.

"Never look at their faces," she says, "or you'll wake them up. Just drift through their room as though you're part of their dreams."

I have to agree when she tells me that times are harder than ever because of modern technology with its surveillance cameras, its computers. Just the same for me. When I first started switching diamond rings, a cubic zirconium was something straight out of a superman comic; if it cut glass it was definitely a real diamond. Now they actually advertise zircs as an alternative to real diamonds. And computers? Well they're the real killers. I used to be able to buy duplicate car keys from any decent hardware store. Now I need a bent key man from a main dealership, or at least a computer genius to re-chip them.

Her eyes are beautiful, I pour her another glass of champagne and suggest that if we at least push the twin beds together we'll be less likely to fall out. Even though she stiffens as she says she won't entertain the idea of such closeness, something, just something in her expression, something in the way she avoids my eyes, makes me believe that if I'm just patient enough, I'll have her and that, when I do, it's going to be the most wonderful experience of my entire life. She closes the bathroom door to get ready for bed. I'm already beneath my blankets waiting for another glimpse of that beautiful olive skin, eyes trained on the bathroom door, but she emerges swathed in a double XL hotel dressing gown. I remember cursing the Adelphi for providing such a passion killer. I lay in the darkness just a couple of feet away from her, longing for a taste of those lips. She mumbles and snores lightly in a very female way, then I'm asleep.

Rutter Gets On The Case

The Bull, a dockland pub situated on the corner of Great Howard Street and Dublin Street in Liverpool, had been closed for several years before Johnny Pettit took it over. Due to his comprehensive criminal record, Pettit didn't even bother applying for a licence. Instead he got his brother in law to front it. To say that John liked a drink would be something of an understatement, and buying his own pub just a few hundred yards away from where he was born, had been a lifelong ambition. Pettit's six-bedroomed luxury house along the coast in Freshfield had almost been forgotten and, since reopening the Bull, he spent most of his week in the flat above. He had been married to Irene since his release from borstal in 1972. Everyone said that it wouldn't last but twenty-five years down the line and they were inseparable. One son was away at university and the other, aged nineteen, was quite happy to babysit their family home with his girlfriend.

It's been a hell of a week for Johnny. There's a great deal to celebrate as earlier today they were paid out in full for the BMK and his share is more than enough to retire on. As soon as he's straightened his cash through the scrapyard and pizza operation, he'll sell both businesses and just relax. It's 11 p.m. and everyone's gone home the bar is empty; he presses a glass against the whisky optic and comes from behind the bar to sit next to Irene.

"You sure you don't want another drink love?"

She shakes her head and smiles as she attaches herself to his arm and snuggles in.

Rutter's headlights illuminate the derelict warehouses as he turns the Audi to park outside the Bull. He steps out on to the dark empty street, slides his arms into his suit jacket and straightens his tie. His red hair and pale, emotionless eyes are visible by the light shining through the pub window; he walks inside.

"This still open?" he asks, being careful not to recognise Pettit too quickly, while glancing over the bar as though looking for the staff.

Johnny Pettit instantly recognises him and smiles.

"It's open for you Mr Rutter." He's delighted now he's got some drinking company.

"Well bloody hell, if it isn't Johnny Pettit. Never thought I'd see you working in a pub. What's it been, ten years?"

John lifts the counter hatch and moves behind the bar, tops his own glass up and selects another.

"I don't work here Jimmy, I own the gaff. What are you drinking?"

Irene Pettit gets up from her seat smiling weakly, resigned to the fact that it will be a few more hours before John finishes drinking.

"I'm off to bed now, love."

John hugs her and kisses her cheek.

"Slip the bolt on before you go up love," he says fondly as he pours Rutter a whisky.

Rutter sips the drink.

"Cheers John. You must be doing well these days, your own pub and all."

"You don't know the half of it Jimmy, I must be the luckiest bastard in Liverpool."

Rutter suppresses a smile; nothing could be easier than this. Never fails to amaze him just how stupid ex-cons can be. He is being given instant trust, by virtue of the fact that he shared a cell with Pettit ten years earlier. Pettit could, very suddenly, become the unluckiest bastard in Liverpool.

Tony

The Adelphi Hotel's Sefton Suite is a monster of a space; it's an exact replica of SS Titanic's first class smoking lounge. With its high ceilings, ornate mahogany panels and massive marble columns, it was always my favourite place to breakfast. Even if I wasn't staying in the hotel, I often walked in for a fry up and no one ever presented me with a bill.

OK, we may have been pressed into service by the McGregor brothers but, now that I'm not being strangled and half stabbed by Billy, he seems far less of a worry. A little distance is a good thing and time is a great healer. A plan is beginning to take shape. I figure that, by the time Rebecca and me have got the required £150 grand, she'll be so impressed by my way of operating, she won't be able to help herself. She said she wanted to learn a few new moves and, by the time she does, she'll be in love. I can feel it. I can see the signs. She's fighting it but, in the end she'll capitulate and, when she does, we'll buy a couple of tickets for Grenada then take the ferry to Moses' gaff in Carriacou.

She glances up, eating nervously, a few crumbs of scrambled egg roll off the back of her fork and she reddens with embarrassment, I never saw anyone this awkward about eating. She puts her knife and fork down and uses a serviette to remove the spilled egg from the tablecloth.

"Leave it," I insist.

"We've paid good money; we're allowed to make a little mess."

She parks her knife and fork on the plate, says she's had all she can eat and goes back to dabbing the tablecloth. I try to take her mind off it.

"Great room for breakfast eh?"

"Too big," she replies, "like a railway station."

"It's meant to be big; it's a replica of the Titanic first class lounge."

"Really?"

"So you're one of the few people who ate breakfast on the Titanic without having to drown."

Even though she survived the Titanic, she still doesn't respond. Maybe she's brooding over our problem with the McGregor brothers.

"Worried about the dimwit brothers? Don't, they're miles away from us. Won't hassle us for a month. And they're busy with a deal that'll make them so much money that our hundred and fifty grand will just seem like small change."

She looks worried. "We are going to get them their cash back aren't we Tony?"

"Definitely" I reply. "Don't worry, we'll do it as long as we're careful not to get lifted"

I'm dying to tell her that I'm ready to bump them again and keep their money. They're bastards, terrifying a helpless little woman over a few quid. If anyone deserves to get turned over, it's the McGregor brothers. I wonder if I'm finding a way to justify parting another couple of mugs from their cash. Either way, they're just a pair of drug dealing morons. They definitely deserve it.

"Come on," I say, "let's get moving. We've got a lot of work to do if you want to get the cash together."

We walk through town towards Fat Andy's chat-line office next to Radio City in Stanley Street. Something of a long-firm specialist and serial bankrupt, Andy's a good friend these days. Decent enough kind of a bloke, even if he does fancy himself as a crook. Kenny always says he's got more front than the Empire State Building, which is something of an exaggeration.

I first met Andy about ten years ago at a party and 'Tweedled' him. You know the old trick with the diamond rings? Tweedle Dee and Tweedle Dum; dumb being the operative word. Andy was the perfect mug, couldn't keep his eyes off that chunk of a diamond sparkling away on my pinkie. Within five minutes I had him trying it on, holding it up to the light. Funny the way they all become gem experts, revelling in the beauty of light reflecting off facets. As it happened, he was celebrating his recent coup on the Liverpool Meat market when, after only a few months of trading as a butcher, he managed to turn them over for a fast eighty grand.

He had to have that ring but wouldn't trust me so, after checking his credibility with Kenny, I helped him along. As soon as Kenny vouched for his honesty, I let him take the ring for a few days, get it valued and make me an offer. Greed always gets the better of them and, if it's not greed, then it's meanness. That ring was worth five grand all day long but all he offered was two. Completely insulted by such a bid in the bollocks, I snatched it back. He didn't even watch my hands as I switched Dee for Dumb. I'm still indignant when he ups the offer to two and a half.

Sensing he's not going to go much higher, I reluctantly accept his final offer of three grand. Just to rub it in, I remember holding each one of his twenties up to the light and asking him whether they were snide. In those days, not even the gold was genuine, just yellow metal with an 18k stamp so, a few weeks later when his pinkie turned green, he realised he'd parted with three grand for fifteen pounds' worth of costume jewellery.

Some time passed before Kenny called, telling me that Fat Andy was threatening murder. There was nothing to do but front him up. I denied it as always, saying that it was definitely the genuine article when I gave it to him and blamed the jeweller. He might not have believed me but what could he say? A few months went by before I met him again up at Kenny's farm and my little deception hardly got a mention. He makes his living knocking people, just like I do. Easy come, easy go, time's a great healer so, after a few whiskies, I owned up and he was decent enough to take it with good grace. He just laughed it off. Since then, we've been mates, sharing stories of our conquests, failures and successes.

Fat Andy's latest project is a telephone chat-line and he's pulling sixty grand a month with a staff of three. It didn't take him long to figure that the revenue from premium rate telephone lines is generated by advertising and therefore, advertising credit is a licence to steal from any publication stupid enough to trust you.

He was disappointed to discover that national newspapers are very careful about vetting credit applications, so he got hold of the yellow pages for each major city in the UK and began placing five hundred pound adverts in every free and every provincial evening newspaper. Call 'Cherry Red Lips, Les Girls,' or 'Dial A Date Dating Agency' and you'll be charged 38 pence a minute for the privilege of listening to long drawn out recorded stories, or interacting with recorded messages which were set up to get you dialling more premium rate numbers in your search for romance. Dial 'Secret Whispers' and you're connected to his two girls who are willing to share their secrets with you, what they're wearing and what they're not. You might even get connected to Andy, who says that a whispering man sounds just like a whispering woman, and he's the last person to refuse revenue.

Now he's set up with a serious full time secretary working eight-hour days, opening accounts and placing adverts in as many publications as possible. She never bothers with all of those Yellow Pages having got hold of a copy of B.R.A.D.

Andy's chat-line operation trades from a couple of rooms in an old sandstone bank headquarters which has been partitioned into small box rooms in lease-free rental units. The sign outside reads, 'Fully serviced offices available'. We walk into the oak panelled hall and approach the receptionist, a smart, efficient thirty-something blonde.

"Can I help you?" she asks smiling politely.

"Yes, my name's Hurley and I need to see Andy."

"Andy? What company is he with?"

"The one that doesn't display its name."

She glances up at the sign, a black and white plastic list of room numbers with company names, more specifically to the two blank spaces next to rooms fourteen and fifteen.

"Ah yes," she replies picking up the phone, "you mean Andy from the telephone company," and into the mouthpiece, "I've got a Mr Hurley in reception. Should I send him up?" He's obviously made some kind of a crack because she's struggling to supress her laughter.

"Do you know where to go?"

Rebecca follows me up the wide stairway on to the third floor. We're here for the use of Andy's yellow pages. Might as well claim an identity for each car in a different city and, if she's about to become the 'Company Secretary disposing of the Managing Director's Mercedes', using a genuine company name each time will add to the authenticity, and that's so very important. If you simply invent company names, you're forever wondering whether they sound genuine enough and that can really rattle your confidence.

We walk in without knocking. Fat Andy gets up from his chair to greet us, shakes my hand and smiles at Rebecca. To be fair, he isn't as fat as his name might suggest. He is large, about six foot and overweight but carries it well, looking like a Viking with that long hair and fiery red beard. The two girls sitting at the worktop built along one side of the office are too busy to even look up; each has two punters on the go, two phones apiece.

"Hi Tony."

"Hello Andy this is Rebecca. Rebecca, Andy."

"My word Tony you've excelled yourself this time. Are you a model dear?"

Rebecca doesn't respond other than to stiffen slightly; she was never amused by such banter. In fact, she found it demeaning. I ask him if we can have the use of his library of Yellow Pages and, as always, he's glad to assist.

"Follow me into Mission Control."

He pushes open the adjoining door. Pat, his secretary says "Hello", gets up from her desk, smiling, and pushes a red pin into Kidderminster on the wall mounted UK map; the red dot instantly lost in the forest of coloured pins which already pepper the country. She offers to make us a coffee, very efficiently takes the order down on her pad and goes out to make it. Andy approaches the map using a pen as a pointer. If it wasn't for the beard and that hair, he could be Winston Churchill pointing at a war map.

"OK ," he says, "I can see you're curious. This is how it works here in Mission Control. Red pins represent 'advert placed awaiting publication'. Green pins represent 'advert up and running'. Yellow pins mean 'Houston, we have a problem, newspaper threatening to pull advert due to lack of faith in our promises to pay bills'. And the saddest colour, black, means 'advert stopped, collections department ready to begin court proceedings'. Good system, eh? All legal and above board."

When Pat returns with the coffee, I take mine and ask, "I hate to be kill-joy Andy but what happens when most of the pins turn black?"

"It's all in hand," he replies enthusiastically. "Got another office in Manchester and I'm about to set up in my wife's maiden name. Think about it Tony, you should've listened when I told you to get one of these going. Sixty grand a month for the past year and it's not over yet. It's a lot of money; it's not too late to open yours. I'm not even half way through B.R.A.D yet."

"Brad?"

"Yeah it's the advertiser's bible, every publication selling advert space is in it. OK this is a serious amount of cash. I'll definitely have to end up bankrupt, that's why I've done it properly, kept books, got a good accountant, ex VAT inspector, says it's your duty to claim the VAT back as soon as you've received the advertising bills, doesn't matter that you haven't paid them."

"Deliberately having the customs and excise over? They'll never let you get away with that."

"Tony, as long as you're not a limited company and all the cheques are made out in your name and paid into your bank, the cash is yours to spend. As soon as someone puts a writ on me I'll just roll over and admit I'm a failed alcoholic businessman with a hopeless gambling problem. There's absolutely nothing they can do about it. No crime committed. Anyway, that's enough about me, what are you up to using the Yellow Pages? I thought you were grafting with the McGregor crew?"

Rebecca chips in. It's as though I've been upstaged and she's coming to my defence, or perhaps she's simply paying him back for the 'model' remark.

"He became self-employed again, met me and we formed a partnership, its new venture."

Andy's gagging to find out more.

"New venture?"

"Yes but that's all I'm prepared to say at the moment, you'll get to know in due course."

"I like her, a bit special isn't she."

"She's very special," I reply flicking through the Guildford Yellow Pages. "One of a kind."

She picks eight company names and I choose another seven; before we leave he mentions that he's been invited to a celebration at Kenny's farm and wonders if I'll be there. I tell him that we'll both be there, thank him for the help and leave.

"What an overblown ego," she says as we step out into bright sunlight on the street.

"Yeah he's full of shit at times but he's a nice enough bloke, doesn't hold grudges and always willing to share. Besides, he's right you know, if I'd teamed up with him when I got out, you and I wouldn't be in this mess."

"That's true", she says.

"If I got a chance to step back into the past though and do things differently, I wouldn't bother."

"Now I know you're mad," she replies.

"I really wouldn't," I continue, "because it'd mean that we would never have met and, like Andy said, you are bit special."

She never reacted to that remark straight away but later, when we were driving out of town headed for the Dave's place on the Kirkby Industrial Estate, she reminded me.

"We're partners in crime Tony and that's all we'll ever be."

She didn't look as though she meant it, so I didn't believe her.

The Kirkby industrial estate on the outskirts of Liverpool was built in the Second World War as a munitions factory. Rusted, overgrown rail tracks run to forgotten bunkers, these days no more than grassy hills on the landscape at the rear of the estate. Later, manufacturing premises built in the boom years were a collection of large, heavy industrial factories, some just abandoned when bust followed boom and others demolished. These days it is a collection of yards with one or two office buildings fronting them. Car repair garages, spray shops, scrap yards and pallet yards.

When Danvir Shankar moved into the yard on Hammonds Road, he moved in with a plan for a different kind of enterprise. 'Dave', as he is known to his British friends, has been copying and wholesaling designer clothing since the early eighties. In the beginning, producing such goods wasn't even considered criminal. He ran his Manchester factory, openly employing thirty women full time, printing copies and replacing tee shirt neck labels. In 1991, his silkscreen print carousels were replaced by robot embroidery machines and business boomed, producing perfect copies, even down to the swing tickets and packaging. He was supplying a national network of distributors and making inroads into France and The Netherlands, when the police arrived to close him down.

He considered an early retirement but the phone wouldn't stop ringing with orders, so he flew to China. These days, if you buy one of Dave's copies, there's a fifty per cent chance that it was made by the same employees working in the same factories that produced the genuine article, the only difference being the fact that the copyright holder receives none of the revenue. Nothing could be easier than sub-contracting the work and his lines grew in number to include watches, handbags and very smart suits. The riskiest part of Dave's operation is receiving each container of contraband without having it confiscated by customs and ending up arrested.

It's about midday when we pull up outside his new place. The sign above the gate reads, 'Dave Shankley's Secure Storage Facility. Rates From £10 a Week'. The place definitely looks secure, being enclosed behind a ten-foot fence topped with coils of razor wire, exactly like a prison fence. I press the button to introduce myself over the intercom, then the gates slide apart and we drive straight in. Dave's smiling when he comes out to meet us, I don't think I ever saw him look miserable. It's infectious, even Rebecca looks happy when I introduce her.

There are two long rows of forty-foot shipping containers and two more of twenty footers laid in neat lines running down the yard away from the main building. We follow him inside. This building was once a welding shop but now it's partitioned into dozens of small wire mesh security cages. In the corner, there are two Portakabin offices and, everywhere I look, surveillance cameras. This is the first time I ever saw a set up like this and can't help wondering if anyone would pay to rent such tiny cages or old shipping containers. It's definitely the first of its kind in Liverpool. I always saw Dave as kind of cool; an Indian with his own Guru, reminds me of a younger, darker Omar Sharif. I don't know exactly what his religion is; I was never rude enough to ask but there was always serenity to him a kind of contented peacefulness. He offers us a seat and settles into his leather swivel chair behind a massive, shiny desk. When he casts an enquiring glance in Rebecca's direction, I quickly let him know she's OK and that it's safe to talk.

"I thought you might have turned up sooner Tony, I've been open for a couple of months."

"Sorry Dave, I've been running around like a headless chicken since I got out. Still getting sorted. I just teamed up with Rebecca here on a little venture."

"Anything I can help you with?"

"There is, if you can you still get those photo driving licences?"

"Yes I can but you know, there's work involved and they're a hundred and fifty a piece, not cheap."

"How about if I wanted fifteen."

"Still the same amount of work. Fifteen photos to take so they'd still be a hundred and fifty and there wouldn't be much left in that for me."

"Even with fifteen identical photos?"

"You are on a 'little venture' aren't you Tony? A grand would cover it, that's just sixty-six pounds sixty-six pence apiece, less than half price."

"Great, how are we fixed for credit?"

Dave smiles. "Do I look as though I just rode out of The Bengal on an elephant?"

It's embarrassing begging in front of Rebecca but what else can I do?

"Come on Dave, help us out we're in trouble here, give us a break."

There's a long silence as he sits deep in thought with his eyes closed, then, "Here's the deal. We make the fifteen today, I show them to you and, if you're happy with the final product, I'll let you take the first one to get you working. Then, as soon as you've used it on your 'little venture', you'll come back, collect the rest and let me have the full payment."

I get out of my seat to shake his hand then so does Rebecca.

"Dave, you're a star mate; I knew we could count on you."

He picks up the phone, dials and has a short conversation in what I think is Urdu or Bengali, then hangs up, telling us that we'll have to stick around for a little while. Soon after which the intercom buzzes and we hear a man speaking that same language. Dave glances at the gate monitor and presses the opening switch saying, "Here he is, the Lord Snowden of driving licence photos. Have you got the details?"

Rebecca passes him her list of chosen names, birthdays and addresses then fishes a hairbrush and some make up out of her shoulder bag. Her short black hair looks perfect to me but you know what women are like and she disappears into the ladies room. Lord Snowden comes into the Portakabin, shakes Dave's hand and they converse in their own language. Snowden's eyebrows rise slightly and he gives me a curious look; I guess that must be at the part of their conversation when Dave tells him we need fifteen with the same photo, which is something of an odd requirement. Rebecca comes out of the ladies looking exactly as beautiful as she did when she went in, which is very beautiful, and Dave gets her to stand close to the white wall. Bailey takes no more than a minute to shoot a few facial shots with his digital camera then says something to Dave and leaves. Dave apologises for his friend's apparent bad manners by explaining that he can't speak any English, and goes on to tell us that he'll be back with our licences in about an hour.

"In the meantime," he says, "I might have a few other odds and ends you'll be interested in."

We follow him out into the bright sunlight of the yard and along to the closest forty-foot container. He opens up, steps in and flicks the light on. It takes a moment for our eyes to adjust, then we see that the whole thing is racked out with rails, carrying thousands of men's and women's designer suits each in its own suit carrier.

"Women's on this side," he says pointing to the left, "Versace suits and Christian Dior dresses." Then, pointing right, "Men's over here, Armani, Hugo Boss and the rest. They stand me eighty apiece across the board. Yours for just a hundred."

He steps back into the sunlight and talks, walking away. "Take as long as you want I'll be in the office when you're ready."

I've always liked a suit, in fact there's a couple of dozen of mine hanging in Kenny's wardrobe. He was kind enough to rescue them from my flat last time I was arrested, so I only picked one from Dave's selection. The grey pinstripe Hugo Boss was an almost perfect fit; trousers too long but only slightly. She's so shy she sent me out of the container while she was having a try on, even insisted that I stood guarding the door.

My new suit in its carrier gets heavier by the minute so, after changing hands a few times, I end up hooking it on the wire fence. What seems like an eternity passes before I finally hear her little tap tapping on the container door and she steps out dressed in a dark business suit.

"What do you think?" she asks twirling to give me the full three sixty.

"Perfect company secretary." I reply, then, glancing down at her bare legs, "You're going to need some stockings."

"Tights," she replies curtly, never missing the chance to find innuendo when none was intended, well there may have been a little but, hey, I'm not a monk.

An hour later, we're finally on the road driving to North Wales for Kenny's party with the first of fifteen perfect driving licences, one Hugo Boss suit and three assorted ladies' outfits. That shopping trip really wore me down so I let her drive, I think she likes driving it always brings a smile to her face.

"Seems like a nice bloke that Dave", she says in her slight South London accent.

"Yeah, he's a good one.'"

"Taking a risk giving you credit."

"I've known him for years Becky, I'd never knock him; just like Kenny."

She looks unconvinced, "But you could if you wanted."

"There's a golden rule Becky and this is it; there are sixty three million potential mugs in the UK. You're allowed to let a few off. If you don't, you'll end up having a very lonely existence."

Driving through Liverpool City centre, we get caught in the rush hour traffic. Sitting waiting at the Mersey Tunnel Toll she gives me a very sheepish look and says:

"I know that I'm always having a go at you over things and well, I know you're a nice guy really but, do you mind if I tell you about something that's been bothering me?"

"No, fire away."

Perhaps this is the start of a relationship; I've just been upgraded to 'nice guy'. Maybe she's about to tell me she doesn't like my aftershave, in which case I'll just ask her what kind she likes and buy a bottle.

"It's that name, Becky. I hate it when people call me that. Someone else used to call me that a long time ago."

There's look of pure hatred in her eyes as she stares through the windscreen, so powerful that she's almost crying in frustration.

"No, no problem, sorry, from now on it's Rebecca."

By the time we're driving out to the other side of the river, she seems to have let go of whatever sad memory had upset her and she's busily pressing buttons, channel hopping on the radio as she's driving, past the urban sprawl of Birkenhead into the green Welsh countryside. Over the radio comes a Leonard Cohen song about some drunk in a midnight choir. Curiosity gets the better of me and I just have to ask, "Who?"

She gives me a blank look.

"Who?"

"Who used to call you that name?"

"Oh that. I might tell you one day, just forget it for now."

That really gives me a boost. The fact that she said she might tell me "one day" is a clear indication that she sees some kind of long-term future. At that point I'm certain that she's growing to like me far more than she intended.

The Major

Patterson spent last night in Liverpool observing Rutter, he watched him enter The Bull, then silently stepped out of his Range Rover and stood a few metres along from the pub in Dublin Street, from where he could hear the bolt shooting on the bar door and see a light being turned on upstairs. Moving silently, he walked around the corner of the pub to its front on Great Howard Street.

Fortunately, this is a dead part of Liverpool and the street was deserted; all perfectly still apart from a newspaper drifting, scraping along the pavement, lifting on the breeze. The large brown VentAir window fan blades had been frozen in time since the motor burned out twenty years earlier.

Leaning on the wall close to the window, Patterson strained but managed to hear every word of Pettit's slurring confidences to Rutter as they drifted through the stationary fan. A freely offered, ego fuelled, blow by blow description of the BMK robbery, the culprits, the barrel reconditioning yard, everything except the name of whoever commissioned the job and where the chemicals finally ended up. Uncomfortable with his own decision to let Rutter run on for a little longer, he drove off and booked into a hotel for the night.

This morning he got up at five sharp, showered, breakfasted and drove to the ICI plant where he intended to validate Pettit's indiscretions. First, he walked the outer perimeter of the security fence; the ground beneath the grass had been dry for some time and was hard. Eventually he came to a place where remnants of tyre tracks were still faintly visible on the grass. Walking around to the gate the thieves used for their exit, he counted the fence posts, then entered the plant and navigated his way to the same position within the fence. From there, he combed his way back through a minefield of hissing, stinking pipes towards the security post. He realised that maintenance of such a plant would be an on-going and intense operation so, seeing a couple of ladders lying on the ground was no surprise. However, when he went behind one of the large vessels, he discovered a ladder with hooks on the top and the ladder just happened to be the same height as the fence.

"So Pettit was telling the truth," he thought, "but why hadn't the police noticed the ladder?" They wouldn't really, not when it's one of so many, and that thought led him to the barrel recycling yard next to the river.

Now, sitting next to the yard looking through the fence at the thousands of barrels, he's certain that every word Pettit said is the truth. His thoughts focus on the creature at the end of his string, Rutter, that treacherous wholly despicable, murderous excuse for a human being. Inside the Range Rover glove box there's a GPS tracker and, covertly installed on Rutter's Audi, is a live transponder. He opens the glove box and pings the car, to be surprised by the fact that the Audi still hasn't moved, having been parked outside the Bull all of last night and today.

Had Patterson lingered outside that window for just a few moments longer, he would have heard about the party at Kenny Robinsons and things might not have turned out quite so badly for Rebecca; as it is, the puppet, albeit temporarily, has slipped free from its strings.

The Celebration

It is early evening when Kenny Robinson settles into his big old leather armchair. He's just finishing his mug of tea when the phone rings.

Janice picks up in the kitchen and shouts, "It's Tony for you Kenny."

He picks up the phone.

"How's it going Tony?"

"Not bad, I've got details."

"Good, where are you?"

"I'm in that garage just down the road from you."

"Well then why don't you come up early, you know we're having that party tonight, celebrating our Wayne's bit of luck. You'll have to stay the night; it'll be a good do."

"I'm not alone though Ken, I've got a friend with me."

"What's her name?"

"How do you know it's a she?"

"Usually is, isn't it? Don't worry, you can bed down in one of the caravans. Rattle the bed as loud as you like out there."

"OK, Ken. See you in about ten minutes."

Kenny's grandson crawls across the floor and begins tugging at his ankle. He lays the phone back on the receiver, reaches down and lifts the infant on to his knees. The sweet sickly baby smell strips away the years. The boy looks exactly like his father and, for just a moment, he could be bouncing Wayne on his knees. He wonders where all that time went. The world's so different these days, how can a few barrels of oil be worth half a million pounds? But they are; still, now that Wayne's all set with enough money, Kenny's fatherly duties are over. He'll be able to sell the farm and move to the Algarve with Janice. They've been looking at a place on a sandy delta just outside Almeria; fifteen acres, an eight-roomed farmhouse with a few outbuildings, the perfect place to retire in the sun.

Hearing a car coming up the lane, he looks up at the wall mounted security monitor. Tony's silver Mercedes coming into view brings a smile. He's got a lot of time for

The Bumper, such a hopeless case, always in a mess over one woman or another, always avoiding one victim or running away from his own comeuppance. In his time The Bumper must have had millions through his hands but, no matter how often Kenny tried to get him to hang on to some of the proceeds, he always ends up broke. "That's your trouble" Kenny often tells him, "money just doesn't stick to you, it flies away." He gets up and imprisons his grandson safely in the playpen before going out into the yard.

Lifting the latch on the heavy five-bar yard gate, he gets his first glimpse of Rebecca sitting in the passenger seat. 'Nice' he thinks, pulling the gate open to let the Mercedes through, 'very nice'.

Tony

Kenny's pack of Ridgebacks milling around us unnerves Rebecca, their wet noses sniffing and nudging our legs as we follow Kenny towards the kitchen door. She looks genuinely scared and grabs my arm so tightly it hurts.

"Please tell me they don't bite," she pleads.

Kenny puts his arm around her with more than a little mischief in his eyes.

"They do but they won't bite you love," then loudly at the pack, "because they only bite coppers!"

The dogs become more animated and growl. Then Kenny primes them further and even more loudly. "Don't you lads, Coppers, you bite them Coppers!" At which the pack of dogs go berserk, racing away from us towards the gates, growling and barking, looking for anything in a blue uniform to attack. Janice swoops in, rescuing Rebecca.

"Stop it Kenny, you're terrifying the girl. Come here love, take no notice."

Rebecca looks awkwardly in my direction but I offer a quick introduction and abandon her to Janice's recipes, remedies and gossip.

I always loved that main room in Kenny's house. You need to duck beneath the rough oak beams, all of which are loaded with ornaments antiques and souvenirs. The stuffed fox, the badger and the police helmets, there's a story attached to each object. I take a seat opposite Kenny in front of the crackling, hissing log fire. His intense blue eyes give me one of those all-knowing looks which never fail to disarm me.

"This Rebecca, is she the one that ripped you off in Brighton?"

I clam up. How could he possibly know what she's done to me? Until he continues "Wayne said Joey McGregor told him you'd given them the rip and she gave it to you. What were you thinking of turning those two crazy bastards over?"

"I was off to the Spice islands. Just didn't work out that way."

"You mean when she turned you over?"

"No Ken, she was just looking after the money until a copper stole it."

"Yeah, if you say so Tony, she's certainly pretty enough to catch a man with his pants down."

I change the subject by handing him the details for the car identities and follow him into his office next to the bedroom. As we chat, he types the details into his computer, engine numbers, registration numbers and chassis serial numbers. He looks over the screen at me.

"You want me to keep first date of registration the same on all of them?"

"No, make them random; got to keep all the docs as different as possible, they're all registered in different areas. The less chance of being linked, the better."

"Got the new Windows 95, Tony, it's a great program, you can do anything with it. You should get one, that's where the future lies son; information technology."

Don't know how Kenny got to be this clever with his computers, but he is. He reads though the details, loads the blank logbooks into the printer, moves his cursor over the print button and presses enter.

"Amazing these modern printers too," he says and I'm impressed as the perfect logbooks pile into the document tray. He pulls up the tax disc file, types twelve registration numbers, twelve dates then selects 'Print' and two A4 sheets of tax discs land on top of the logbooks.

"You want to pay me now or later?" he asks, then agrees to defer payment until we've had our first couple of sales.

"Come on, I'll show you around the caravan, you can put your luggage in while we're at it. How long will you be staying?"

"Just tonight, we need to get busy."

Going to the yard, we pass through the kitchen. Rebecca looks perfectly at ease now, sitting at the long oak table peeling potatoes. The air in the kitchen is uncomfortably warm; a few silver strands have escaped from Janice's bun and are clinging to the side of her round red face. She blows sideways, trying to dislodge them and smiles up at us from her position crouching in front of the open Aga door where she is basting a massive leg of pork.

Geographically close to Liverpool, within a few hours' drive from Manchester and Birmingham, the North Wales coast has dozens of caravan sites. Thousands of static caravans, too large to tow, become impossible to sell when they are being replaced by newer units. Kenny has deals with several sites to shift their redundant caravans free of charge. If the caravan is too rough for re-use, he gets his lads to quickly chop them down for scrap. If they are still useable, which most are, he plants them on the top field and struggles trying to knock them out. Sales aren't very frequent, so the number steadily grows until the field is completely full and he's forced to have a cull.

Walking through the gate into the field, I'm pulled up by the sheer number laid out in front of me.

"You do like a caravan don't you Ken?"

"Yeah, pity no-one else does, they're a bastard to sell. Be a shame to give this lot the chop."

He connects a blue outdoor 240-volt lead to the socket on a large pale green caravan and we go inside. The florescent lights flicker to life, disclosing someone's perfect home from home. Beautifully crafted teak furniture with spotless upholstery, the white sheets on the double bed turned down.

"When you said you'd be coming I got the dragon to change the bedding."

"You got this for nothing? Free?"

"Yes"

"You've got your own little caravan site here. Why not rent them?"

"Strangers are the last thing we want here Tony."

"Yeah suppose you're right."

"Put this in earlier," he says, opening the drinks cabinet, taking out two glasses and a bottle of Jameson's Irish Whiskey.

We spend an hour sharing stories of times passed, successful scams, old friends and the times we nearly stole enough. Halfway through the bottle, he gives me another one of those sideways looks of his and says, "She did bump you, didn't she?"

I'm truly embarrassed but I'm also a realist and, when there are no excuses, when you can't invent a believable lie, the only thing left is the truth, so I just admit to my own stupidity. He might be my best friend but he's an awful piss taker.

"A hundred and fifty grand," he wheezes, laughing so loudly he almost chokes.

"That's got to be the most expensive fuck in the world."

Perhaps it's the way I can't look him in the face and don't come back with a wisecrack of my own, but he gets straight on to it.

"You haven't, have you? Haven't even given her one. Jesus Christ, kid!"

That's the trouble with close friends; if they know you too well, they can almost read your mind. Finally, he stops laughing and shows a little sympathy.

"Jesus what a fuckin' mess kid, you back on the car job? You're not going to get away with that."

"Not me Kenny; her, I'm just going to do the snatching."

"So," he says after another sip of whisky, "if she's lucky enough to get away with that many bumps, you're

118

just going to hand them back their hundred and fifty grand?"

"Haven't decided yet."

This really gets him laughing again. "That'll be a first, someone getting their money back out of you."

"Just promise me one thing, eh Kenny, don't talk about this to your Wayne. Just say she was minding it when that copper nicked it. I'll say the McGregors are lying."

"Your secret's safe with me, kid."

When the bottle was finished, we stepped out of the caravan on to the dew-soaked grass, barely sober enough to get the number plates sorted. Kenny wasn't enthusiastic about the prospect of more work but agreed it was best to get it done.

Walking down the path towards the rough stone workshop, I pause for a moment to take a deep breath of the clean country air. We've spent the last half hour discussing the way that the authorities seem to be on a mission to make it impossible for a man to earn a crust. It's as though all the money in the world is like a liquid contained in giant government vessels. They'll let you lick up a few drips by working for peanuts, as long as they manage to extract their tax but, as soon as you drill any holes and start to milk it, giant fingers come down to plug the holes.

When I ran my first motor job, you could buy a set of plates in any car shop or garage, no questions asked. Logbooks were simple green documents filled out by hand and authenticated with a post office stamp. Those stamps were so easy to make and no one ever scrutinised the paperwork when you sold the car. In fact, if you bought a stolen car in good faith and could show the advert you answered, you got to keep the car and the insurance company paid the punter.

On the first of November last year, the giant's big fingers landed to crank the screw down even tighter by licencing all the number plate suppliers. Since then, it has been an offence to supply number plates without such a licence and it is impossible to obtain your new plates without proof of your identity and the car's logbook; just to add insult to injury, every purchase is recorded and passed to the DVLA. Fortunately for me, Kenny saw it coming well in advance and bought a whole number plate lamination system, so it's no problem to make our own. He's holding enough stock to create a few thousand new plates, though I imagine that, eventually, those big fingers will land again to alter the actual format, then we'll all be stuffed.

The most important thing you need to remember, when switching number plates, is very simple; you need to drill the holes for the securing screws in exactly the same place as the original number plates. All plates are fitted by the dealer rather than the manufacturer. They simply zip a drill through the plate into the body and wind in a screw, then repeat the process on the other side. It's a haphazard way of doing it, the holes in the body seldom get drilled in exactly the same place and you don't want to end up with the car nosed into some farmer's gate on a busy main road, wishing you had a drill with you to make a fresh hole.

I left Kenny and went down to the Mercedes. It's impossible to keep the crease in your trousers while kneeling, so I took the kick mat out and stood on it to take them off, then folded them neatly and laid them on the back seat. Working quickly, keen not to be caught in my shorts by the headlights of any arriving guests, I got the number plates off in record time, slipped back into my trousers and rushed back up to the workshop.

Walking back through the doorway, I see that Kenny is well on with the job. Plates are beginning to stack up on the workbench next to him.

"How are we fixed for screws?" I ask, showing him one. I already know where he keeps his selection of self-tappers; I'm just being polite getting his permission to go rooting. The workshop is neat and very well organised, next to the wall on which hangs a full set of Snap On spanners, a storage cabinet with dozens of drawers containing bolts, nuts, washers and screws; on the end of each drawer, a life-size illustration of its contents. I pocket half a dozen of the same size and the next size up; car bodies are thin metal and you can never tell when the hole's about to strip. Kenny has already loaded the pillar drill with the first five number plates, he places one of my original plates on top then closes the vice clamping them all into position.

"Jesus I could do with another drink," I say gripping the end of the stack tightly to be certain the plates don't slip then, as the drill winds through our template into the new plastic.

"Did you read the headline about that lunatic who escaped from the asylum and raped the woman in that laundrette?"

"Yeah," he replies dryly, while drilling the other screw hole, "Nut Screws Washer and Bolts. It's older than me that one, Tony. Now fucking concentrate, they'll all be arriving soon and I'm not doing this twice."

Always gets serious when he's doing something like this, fancies himself as a bit of a craftsman.

Before attaching the set of number plates to the Mercedes and sticking a new tax disc in the windscreen, Kenny let me change into one of his overalls. He's six foot four and I'm eight inches shorter, so I guess I must look a proper idiot, like a kid trying on his father's clothes. I've only just finished doing the plates and tax disk, having been constantly hampered by the long sleeves, when the yard is suddenly lit by headlights at the gate. Being loaded with fifteen sets of plates and the paperwork makes the holdall heavy as I hoist it into the boot. Thankfully no one sees me rushing back to the workshop to get changed. Obviously I don't want to get seen looking like this, but neither do I want everyone in the world to know I'm back on the car job, and the sight of me holding a screwdriver anywhere close to a number plate would definitely be something of a clue. Wayne, Billy Jones, Ronny Hill, Billy Longhair and Sid the Chink, all highly trusted friends, but you can never tell with the wives. Women's honour is far shakier than men's. If one of them, for instance, fancied me and became jealous of Rebecca, anything might happen. About a quarter of the guys I met in prison had been thrown in by their women, so why tempt fate?

The dogs arrive at the gate just before Kenny and, from the workshop, I hear him treating Ronny Hill's wife to the dogs and coppers routine.

The silk lining in my trousers slides cold against my skin as I pull them up and fasten the belt. I pull my jacket on, straighten my tie, then kill the workshop lights and stand waiting in the doorway. Just a moment goes by before the pack of Ridgebacks runs howling towards another pair of headlights at the gate with Kenny close behind. In the interests of survival, I call out to him but it's only Wayne, and the dogs calm after greeting him.

More guests arrive, mostly couples who greet each other in the main room then, one by one, the females peel off into the kitchen leaving an ever-increasing arc of men, some sitting, some standing, all drinking around the fire. I slip back from the crowd and plant myself on Kenny's old armchair, sipping a whisky, watching the news. It's another report about The Home Secretary promising to employ MI5 in the prosecution of serious criminals.

"Now that's a very large bunch of fingers to come down plugging holes", I think. Then, distracted by loud laughter, I look across at the crowd to see Kenny has just entered the room wearing a police helmet.

"You're all fucking nicked," he says, doing his best impression of that flat emotionless police way of speaking. Wayne comes over and sits next to me, I wish I still had a head of hair like that, not that I ever did, not that blond. I almost resent him for looking the way he does, same blue eyes as his dad, but you can't resent someone you've known so long. I suppose Kenny and his kin are the closest thing to family I ever had, though I'd never let on to them about that. Grinning, he opens a bag of Charlie to show me the contents; it looks like a bag of sherbet I might've bought him years earlier. Then he wipes the glass topped coffee table with one of his mother's tea towels and pours about 20 grams out, quite a lump, talking as he chops it into rough lines with a playing card.

"A bit dumb Tony, bumping the Ugly Brothers."

"They'll get over it."

"Yeah but you mightn't. Did they do that to your face?"

"It's only a scratch", I reply running my fingers over it. "Nothing."

He bends down to the table, hoovers a line, straightens up and sniffs loudly, brushing a nostril with the back of his hand.

"It's a good one Tony." That sudden over-confidence is on his face, his blue eyes glittering.

"No not now thanks, I'm on the whisky, maybe later."

Don't get me wrong, I've got nothing against cocaine, in fact I do have a very occasional go at it but the last thing I need to do right now is feel as though I'm cleverer than I really am. Things have gone badly wrong, I need to get working and make some very serious decisions.

Then Wayne does something completely out of character. He puts his hand on my shoulder pulls me close and stares straight into my eyes.

"I've told those two bastards, whatever they do to you, they're going to get straight back off us, guns, knives, whatever; hurt you and we'll pay them back."

He releases my shoulder and takes another dive into the sherbet.

"What did they say about that?" I ask as he vacuums enthusiastically.

"Joey's a total bread head, doesn't want anything to fuck up the few million they're about to make out of that BMK; Billy's the one to worry about."

"I didn't want to drag you into this, it's my mess and I'll sort it out."

Wayne straightens up grinning.

"Sure you don't want a go at this," then, gesturing towards the group around the fire, "before the vultures land?"

I decline his offer, pouring myself another whiskey.

While it's definitely true that I would never wish to involve him in any of my disasters, his promise of retaliation might just get me out of this mess. He's right about Joey, like all non-addicted drug dealers, the prick is an absolute bread head. Being faced with Wayne's threat might just convince him to wipe his face and get on with the business of collecting his millions. That's the way it usually works with his kind and, the more time that passes, the less they feel insulted over being bumped. They can promise to kill you a thousand times but, in my experience so far, their promises fade to nothing, being overtaken by the desire to grab more and more money, nothing else matters to them. The unlucky thing for me is the fact that they caught up with me too soon while their anger was still fresh. The less violent types sometimes promise to put a contract out on you but eventually, they decide not to throw good money after bad and just get over it.

Even if the McGregor brothers do decide to use an out of town contractor, Wayne's crew will know where it came from and world war three will begin. I figure that my future depends on one thing and one thing only, Joey's ability to keep the reins on The Piltdown Man, that amoeba-brained brother of his. Wayne glances up at the security monitor; a seven series BMW lit up in the gate lights.

"The Pettits are at the gate," he announces loudly as he gets up to let them into the yard and, since it's just

Wayne opening the gate, the Pettits with their guest miss out on the dogs and coppers routine.

A very drunk looking Pettit gets out of the front passenger side and opens a rear door to let Irene out, then Rutter smiles at Wayne over the car as he shuts the driver's door. John Pettit notices Wayne's discomfort on seeing Rutter.

"He's cool, don't worry."

"Hope you've squared it with my dad?"

"No need to Wayne, this is Jimmy Rutter, we go back a long way, I'm sure your dad knows him too."

Listening to John's slurred words multiplies Wayne's discomfort. It's very disrespectful to turn up at someone's party when you're already drunk and it's the height of cheek to invite someone to the farm without consulting Kenny; even he wouldn't dare to do that. He opens the kitchen door, filled with dread, and follows them inside.

A moment after Wayne left the room, Billy Jones and Sid the Chink swooped down on the coffee table. Now they're both on their hands and knees, having turned from vultures into pigs around a trough; they both look up at the door as Johnny Pettit and Irene walk in, Sid's black moustache now dusted white. A light almost cheer of greeting from all of the men, handshaking, even Kenny pats Johnny Pettit's back, so what if he has turned up drunk? He's had it bang off with that BMK, got a right to celebrate. Jan's smiling face pops through the doorway inviting Irene into the kitchen, then Rutter walks in and a black cloud of silence descends on the room. For just a moment I can hear the antique cuckoo clock ticking against a background of the crackling log fire. Drunk or not, Pettit suddenly realises that bringing a stranger to this gathering is definitely a big mistake. His uncertain, faltering voice breaks the silence.

"This is Jimmy Rutter, we did a bit in in The Scrubs together. We shared a pad. He's sound. Sorry I didn't mention he was coming. I think you two know each other don't you?"

Rutter is calm, his thin lips smiling as he leans forward to offer Kenny a hand.

"Yeah you remember me Kenny we met in Long Larton. I think you were doing a five weren't you?"

Kenny shakes his hand saying. "I remember; didn't you get shanghaied for thumping a couple of screws?"

"Correct, I was in for a lorry full of Benson and Hedges; I was totally fitted up, ended up walking at my appeal."

If only Kenny had just booted the two of them out there and then. Pettit was definitely taking the piss. He probably would have called Kenny the day after and apologised, then the future would've panned out differently for Rebecca, but things like that are easy to say with the benefit of hindsight. In reality none of us could have guessed what was about to unfold. I've known Kenny for a long time and, even though he's good at disguising his feelings, I could tell that he was unhappy about the situation. Even me, it was nothing I could put my finger on but just something about Rutter was wrong, terribly wrong.

When the women return to the room, Rebecca hands me a plate of food and perches next to me on the arm of the chair, so close I can feel the warmth of her body and smell her musky perfume. She's been having a great time out there with the other girls. She likes Jan, loves her elderberry wine, likes the other girls and loves the farm;

even the dogs, now that she's been stroking them and experienced their affection. There's a sweet girlish innocence about her one second, and a smouldering sexuality the next.

"Jan's been telling us about her new place in Portugal," she says as though she and Jan have been lifelong friends. "Pine trees next to a river flowing out over a sandy beach, looks beautiful, got its own well for fresh water have you seen the photos?"

"No not yet, but Kenny said I'd be welcome to stay over there any time I wanted. If I do go you'll be welcome to tag along, I mean when our trouble's over."

She turns away as though avoiding the subject.

"What do you think?" I prompt and she replies "Maybe."

Before I can build on the possibility of her "maybe," Kenny calls me into the office next to their bedroom. Wayne and Pettit are with him and Pettit seems to have sobered up. All of Kenny's good humour has evaporated.

"So" he asks Pettit, "when did the prick turn up?"

Pettit goes on the defensive.

"You've got him wrong he's an old mate, straight as they come."

"I asked you when the prick turned up."

"Last night."

"And that was the first time you saw him in ten years?"

"Yeah."

"This whole thing fucking stinks. You heard about Fat Tommy's crew getting busted over in Manchester didn't you? No? Well I'll tell you all about it; when they got nicked, Rutter was there but managed to disappear with the cash. Fat Tommy was lucky enough to slip through a side door and get off on his toes. Phoned me up and told me the whole story, said this blast from the past Rutter prick had just turned up, bent himself on to their firm and, the next thing, the whole crew are in fucking handcuffs, a few days after which Fat Tommy turned up dead."

Starting to realise what an awful mistake he's made, Johnny Pettit begins backing up.

"Well if you're right, what the fuck are we going to do?"

Wayne interrupts. "That depends what you've said to him. Have you told him anything John?"

Johnny Pettit looks down at the floor as he replies. "Yes."

Kenny is disgusted and takes a deep breath. "So", he says very calmly, "has he talked to anyone else since you told him?"

Pettit shakes his head as he answers.

"No we were drinking all night, then again today; he hasn't been out of my sight."

Wayne almost gives in to his desire to thump him.

"You're a fucking piss head Pettit" but Kenny remains calm.

"Keep a lid on it Wayne, arguing amongst ourselves isn't going to get us out of this shit. First thing we need to do is find out how much they already know. Then we can decide what we're going to do. At least if they have sent this prick, it means they don't have any evidence. Here's what we'll do, we'll give him a smoke of that Dutch stuff, that'll open him up."

A few months earlier, it was just after I got out of Walton, one of Kenny's friends came over from

Amsterdam trying to sell a new kind of weed. It was a genetically engineered kind of skunk but I guess they'd overdone it somewhere along the line because it was way too heavy, one smoke could floor a charging rhino. The fact that it was miles too strong made it impossible to sell. Wayne builds four joints, three with just tobacco, one with the head banging gear, and we join Rutter who is still sitting by the fire. No one is talking about anything recent, even Sid's caught on to the fact that something about Rutter stinks.

Rutter inhales his first lung full of the mad scientist's product and wheezes. Kenny takes a long draw of tobacco and copies his wheeze.

"Good smoke, eh Jimmy?"

Rutter agrees and draws more fumes down. Wayne relaxes his face muscles and manages to look mildly stoned. Pettit's far too worried to contribute, he might be part of this charade, but all he can do is sit staring into the orange glare of flames leaping up the chimney. I remain silent, watching, sipping my whisky, listening. You can tell by the uneven tone in Rutter's voice that the weed has almost done its job.

"You're right about this," he says, "pure cat's piss though, stinks. Smells more like a whiz factory."

He takes another deep draw on the joint, then studies Wayne through glazed eyes for a moment before continuing, "Didn't put any of that BMK in these joints did you Wayne?"

Wayne shares a moment's eye contact with his father; they are both mildly appalled but not altogether surprised by Rutter's remark. That over engineered smoke is performing perfectly; Rutter's as helpless as a cold war spy with a head full of Pentothal. They drop their act and Kenny begins the gentle inquisition.

"In a way it must like being a copper Jimmy."

"Yeah, none of the bullshit and all the benefits."

The joint drops from his fingers on to the stone paved floor; he doesn't even feel it go. Kenny's words are just part of some beautiful safe dream. He's barely audible as begins to ramble.

"Money in the bank every month, they never miss."

"When did it all begin Jimmy?"

Rutter feels as though Kenny's words are his own, some self-inquiring thought, created by his dreaming mind and, as he replies, he feels as though his own words are safely contained within his head, just part of that same beautiful echoing dream.

"Ten years ago, when I walked at that appeal; bang to rights really, that was the deal, I said I'd turn, it was all sorted.

He reaches down and lifts the joint from the floor and takes another draw without realising that it's no longer alight. He wheezes a little, then his quiet whispering eureka moment escapes; we all manage to hear his words.

That's it yeah, that's why Pettit wouldn't tell me who they robbed it for, they're cooking it for themselves".

His eyes close for a moment, when they open, he looks at me first then, one by one, he looks at all of our faces. Suddenly lucid, he forces himself out the dream and becomes paranoid.

"What did I say? Was I talking about something there? Did I say something?"

His eyes go from terrified to furious. Suddenly there's a gun in his hand. The gun points at Kenny's face. Wayne grabs his arm and forces it upwards. A loud crack and we're showered in plaster as lead smashes into the ceiling. Pettit's fist smashes into his nose. Blood spatters on to our faces. Rutter gets his arm free. He fires three more crazy un-aimed shots. The bullets fly into the women's end of the room. Wayne wrestles him to the ground. Fists fly and shoes thump into Rutter's body. Kenny shouts.

"Get him into the yard!"

I snatch the gun from the floor, pocket it and race in the other direction to the group of women, Irene screaming, Rebecca's face white as a ghost. Two of the three bullets went through Kenny's vacant armchair into the wall. The other bullet flew past and smashed the top rail of the empty playpen. Rutter's limp feet disappear through the door as they drag him out into the yard. Janice is over by the fire on her knees in front of where Rutter sat, in her hand a tea towel scrubbing at the blood spoiled Moroccan rug.

My arms automatically go around Rebecca and pull her close.

I say to her, "Thank God you're alright. There now it's over, it's finished. Everything's going to be alright."

She's trembling. "Over?" she shouts, "They're fucking killing him out there."

The sound of barking dogs and angry voices invades the house through the open doors.

Outside in the moonlight Rutter's unconscious face is a bloody mess. Excited by the smell of fresh blood the Ridgebacks are snapping at his limbs, tearing his clothes.

Kenny punches one of the dogs and roars, "Go on, get out of here you bastards" and the dogs retreat a hundred yards and crouch salivating waiting for their master's permission to attack.

Wayne's boot stamps viciously down on Rutter's ribs.

"Die you fucking bastard," he hisses. "Die!"

Another stamp crashes down on Rutter's ribs. Kenny pushes Wayne away then stands guarding Rutter's body.

"Stop it! That's enough now."

Pettit's voice trembles as he speaks, knowing this whole sad episode is entirely his fault.

"What are we going to do with him?"

Then Wayne replies.

"He's such a decent kind of a fella. Why don't we just take him down to the Crown and Cushion and buy him a fuckin' pint? We're going to off the bastard. Take him up to the old quarry and push him off."

He attempts to get another kick past Kenny but ends up swiftly and firmly pinned against the wall, he could almost certainly break free but that would mean disrespecting his father and he'd never do that.

"OK Dad, take it easy," Kenny releases him.

"Right Son, do we all agree that the prick was sent here by the filth?"

They both agree, he continues, "So when he doesn't check in, report back or whatever he's supposed to do, the first place they're going to look for him is here."

Neither man disagrees as Kenny continues with his estimation.

"A good hiding's one thing but a murder charge is something else. No, rather than kill him, we need to be praying that this bastard survives."

Pettit repeats his question, "So what are we going to do?"

Kenny thinks for a full minute before delivering his verdict.

"You brought him here John; you'll have to take him away. We'll put him into your boot. You'll drive about twenty miles, let's say the outskirts of Chester, and leave him somewhere they're going to find him easily. One of those bus stops with a wooden shelter, there's a few of them just before the start of the suburbs."

"Sounds like a plan Kenny but Irene's not going to have any of that."

"She'll just have to stay here and help with the clean-up then, won't she. You'll have to come back for her." Pettit agrees, Kenny continues, "And while we're on the subject of cleaning up, we're all covered in blood; the clothes need to be burnt. Wayne you're about the same size as John; any of your clothes still on the farm?"

"Yeah I'll sort that."

"Right then, when you come back for Irene we'll burn your clothes. Did this prick arrive in a motor?"

Pettit nods, "Yeah an Audi."

"Get his keys and check him for a wire."

Pettit gets down on his knees and searches the keys out, discovering of course that Rutter isn't wearing a wire; Super Grasses don't work that way.

Kenny continues, "First thing you do when you get home, John, is get rid of his motor; the second is you get rid of your own."

Pettit protests. "My own? Jesus Kenny I only just got it, it's brand new."

"It won't be brand new when you get back here with that bastard's blood running down all the cracks in the boot. He's had a good pasting; he's unconscious what if he doesn't wake up?"

Pettit agrees that his BMW will have to spontaneously combust and they hoist Rutter's limp body into the boot. Wayne lets the BMW out of the gate and stands watching the red tail lights disappearing down the lane. It's all quiet again, almost as though the violence hasn't even occurred. His father stands next to him and speaks in a quiet measured tone.

"Didn't ever kill anyone, did you son?"

Wayne sighs. "No Dad, never."

"Good, I reckon if you start that shit for a few quid or to save doing a bit of bird, then you might as well just do the world a favour and top yourself."

"Dad..."

"What?"

"Thanks for stopping me."

"Don't mention it son. Now get yourself inside, burn those clothes and have a shower. Scrub every fingernail and your face; don't leave a trace of that bastard anywhere."

I never liked this kind of violence, even when it's as justified as this; it makes me shake like a leaf. I'm just not made that way I suppose; I'm probably something of a coward. That's why I rushed to the women's end of the room instead of going outside with the men. To tell the absolute truth, I've been dying for an excuse to get out of here ever since it all started, but just deciding to leave would look and feel as though I was deserting my friends. When Kenny comes back into the room and Rebecca tells me loudly that she wants to leave, Jan gives me the out. She's abandoned the task of cleaning her eight by four Moroccan rug; it's rolled up standing next to the fire. Her and Irene are on their hands and knees bleaching blood out of the York stone paving in front of the fire.

"Kenny," she says, "will it be alright if Tony gets rid of the rug? It's too big to go on the fire."

"As long as he doesn't mind," replies Kenny looking in my direction.

"Of course I don't mind," I reply, adding, "It's probably best if I get off now and stay away for a couple of days with that stuff in my car."

I don't waste any time loading the rug into the Mercedes boot; a few minutes later Rebecca stops the Mercedes at the gate so I can talk to Kenny through the open window.

"Thanks for all the help Kenny and the party would've been great if Rutter hadn't turned up."

"Yeah and if my aunt was a man she would've been my uncle. Go on Kid, get yourself out of here in case it comes on top."

Then he stoops to look past me at Rebecca in the driver's seat.

"Sorry about that bit of trouble love."

"Not your fault Kenny" she replies "Tell Janet I'll be back in a few days."

Kenny smiles at me as we drive past him on to the dark lane. Once safely out of earshot, she repeats his words.

"Bit of trouble? I'd hate to see some really serious violence."

"That's Kenny for you," I reply. "Never likes to overstate things, he can't stand drama."

The fact is that over the next few days, he'll be expecting a visit and if it doesn't come, the whole episode will fade into the past. On the other hand, if his front door does get knocked down, he'll just deal with it; he's had far worse worries than this one. They can knock your door down as many times as they like but if there's no evidence hiding behind it, they're wasting their time. I imagine that, as we're driving through the dark lanes to the A55, he'll be shifting anything iffy off the farm over to his cousin's house and that, by now the room where the gun went off will be cleaner than a BUPA operating theatre.

It's around midnight when we reach the A road and turn south in the direction of Conwy and Llandudno, her face changes colour as we pass though pools of yellow produced by the new highway lights that have just been erected. At any other time, I'd be lazing sideways in the passenger seat feeding on her beauty but as it is, I'm looking straight ahead, concentrating on giving her directions.

Llanddullas beach is a windblown desolate place in the daylight, but on a night like this, it's as lonely as the moon. The steep shingle beach slopes straight down into deep water and even a slight swell produces a roar, as tons of pebbles clatter against each other in a giant natural washing machine. Tonight, with a high tide tormented and fortified by a following wind, foaming waves break a long way up the beach and rake a few million extra stones down into the machinery.

We turn right off the A55 on to the lane which crosses the railway track, then bends left and runs parallel to the beach; wipers swishing fast across the screen, struggling to deal with the horizontal sea spray. For a moment it looks as though she's expecting a kiss but I figure that she's been upset by what happened tonight, so I stroke her cheek very gently and do my best at providing a little reassurance.

"It's going to be alright. What I mean is that we're going to be alright."

In return she smiles weakly as though she's dying to believe me; the evening's events have definitely taken their toll on her spirit. Her hands are cold to the touch when I give them a gentle squeeze and ask her to wait in the car; then as I step out, a gust almost takes the door. By the time I get Janice's rug out of the boot, I'm already soaked; walking across the pebbles into the wind, I taste the salty spray.

That reminded me of my childhood tears, perhaps it was an omen; on reflection it probably was. If only I'd have been smart enough to see it.

At first the Moroccan rug looks like a magic carpet flying over a cloud, as it's drawn up and down the beach by the white hissing foam, until a retreating wave drags it into deep water and another breaks over it, taking it down beneath the surface. I'm out of her line of sight when I get take Rutter's gun out. She missed me picking it up and I saw no reason to give her anything else to fret about. First, I slip the bullet out of the breech, pull the magazine out and hurl them into the waves. I try very hard to break it down further but, half blinded by spray and buffeted by the wind, I soon give up and hurl the whole gun into the sea.

I must look a mess getting back into the car. She's amused, almost laughing at me.

"You look like a drowned rat."

Not that I mind, at least if she's laughing at me, she's not busy with feeling sad about herself. We sit for a while in silence with the heater on full, the wipers swishing, just watching the clouds driven by the wind as, one by one they slide over the moon.

"I like it here," I tell her, "especially when it's wild like this."

"That's one thing we've got in common," she says. "I love places like this too, especially when there's no one else around. Like as though we could be the only people left in the world."

I'm about to get closer when she turns the radio on and station hops until she finds some loud music she likes, then we lose the intimacy completely as she changes the subject.

"We'll need to book in somewhere for the night and it's late."

"Well," I reply "it's either Chester or Llandudno. What'll it be?"

"Llandudno."

"Llandudno it is then. When we get back to the main road, turn right."

Pettit

John Pettit had been drinking whisky for more than twenty-four hours but, as he pulled up alongside the rural bus shelter, it was as though all of the alcohol had somehow evaporated from his system; such had been the sobering power of the evening's events.

His heart beats faster and faster as he stands next to the BMW boot, waiting for a clear road before opening the lid. Dragging Rutter's body into the wooden shelter, one of his shoes sinks into the soggy grass verge and he makes a mental note to burn them at the same time as his clothes.

Rutter, now half-conscious, groans weakly as Pettit hoists his shoulders leaning him on the timber shelter wall. Since Rutter might come to, he takes a few steps away before turning his back on him to look out along the road.

A pair of headlights flies past, illuminating the shelter, followed by another. He looks around and sees Rutter's shape but being still blinded by those bright headlights, doesn't see the open eyes. The BMW wheels turn and he accelerates away, half a mile down the road he uses a pub car park to spin around and head back towards the farm.

From his position sitting on the cold cement floor in the corner of that shelter, Rutter sees Pettit's headlights flying past, without realising it's him. Though he can see clearly through one eye, the other is blurred, swollen and beginning to close. Congealing blood feels like two concrete plugs inside his nose and when he coughs to expel a mouthful of blood and keep himself from choking, a sharp, stabbing pain pierces his cracked ribs. Running his tongue around a broken tooth, searching for the source of the blood, he realises that it is in fact pulsing from the tongue itself.

Keen to avoid any more torturous coughing, he pokes the split tongue out of the corner of his mouth to let the blood escape. And, as the blood runs down his chin, he thinks, "You bastards are going to be sorry you never killed me; very fucking sorry."

As John Pettit drives away along the A55, Kenny's words play over and over in his head.

"We need to be praying that this bastard survives, he's unconscious, what if he doesn't wake up?"

A few miles down the road he decides that the sooner Rutter is discovered and gets some medical attention, the better it will be for everyone, so he pulls over at a telephone box and dials 999.

"Yes, send an ambulance please. There's a man in the bus stop at the junction of the Capenhurst road and the A55. Looks very ill, he's unconscious."

Then he hangs up, wipes the phone and continues his journey back to Kenny's.

He dreads walking back into that room on the farm and, when he does, all of the other guests are gone. Just the Robinsons remain with Irene who is sitting waiting for him with her coat on. He apologises to Kenny and Janice but, though they acknowledge his admission of guilt, no one wants to hold a conversation with him, not even Irene. Filled with shame, he changes clothes as quickly as possible, eager to be out of there.

Kenny comes out to see him through the gates and says, "Don't forget those couple of things you're going to do, will you John."

"No I won't forget," he replies, then drives away. A few long, silent minutes pass before Irene speaks.

"I told you your drinking would get you in trouble one day, didn't I."

"Oh shut up Irene," he shouts.

"That's right John take it out on me, it's definitely my fault, isn't it."

Then she gives him the silent treatment all the way back to Liverpool.

Once inside the Bull, she goes upstairs without even saying goodnight. He pushes a glass up to the whisky optic, drinks the double in two gulps, instant warmth deep inside. A smile begins to form, "she'll be all right by the morning," he thinks and then, instead of giving in to his desire for another glass, he pulls on a pair of leather gloves, goes out of the pub and walks along Dublin Street in the direction of Rutter's Audi.

It's still dark, the early morning air is cold and all along the street, puddles left by the earlier downpour reflect the streetlights. He ducks into the driver's seat, pushes the ignition key into the steering lock and starts the engine. "Good," he thinks, seeing there's plenty of fuel, then he stops the engine and opens the glove box for a search. He takes few papers out and a business card drops on to his knee. He picks it up for a closer look. On one side 'Detective Chief Superintendent Commerford' and a phone number, on the other side is the coloured artwork of the official Sussex police badge. "Jesus Christ," he thinks, "What an absolute prick". If there had been any doubt in his mind, that business card took it away. The interior light times out, so he reaches up and turns it back on to look through the papers. Nothing of any interest other than a five-year lease for a property on Anglesey. He drops the papers on to the passenger seat, gets out and shivers as the cold breeze blows though the open neck of Wayne's shirt. His interest is primed when the boot flips up and he sees the full carrier bag but, when he opens it to discover that it's stuffed full with ecstasy tabs, the shivering stops; a nice few thousand pounds' worth.

Under the spare wheel cover, he finds another carrier bag, next to it an ugly, battered sawn off and a .32 Beretta. He looks nervously back up the street before opening the bag. Suddenly he is startled by feel of something scratching over his foot, he kicks, feels the weight and jumps back to see a fat rat scurrying through a hole in a warehouse door; that gets his heart is thumping. He goes back to investigating the bag which contains two boxes of shotgun cartridges and four boxes of .32 bullets; he moves the ammunition aside and finds cash, all in bank wrappers, new fifties and twenties, looks like quite a few thousand. "Every rat has a silver lining, even you Rutter," he thinks, smiling as he hoists the bags out of the boot and starts back towards the pub. It's 3 a.m. but he'll call his brother in law, a couple of grand should get that lazy bastard out of bed and those cars are best sorted while it's still dark.

The Major

Patterson was a patient man. Years spent on observation duties in various desert, jungle and mountainous posts made him that way. Since returning from his trip around the BMK crime scenes, he had been cat napping in the Range Rover parked in the road parallel to Dublin Street. But, when Pettit started Rutter's Audi, his tracker alarm sounded and his eyes flashed open. Within a second or two, his reclined seat was upright, his gun was on the passenger seat and the Range Rover was moving towards the Dock Road. When his tracker informed him that the Audi engine had stopped, he pulled on to the kerb next to the Langton dock wall, parked and re-holstered his gun. Having spoken in depth to Chief Superintendent Commerford about Rutter's recent activities, he had made the decision to let him have a double tap, and the very deserted area around Dublin Street would be the perfect place for such a strike.

Now from his position in the Range Rover, he has a clear view straight up Dublin Street to Rutter's white Audi and past it to the Bull pub. "Missed you," he thinks, reaching into the glove compartment for his field glasses. No need for the night vision monocular; the streetlights are more than ample to provide his glasses with an image. First he focuses them on the Audi and sees straight through the front and rear windows, if there's anyone inside, they'd have to be lying down. He quickly lets go of that idea and focuses on The Bull. A pool of light reflecting on the wet street tells him that the pub lights are on, Rutter must be in there.

He lays his field glasses on the dashboard, opens his stainless steel flask and pours a mouthful into the lid; as he does, steam floats up straight into his binoculars, misting the lenses so, after quickly screwing the stopper back into the flask, he uses a tissue to clean them. As he does, his mind wanders back to that incredibly hot summer in Oman when he used to tell his men to wipe the sweat from their eyes, saying that a steamed scope might just as well be a blindfold. He takes a sip of the hot, black Turkish coffee, savouring the dense, strong, unsweetened taste. After finishing his drink he replaces the lid and rests his head half sideways on the headrest, looking along Dublin Street towards The Bull.

He doesn't wait long before he sees two men leaving the pub and walking towards the Audi. Even at such a distance, he knows that neither is the subject, both being a different build; through the glasses he recognises Pettit getting into the Audi and a shorter, bald, fatter man getting into Pettit's BMW. The headlights come on and they drive towards him then turn right on to the dock road. He lets them get out of sight before starting the Range Rover and uses the tracker to follow them. The display shows the Audi turning off the road between the gateless pillars of The Collingwood; a disused deserted dock.

Parking the Range Rover on the pavement next to the pillars, he hopes that they've gone to collect his target and waits, watching the Audi's progress on the tracker display. The Audi stops momentarily, perhaps changing drivers, then it proceeds slowly west, before curving gently north and maintaining a northerly course at a steady three miles an hour until the signal disappears as abruptly, as if someone had discovered and destroyed the transponder. Sitting with the driver's window open, he hears Pettit's BMW crunching gravel towards the gateway then sees its headlights.

From his viewpoint parked close to the wall, he watches the headlights beam out across the dock road and pan along the front of the buildings opposite then, as the BMW passes, he gets a good look of both occupants. Pettit is driving and the bald man in the passenger seat is definitely not Rutter. For just a moment, the tracker comes back to life, displaying the Audi still moving north at three miles an hour, then the signal disappears from the screen. He quickly un-holsters his weapon, starts up and drives on to the abandoned dock; they must have delivered the car back to Rutter, he's almost certainly driving it and this is an even better location in which to conclude his operation. Following the exact route as shown on the tracker display, he stops at the quayside and gets out. Realising that the whole dock is fenced off and there are no other obvious exits, he looks along granite copings to an old slipway, then out on to the river.

Thousands of bubbles stream along the water's surface, disclosing a track where the powerful tide is dragging the submerged Audi north towards the Irish Sea. He stands for a few minutes thinking and reaches the conclusion that Pettit has done his work for him. "Mission accomplished by person or persons unknown," he thinks, then returns to the Range Rover. He pours the last of his coffee and sits watching a dredger moving downriver on the ebb tide; even though the drink isn't exactly hot enough, he enjoys it and finishes every drop before starting up.

He's quite pleased, thinking that this part of his mission is over, especially since the Rutter problem appears to have solved itself. He hates having to spend time in the north. With Rutter removed from the equation, he'll furnish the police with whatever help they require in matters of remote surveillance but should never be required to make a personal appearance. There's an orange glow in the sky above Dublin Street. He cruises slowly along the dock road and stops at the end of the street to see Pettit's BMW fully ablaze, black smoke rising into the pre-dawn light. The burning car is a welcome sight serving to reinforce his theory that Rutter has been killed; destroying the car is almost certainly part of a clean-up operation.

As Patterson follows road signs out of Liverpool for the M6, Rutter is being wheeled into the Countess of Chester's accident and emergency department. Almost every part of his body hurts but, even though he's got a face like a pumpkin and he looks as though someone has been chopping firewood all over his body, a long examination reveals that, apart from several stiches to his face and tongue, most of his injuries are superficial;

bruised ribs, a broken finger, broken nose and concussion. In the light of his concussion the doctor decides to admit him to a ward overnight.

It was one in the morning when Tony and Rebecca arrived at the Imperial Hotel. He wasn't surprised when she insisted on a twin rather than a double and didn't protest; at least they'd be together in the same room. After spending an hour in the bar waiting for him to finish his nightcap, her patience finally failed and she took herself off to bed. Several of his drinks for the road later when he arrived at the door, she lay pretending to be asleep but peeped through hooded eyelashes as he crashed in, fumbled his way through the darkness, stripped and flopped on to the bed. Within a short time, he fell into either a deep sleep or passed out, he had certainly downed enough whisky for it to be the latter. After quietly slipping out of bed to open a balcony door, she settled on the side of her bed watching his bare back rising and falling in the moonlight with each breath, then she reached over to pull the covers over his cute bottom. She was beginning to care for him more than she intended, more than she was comfortable with.

The Llandudno Imperial is one of the better British seaside hotels and always reminded Tony of Brighton's Grand. When you pull up in a car, you're directed to the car park at the rear, not greeted by a porter wearing a top hat but it has a similar kind of listed architecture and offers much better accommodation. Members of staff are always friendly and polite with none of that out-dated upstairs downstairs attitude.

Rebecca was up and dressed for the gym at seven, then changed and breakfasted by eight thirty.

She throws the curtains wide then opens both balcony doors, pinning them back on the cabin hooks and walks towards Tony's bed, grinning.

"Come on sleepy man, if you get up now, you might just be in time for breakfast."

He sits up, stretches and yawns.

Tony

I might've been slightly hung over but I always wake up in a good mood, can't help it, just the way I am, bit of a light bulb, either burning bright or blacked out. It really used to piss Joey McGregor off when we were banged up together. He was exactly the opposite, woke up in a bad mood, which got steadily worse as his day deteriorated.

She does look special, so confident, standing proudly with her hands on her hips as though she's achieved something wonderful by managing to get up before me. Why shouldn't she feel good? Better that she feels this way than the way she did last night, witnessing that shitty violence. After telling me she's had a workout and already finished her breakfast, she puffs up even more.

"I'm going down to the shops, anything you want?"

So I ask her to get me a toothbrush and promise to be all fed, watered and ready when she returns. Fed? That's a joke. All I can stomach is a pot of black, sweet coffee and we've got a busy day ahead of us. As soon as I'd showered, I called Kenny and was relieved to hear that they hadn't had a visit from the plod. That's good, even better that there'd been no mention on the local radio stations of any dead men being found on the A55, Rutter must have survived.

The advert comes out tomorrow so we need to get hold of a cheap car, get this one valeted and have the keys made. The world was far simpler before they started installing computers in cars. These days if you want to get a new key for a Merc you need to visit a main agent, unless you've got a Clive.

Clive is in his early twenties and something of a techie who manages to earn a good living at it. He launched his business, 'North West Odometer Calibration', from a single advert in a free paper. Now, three years down the line, he's accumulated a list of regular customers, a mixture of car sales pitch proprietors and 'seldom seen', fly-by-night serial 'private car' sellers. Re-setting the mileage on cars is not a crime in itself, it only becomes one when you sell the 'clocked motor' as having genuine mileage.

Even though he's never committed a crime in his life, he imagines himself to be a serious crook, always whispers in vague terms and never fails to look over his shoulder when engaging in one of his odd conversations. This kid's self-image is so confused, he holds poses and pulls nervous faces more frequently than Mel Gibson. He usually turns up on a high-powered Kawasaki with the hardware in a backpack. He opens the bonnet, plugs in and downloads the necessary information to pair the new keys with the engine management system. Your original key will never work again but that hardly matters. What does matter is the fact that Clive is so incredibly naïve and has no idea that he's aided and abetted me in so many crimes.

He was uncomfortable the first time, thinking I might be up to something shady; in fact he was so concerned that I was forced to invent a story. First I reassured him by pointing out that I was already in possession of the original key and logbook, so I could hardly be stealing my own car. Why would I need twelve keys? I swore him to secrecy, before letting him in on my latest business venture, the 'time share car job'. He was easily convinced that I had a friend living in Marbella who would deal one luxury vehicle to six expats who wanted the use of a status car on a timeshare basis. Each paid a sixth of the cost of car plus insurance, in return, they were privileged enough to take their turn flashing it up alongside the Marbella jet set. I always had to have twelve keys so that each punter received a spare. If you're going be a convincing liar, it's always best to keep as close to the truth as possible; doing so makes you more believable. The time share story is not very far removed from reality, the only difference being the fact that each of my punters get to own the car completely, if only for a day or two, but they do always get it at a knockdown price.

Stepping out on to the balcony, I fill my lungs with the fresh sea air and look out half a mile across the bay towards The Great Orme Cliffs towering out of a glittering blue sea. Not a cloud in the sky, gulls gliding and I suddenly get the feeling that this is going to be a perfect day. A quick call to Clive confirms that he'll be arriving around eleven thirty to do his stuff with the keys. Usually it only takes a couple of hours for him to work his magic, which will leave plenty of time to show her Llandudno. I decide to take her up the Orme on the chairlift and bring her back down on the cable car. It's a wonderful view from up there, especially at sunset.

The Major

Patterson drove home through the night, took a light breakfast and turned in just before 10 a.m, to be woken at mid-day by a telephone call informing him that Rutter had been admitted to a Chester hospital.

Now driving out of Chelsea along the Kings Road, he turns on to Sloane Street then back up towards the Edgware Road. His estimated time of arrival in Chester is four in the afternoon. He is never annoyed when called to action; it's always been that way, he's never completely off duty. However, he really did not expect find himself following signs for The North quite as soon as this. Cruising through light traffic along the North Circular, he calls Commerford and is surprised to discover that he doesn't know about Rutter's little setback. This fact presents two possibilities; either Rutter is too badly injured to call his controller or he's got wind of the plan to remove him and gone to ground. All the evidence indicates that it's probably the first; Rutter must certainly be quite badly injured if Pettit felt it necessary to get rid of both vehicles. Accelerating up to eighty along the motorway with a clear road ahead, he clicks the CD player button and muses that he won't be taking much jollity to Rutter as Jupiter begins playing.

"Well at least it's Chester," he thinks, "not Liverpool Manchester or, even worse, Birmingham."

He likes Chester, sees it as a northern outpost of civilization, much the way the Romans might have; an oasis of culture in a land of barbarism. He decides that, assuming the operation plays out smoothly leaving no loose ends; he'll book into the Blossoms and spend a few days wandering around the city walls and arcaded shops. Swinging gently on a hanger next to the rear door pillar is a pristinely ironed white doctor's coat. On the passenger seat next to him is what looks like a perfectly innocent stethoscope. However, if you're unfortunate enough to have your chest sounded by anyone wearing this particular medical instrument it will be your last examination before the pathologist. Cold discomfort of stainless steel pressing on your bare skin helps mask the feeling of the minute needle springing in and out of your flesh to deliver the pellet.

The tiny shard of frozen Ricin melting in your body never fails to induce a fatal heart attack and leaves no evidence, other than the tiniest of red spots which is soon lost within the bruising caused by attempts at your resuscitation. The effects of this weapon are so fast that you may just have time to see that white coat disappearing though the doorway.

Tony

When I'm grafting, I always think it best never to trust anyone with information that's not necessary to their part in the bump. That's why I arranged to meet Clive on the promenade rather than at the hotel. Sitting on a wall that encloses one of the seafront flowerbeds, I brought Rebecca up to speed with the disinformation I'd been feeding Clive about the Marbella car job. She seems to be almost as naive as him. Not only does she believe that the McGregors are going to get their cash back, which suits me, so I don't mind, but she suggests that maybe I should start 'time sharing' motors as a genuine business. Who on earth would waste their time talking six punters into buying one car? Six times the work for a sixth of whatever the profit might be made out of one legal motor. Still, it's not her brains that are attracting me, it's several other things, like the way her vulnerability plays against her independence, the cute way she gets nervous when she eats, the way she reddens when I catch her looking at me with a little desire and, of course, her dark eyed, dark haired beauty. Sitting on that wall, surrounded by red and white geraniums with the blue sea for a backdrop, she might be some Polynesian princess or an Aztec queen. She gazes up at a large gull gliding on the breeze.

"Look at him," she says, "just hanging there effortlessly, isn't he beautiful?"

"Yes," I reply, "but how do you know it's a male?"

"Must be a male, spends most of his time shitting on people from a great height."

There you go again, I think, just when we're getting close, you say a few words and completely destroy the moment.

Then, catching sight of Clive I call, "Here he is," and get up to wave his motorcycle down. "Now watch what you say in front of him."

Dressed in a set of powder blue designer racing leathers, he flips his leg over the Kawasaki and pulls it on to its stand before removing his full-face helmet to disclose a contrived smile. When I introduce them to each other, he pulls one of his overly serious faces, meant to give some kind of impression, gives in to a few twitches as he adjusts to a more reflective expression, glances at the Mercedes, then back at me. I wonder what he's really like when he's not trying to be someone else.

"Is this the beast?" he asks. Then, as he's taking the equipment out of his backpack says, "Flip the hood dude."

Dude? He's one joke off the laughing academy. She's in danger of offending him when she tells me, too loudly, that he's exactly as I described him, so I quickly repair the damage.

"I told her you reminded me of a film star, Clive."

Though, to be fair, I never mentioned which star or what particular mannerisms. He smiles back at me and blinks, then begins plugging wires into various sockets around the engine bay. After about fifteen minutes, I figure that he's well on with the job and we get up from the wall ready for a stroll to the pier when his head emerges from under the bonnet and he straightens up with a look of genuine concern on his face.

"Problems?" I ask, then he begins hitting me with what sounds like the start of some very bad news.

"You didn't tell me it was the new model; it's had a serious upgrade. The security system's just about bomb proof; second memory is one thing but even the engine management system's triple coded. It simply refuses to talk to me."

Now I'm seriously worried. "Does that mean you won't be able to do our keys?"

"Not necessarily," he replies, "what it does mean is that I'll need to take the car home with me, hook it up to the main frame while I'm on line, download a few new codes and, well, I might even have to hack a few."

"How long will it take?"

Firstly, I'm relieved to hear that he should be able to do the job in one night then, when I ask him how much extra we'll have to pay, I'm doubly pleased. He tells me that there'll be no extra charge; even though it will take him much longer than usual, he needs to be able to get his equipment communicating with the latest model. The extra time spent will be his own investment, which will return severalfold as he uses the knowledge acquired on our Mercedes to work on subsequent cars. There's just one problem, if we follow him back to his place, we'll be stuck there until the work's finished. But in solving that problem for us, he solves another. He's got an old VW Golf we can use, it's not perfect, having a few electrical problems he hasn't found time to fix, but if we want he'll let us keep it for three hundred pounds and we do need to buy a cheap disposable vehicle. Driving away from his house the Golf displays a few of its faults, the electric windows go up and down one after the other without any prompting then, when we step out of it back in Llandudno, it instantly locks itself then lets the windows down then shuts them. It's like a haunted machine, but it was cheap.

"We'll need to get you a pair of long shoes and a red nose if you're going to be driving this." She says, suppressing a laugh and I think, "What do you expect for three hundred quid, a fucking Ferrari?" A clown car it may be, but we're low on cash and beggars can't be choosers. As long as it starts, goes and the lights work, it'll do the job.

Rutter

Rutter's bed being situated on the end of the ward next to the corridor, meant that anyone entering or leaving passed too close, so that every time a nurse swished by, the noise of her uniform gave him a painful start. Throughout the whole night he was unable to even doze, being constantly disturbed by the mutterings and groaning of a patient in the next bed, as well as whispers drifting across the corridor from the nursing station. Having spent the entire night as nervous as a beaten dog, his thoughts had turned to Commerford and their conversation at that office in New Covent Garden. What did Commerford mean when he said that someone else would be "looking after" him? Ever since dawn, he'd been laying there expecting Commerford to show up. Usually the Superintendent would have stayed close, being eager to keep up to speed on how the operation was going. He tries to convince himself it's just paranoia caused by the lack of cocaine but he doesn't quite manage the job. Just like everyone else in the country he has heard reports that the Home Secretary has pledged to employ MI5 in the prosecution of serious criminals. What if one of those faceless bastards is to be his new controller? Even worse, what if he's already been handed over and they're about to make him redundant? His paranoia spirals off the scale when two local plod walk in to interview him about being attacked. Especially when he refuses to say anything and they talk to him as if he's some kind of petty criminal; it's as though he doesn't exist.

Very slowly, he eases his legs out of bed and lowers them until his feet touch the floor to stand; everything hurts as he straightens his back and shuffles to the telephone opposite the nursing station. With swollen fingers he loads two pound coins into the slot and dials Commerford's mobile but it just rings and rings. He tries again then gives up and, reading from a flier next to the phone, dials a private hire number. When they answer, he attracts a nurse's attention.

"What's the name of this hospital?"

"It's the Countess of Chester," she replies, "but you can't just leave, you need to be discharged."

"Oh I think you'll find I can," he groans, dragging himself back into the ward. In the short time it takes for the taxi to arrive, he gets dressed. His shirt has stiffened with blood, so he tucks the operating gown into his trousers and limps towards the exit. Just as he goes through the door, one of the nurses catches up to him, in one hand a clipboard with a printed form attached, in the other hand a pen.

"Mr Rutter!" Half in the taxi, he turns to face her. She continues, "You'll need to sign yourself out if you're leaving and the hospital can't be..."

He cuts her short hissing, "Just fuck off and leave me alone."

His eyes disclose the fury and absolute hatred that burns inside. She backs away terrified, then turns and walks quickly back into the hospital. He sits in the rear passenger seat and closes the door.

"You know your way to Amlwch Harbour?"

"Anglesey? It's about a hundred quid to Anglesey."

"I didn't ask how much. I asked, do you know where it is."

"All right, keep your shirt on boss" then, glancing at Rutter in his rear view mirror, "So it's a hundred pounds then."

"No problem, just drive."

The minicab driver pulls out of the hospital and turns in the direction of North Wales. Not five minutes pass before Patterson's Range Rover enters the hospital grounds. He drives once around the car park on a reconnaissance and, seeing the security cameras, decides to park outside the hospital perimeter. Stopping out of the way, at the end of a quiet street of semidetached houses, he punches the hospital number into his phone.

"Hello, I wonder if you can help me I'm Peter Rutter, I'd like to visit my brother John Rutter, could you tell me what ward he's in please?"

Coincidentally, when the receptionist puts him through to the nursing station on Rutter's ward, she connects him to the nurse who tried to get Rutter to sign himself out; she has only just stopped crying, in fact she is still holding the tissue.

She tells him that Rutter has left the hospital adding, "If you're his brother, you might want to tell him that I'm thinking of phoning the police. He was extremely abusive."

Patterson sighs, cutting the connection and thinks, "I seem to have missed you again Rutter. You are a slippery one." He replaces the stethoscope safely in its box and plugs its 12v charging lead into a rear cigarette lighter. The Ricin shard needs to remain frozen and the box must be connected to power for half an hour out of every five, in order to prevent it from gaining degrees and softening.

He starts the engine and moves off in the direction of Chester City Centre, having decided to base himself at The Blossoms Hotel.

Ten miles away, Rutter's taxi is driving past the bus shelter where Pettit dumped him. There's a sickening dull ache spreading from his lower back to his knee, then along his shin to the top of his foot. Attempting to find a more comfortable position, he shifts on the seat and winces as the ache turns to a spasm of sharp stabbing agony. Hearing him groan, the cab driver glances in the rear view mirror.

It's a long way to Anglesey and he decides to strike up a little conversation.

"Were you in a car crash mate?"

"No I was attacked by a few football supporters."

"Jesus, did they get them?"

"No"

"Aren't you bothered?"

"What goes around comes around."

"Yeah, well, you'd like to think so wouldn't you," then, recognising a slight remnant of Glaswegian accent in Rutter's voice, "Not from around here are you? Glasgow is it?"

"No, I live in London and I would appreciate you concentrating more on the driving and less on the talking."

The driver isn't offended by his passenger's rudeness, having received much worse from other fares, besides which, he can see that the man's injuries might cause him discomfort when talking. He doesn't reply, neither does he regard Rutter's cold eyes in the rear view mirror; he just concentrates on driving as instructed. Passing the lane that leads off the A55 up to Kenny's smallholding, Rutter silently seethes with hatred. His mind conjures pinprick clear images of their faces; Wayne Robinson, Kenny Robinson, Pettit and Tony the fucking Bumper. They're all going to be sorry for what they've done, very sorry.

Kenny Robinson sits at his desk in the office next to his bedroom concentrating as he draws small, precise rectangles on a photocopied plan. Rutter and the previous night's problems couldn't be further from his mind; the bastard must've survived or the police would've been all over the farm by now. It's a plan of the Portuguese farm drawn at the scale of 1:200 and he's busy with his pencil and scale rule plotting forty foot by twelve-foot rectangles along the riverbank.

It's a fantastic idea. Sounded stupid when the Bumper came out with it, but running a caravan site in the Algarve would mean that he'd always have a regular income. Twenty well-spaced static mobile homes along the riverbank would hardly make a dent on the overall farm area. Just two problems, firstly the geographic one; Portugal is a long drive from North Wales and those caravans will all have to go with a wide load escort. He'll need to buy a flatbed lorry and get the insurance, but that's all doable. The second problem is an unknown quantity. How will the Portuguese authorities react to an Englishman setting up a caravan park in their country? He takes a sip of whisky from his glass, swills it around his mouth and makes his decision. He'll just do it, he won't bother applying for licences, he'll transport them one by one and sort out legalities if anyone bothers to complain. He dials Tony's mobile.

"Hi Tony, how's it going?"

"Fine, just waiting for the keys."

"Remember you were saying I should have a caravan site?"

"Yeah dumb idea, sorry."

"Not half as dumb if I open one in Portugal."

"Sounds like a good one."

"Best idea you ever had. It's a few weeks away but you wouldn't mind driving a wide load escort vehicle for me would you?"

"Yeah, why not Kenny, would it have a flashing light on the roof?"

"Of course it will."

"It'll make a change to have a flashing light on the one I'm driving instead of the one chasing me."

Kenny laughs. "Yeah and you'll be driving a lot slower. Look kid, I'll give you a call in a couple of days; I need to call our Wayne. Good luck with your little project."

Smiling, he pours himself another whiskey. This is much more than just another idea, he feels as though he's standing on the cusp of a whole new life. Janice's main objection to the move has always been the idea that she won't be able to see enough of their children and grandchildren. That's why he chose a farm with so much accommodation. This way, with a row of static caravans fronting on to a river, they'll be spending their whole summer holidays in Portugal; they'll probably want to stay over there forever. He dials Wayne's number. Wayne answers after a few rings.

"Have we got problems?"

"No, don't worry Son, everything's OK; no unexpected visitors. Will you look after the farm if I go over to Portugal for a few days?"

"You know I will."

"Good, because Tony gave me an idea last night. I'm definitely going to buy that farm. It's got space for at least twenty caravans."

"It's a long way to take them."

"All we need to do is get ourselves a big flat bed. You'll help won't you?"

"Definitely, and I'll stay on the farm until you get back. Mandy will have to stay at home and see to the kids though."

"Are you still giving that Angie a seeing to?"

"You're not bothered are you?"

"No, just don't have her or any other little slags in my bed."

"I won't Dad, don't worry".

There's a self-assured smile on his face as he puts the phone down and sips his whisky. It's all sorted. Enough accommodation for twenty families will more than address Janice's reservations about the move. A niggling thought about Rutter creeps into his mind but he quickly dispatches it. Rutter wouldn't dare attempt any kind of comeback, no one's that crazy.

It was raining heavily when the mini cab arrived at the Almwch harbour. The most northerly port on Anglesey, Almwch harbour, once served to export ore from Parys Mountain Copper Mine. The workings ran out many years ago and the mine closed; these days Almwch is a quiet fishing port and a picturesque tourist destination.

The cab driver feels uneasy breaking the silence for the first time in an hour and a half.

"Whereabouts do you want me to stop boss?"

"This'll do," comes a reply from the rear. He doesn't turn to look at Rutter as he stops the cab; instead he keeps his eyes focussed over the harbour on to the grey sea. If his passenger is allowed to be aloof, then so is he.

"So that'll be a hundred please boss."

Rutter doesn't reply when he gets out of the cab and moves to the driver's door. Then, as the driver opens his window to take the two fifties from his pale, veined hand, their eyes meet. There's such a sinister coldness to Rutter's look, the cab driver breaks eye contact as quickly as possible and breathes a sigh of relief as he drives off. Rutter stands for a few minutes looking up the road after the cab to be certain that he doesn't come back and discover his final destination.

He takes comfort from the cool rainwater massaging his cut and bruised face. By the time he reaches the lonely stone cottage on the craggy seafront, his clothes are soaked. The cottage keys, along with the London flat keys, had been attached to the car keys. He curses as he half remembers Pettit fishing them from his pocket at the farm. Fortunately, he never got around to fitting the new hasp and staple to the garden shed. The shovel blade slips into the kitchen door jam and, not without considerable pain, the wood splinters, causing him to almost fall inside. Jamming the shovel against the doorknob and the stone floor, provides some security. He dries his hands on the kitchen curtains before opening the larder door to access the main fuse-box. Throwing the switch gives him another painful start as the television blurts out in the silence. He goes into the room, turns it off and makes his way upstairs. Kneeling painfully next to the bed in the master bedroom, he reaches underneath and lifts the sheet of loose floorboards, beneath which is his cache of emergency supplies. First he takes out one of the automatics and cocks a shell into the chamber then lays it on the bed. Next he tips a plastic bag on to the bed. It contains several smaller bags full of cash, powder and pills. Sorting through, he finds a clear bag containing a small bottle marked 'morphine', opens it, chews two pills and lays down with gun next to him then, when all pain fades to nothing, he smiles as he fantasises the killing of every one of them.

Tony

Day one of the advert. It's not even mid-day and we've had three calls already, one from a punter in Birmingham, one in Peterborough and another in Dover. They're quite spread out, so we've arranged appointments a couple of days apart.

She sneaked out of bed early again without waking me but I didn't much fancy making a fool of myself in the gym. The swimming pool was embarrassing enough, there's me, gasping for breath after one length while she's swimming up and down the pool, underwater turns and all, like some kind of athlete. You'd swear she was breathing underwater. Then she gives me a lecture about drinking too much and what I eat, still, I suppose it means she cares about me, even if she's unhappy about the waistline.

Now standing in front of me, she looks like a real businesswoman in that suit though the blonde wig concealing her short black hair does give her an edge. Perhaps it makes her look a little too horny against the olive skin but we'll have to live with that, who knows what the future holds? If we're unlucky, she might have to stand in a line up somewhere so, the greater her disguise, the better.

I might be a confirmed believer in good luck but your luck does improve when you chip away at it, and I do so by leaving as little to chance as possible. The more prepared you are to deal with a pitfall, the less likely it is to turn into a disaster. Over the past few days I've been making her recite Kenny's address and telephone number. If everything falls apart so badly we end up on foot and separated, we'll meet up there to hide and regroup. If we end up in the same position but penniless a few hundred miles away, phoning Kenny is as good as a sailor calling the lifeboat out; he'll definitely come to the rescue. She's word perfect and I'm more than pleased, at least as proud as any mentor getting the best performance out of an actress protégé.

In her game as a creeper she's never had to deal face to face and convince any of her victims. They've always been asleep and she never even looks at their faces. Now she's got two jobs in one, two goals that must be scored perfectly if we're to pull it off. First, she needs to be wholly convincing in her new role as company secretary disposing of one of the company assets. To improve her luck in that direction, we've been role playing all morning and slowly, gradually, she's become more and more convincing. The second goal is closing the deal there and then, making the sale and ending up with the cash in her hand. I've coached her into how to decline a cheque or bank transfer in favour of cash. It's so easy to accidentally insult people when refusing their cheque and end up wasting your time. There's a clue in the advert 'downturn in business forces sale' and she doesn't want the taxman to get his filthy fingers on the only few quid left in the business. The company overdraft is so great that twelve or fifteen thousand pounds will just disappear into a red bank statement.

It's one thing performing with me playing the role of punter, but quite another on strange ground, on their pitch, doing it for real. Well that's a whole other planet and you need to be calm. Conscience can really take its toll on your confidence and hamper your ability to part someone from their cash. If you're lucky, then you're a cold hearted bastard and this job's a piece of cake but if, like me, you were born with a conscience, then you need to deal with that before you end up red-faced and guilt-ridden, counting your cash in front of the punter. You have to be able to hold your hand out calmly and not recoil from the prize because you feel wrong taking it.

I tell her how I deal with it. So here you are, selling a luxury car worth about £33,000 for fifteen or less. Ask yourself who would have fifteen grand under the bed ready to snap up a bargain. In the past, they would be a collection of fishmongers, butchers, club owners, scrap dealers, and the only thing they had in common was the fact that they were all bent. None of them paid their taxes, all on the fiddle and not one could care less whether hospitals or schools ever got built. Then imagine that you feed them the story that you're only parting with your pride and joy because you've fallen on hard times; will any of them offer to pay the full price? No, they'll all bid you in the bollocks.

Another thing that helps is studying their personalities; many self-made people have found one trick to make money and simply milked it but, more often than not, they see themselves as genius entrepreneurs. Watching the way they talk to their employees can often ease your conscience. If they intimidate their underlings, then you can feel a sense of justice when their golden carriage turns into a fucking stale pumpkin. These days you mostly find yourself turning drug dealers over. Easy that one. Ask yourself what joyful gifts they might bring to the world. Imagine being a teenage kid, strung out, willing to do anything to stop feeling sick and what they'd expect you to do in order to generate their revenue. No question about it, drug dealers don't even deserve the stale pumpkin.

"Do you think I can do this? Do you think I can be convincing enough?"

"Why not?" I reply.

"You're not doing anything they can complain about, letting them have the bargain of a lifetime. You leave them in possession of something they really want. At that point they'll be rubbing their hands together congratulating themselves on cutting a good deal."

She still doesn't look convinced.

"Listen, if it's a question of conscience, well it's just a posh car, they're not going to die of a broken heart when it evaporates."

"You know it's not that Tony, I've been a thief for years. No this is just different, just something I've never done before."

Taking hold of her shoulders I look her in the eyes, she looks into mine.

"Remember when you first saw someone in a swimming pool doing one of those fancy underwater turns? There's a first time for everything and now you're on the road to respectability."

"Respectability?"

"Well you're not exactly sneaking around dark hotel rooms are you?"

She avoids my eyes and pulls away indignant, it's as though she's suddenly ashamed being a professional creeper when only a couple of nights ago she was proudly sharing secrets of her artistry in the field. I was never any good at figuring women out so I don't know why I should feel the need to understand her motives? Just lately, I'm not even sure of my own; no man can figure what goes on in a woman's head, least of all me. One minute I seem to be getting close, the next I'm getting frozen out. Maybe I'm becoming addicted to the knock back, like a prospector spending his lifetime panning for gold but only ever coming up with gravel, without ever noticing that, on the daily walks between his tent and the stream, he's stepping over dozens of nuggets. Am I another blind prospector missing the signs? Or am I buying a lottery ticket and spending all my cash because I believe I'm going to win? Should I just give up? Maybe I will, but not now, it's hard to take my eyes off her swaying hips and those perfect dimples in the back of her knees as I follow her to the car.

"Try not to get too far ahead and try to keep your speed down," I say through the Mercedes window, "that little thing won't go as fast as this Merc."

It was no fun following her in the clown car towards the M6. You definitely get what you pay for when you buy a cheap runner off Clive. The brakes pull to the left, there's a wheel wobble between sixty and seventy but at least the windows are behaving themselves by remaining shut. We're heading for punter number one, a meat wholesaler called George Falkner with a unit on the Gravelly Industrial Estate, Birmingham. It'll be an easy enough place to find, being situated right next to the M6. The fact that he sounds more like an entrepreneur than a drug dealer proves that at least there might still someone out there managing to draw a little milk.

She pulls in for fuel at the Hilton Services and we have our last few moments together before her big debut. This is my last chance to prime her, so I do my best at coming up with anything the punter might ask. Then we sort the paperwork, one logbook, I check that it matches the number plates, and the tax disc; all good. Then there's the blank service book with a dealer's name stamped on the cover. The service book is only blank because Clive was decent enough to wind the miles back to three thousand when he was doing the keys; so here we have an almost brand new car which hasn't even had its first service; what an absolute bargain, a gift at 15K. Assuming that she scores, and I'm confident that she will, she'll ask the punter to give her a lift to the Holiday Inn opposite Birmingham Central's TV Studio. I'll be close by if she needs me when she's in there. It's all good, nothing can go wrong.

George Falkner had been in the meat business since leaving school at fifteen when he got hired as an office boy in Birmingham's wholesale meat market. Initially he'd been taken on with a view to becoming a trainee salesman but, at seventeen, the management decided that he didn't have what it takes to become a successful meat wholesaler and they promoted him out of the office as a meat porter. There was a considerable amount of quick mathematical juggling to do as a salesman; every butcher paid a different rate and deals were invariably quick and sometimes quite complicated. It wasn't just his mathematical inability that excluded him from the job; they didn't think he had much of a personality.

Meat portering is a young man's job, which George hated almost as much as he hated the management for pushing him into it, but he was ambitious and determined not to end up retired at fifty with a wrecked back. At eighteen he bought a motorbike with a sidecar and that was the start of his business. His father's garden shed became a butcher's cutting room and at the end of every shift, a whole side of beef or several frozen lambs would ride home in the sidecar. In the beginning almost every cut of meat he sold was stolen but, as his pub round grew, he began purchasing from the market's other wholesalers. In doing so he displayed an absolute gift for brokering his own deals and, as for the mathematical side of it, well, he bought the latest technology, a clumsy but efficient 1967 desk calculator.

George made his first million by the age of thirty and has continued to accrue his fortune ever since. It has been a long time since George needed to work but he still turns in on a daily basis, simply because he enjoys it. There's no reason for him to buy a secondhand vehicle, he could buy as many new Mercedes cars as he wanted, he's simply infuriated by the instant depreciation a luxury car suffers, the moment you drive it out of the showroom. That's why he hates English main agent car dealerships and once spent the weekend driving to Belgium collecting a new BMW. The Mercedes will be for David, his youngest son, a little birthday present.

Rebecca walks into reception, signs in, is given a visitors badge to wear, then follows one of George's employees into the boardroom. Pride of position on the thirty-foot long shiny mahogany table is the 1967 calculator. George is five foot six, sixty-two years old, slightly built and smartly suited with a very welcoming porcelain smile, which he had fitted in Turkey because English dentists are such a rip-off. He presses the intercom and asks them to send Albert in, then he asks Rebecca for the key and, when Albert arrives, he passes it to him. Since he finds Rebecca, or Joan as she is at that moment, extremely attractive, he treats her to the full story, starting with the portering, the sidecar and ending with his fleet of trucks and the European outlets. When he's finished telling her how to make a million and advising her that she must never give up, he gets around to the subject of the car.

"Tell me about the car dear, how many miles exactly."

"A little over three thousand, George."

"And the interior, what colour?"

"White with red piping; don't you want to look?"

"No it's not for me; I'd like to see the paperwork though."

"Of course," she replies, sliding the forged documents across the table. Albert walks back in with the keys and drops them on the table. George glares at him.

"Be careful will you. I didn't just have that French polished for you to drop bloody keys on it."

Albert reddens with embarrassment.

"Sorry George; the car's a good one, exactly as the advert says."

George gives her a mournful look then watches Albert leaving the room.

"That's the trouble these days, no one cares about how hard you've had to work to get things. So, to the business of the car, what's the bottom line dear?"

Her rehearsals are paying off and she answers straight away, absolutely no hesitation.

"It has to be the fifteen, George. I've got three other people waiting to look at it."

"No reduction for cash right now? You must be able to let me have a grand back for luck."

"I'm sorry George a thousand pounds is a great deal of money to me right now. We paid thirty-one for it just three months ago."

"How about I put the full fifteen on the table right now, you'll let me have five hundred out of it won't you."

"I'd be a fool George but, well, I would be saving myself a load of hassle driving down to Peterborough with it. I'll meet you in the middle, fourteen thousand seven hundred and fifty pounds. I could live with that."

"Right dear we've got a deal then but only because you're so lovely and I'm a foolish old man."

George has spent his whole working life dealing in hard cash and fourteen thousand seven hundred and fifty is just another small number. He uses the intercom and asks Dave to bring it into the boardroom.

I don't mind admitting that I was worried sitting, waiting, parked next to the industrial estate entrance. I timed her, exactly thirty-two minutes is all it took her to part him from his cash but they were a very long thirty-two minutes. I expected her to emerge as a passenger in our Mercedes and only just managed to catch sight of her sitting next to George in the front of a white Range Rover.

Playing snatch-back with a car has always been a great way to earn a fast few quid but, like all good schemes, there are one or two mistakes you must never make unless you like living in a confined space and sharing your accommodation with a shoplifter or a drug addict. The delay between selling the car and whipping it back is crucial, do it too soon and you ring alarm bells, leave it too long and anything can happen. There was one occasion a few years back, when I left a Jag for a couple of weeks, only to discover that they'd taken it on a holiday to France; two weeks turned into four and, when they returned, they put it in part exchange for a smaller car. I ended up having to recover it from the middle of a car sales forecourt and that was truly difficult, especially when the car dealer wheel clamped every car on his pitch.

What's too soon? Too soon is when they can still picture your face, I like to leave it at least four days, which gives them a chance to have it insured and feel as though they really are the true owners. The last thing you want is for the punter to get the idea that there's something odd about buying a new car off a little Liverpool Irishman and losing it straight away. Two days is really too soon but I'm not a one man band any more, I'm in a partnership, one that is being fronted by a beautiful and, by all accounts, respectable young lady. If anyone catches a glimpse of me on the snatch back, they will almost certainly fail to link us. The first time I played snatch back was before mobile phones became common and I used to park up close to a secluded telephone box. These days I use a throwaway mobile, a different phone for every advert, and adverts stopped and replaced after three deals.

Her face is a picture of joy when we meet up in the Holiday Inn coffee shop.

"That was easy," she says through a triumphant smile. "Exactly as you said it would be."

"How much did we take?" I ask and am pleasantly surprised by her answer. It's either beginner's luck or she's better at this than me. I usually aim to take twelve and a half out of a fifteen grand advert but she's nearly got the whole fifteen.

"Clever girl, all we've got to do now is find out where he lives and I'll do my stuff."

That's always a problem when you sell to someone at their place of work, a little patience sitting close to the factory should do it; just a question of following the car to wherever it ends up, then collecting it at a suitable time in the next couple days. If you're unlucky and miss the car coming out, then it's a trip to the local library and a search in the electoral register for his address. I'm pleased reading the typed receipt for the car. 'George Falkner', quite an unusual name, if I miss the car leaving the estate it will be an easy one to track down. Since she managed to collect over two thousand pounds bonus, I suggest that she takes a session in the hotel beauty parlour for 'a treatment', whatever that might be, and I leave her to enjoy it.

When we first bought the clown car off Clive, it had one of those car deodorants swinging from the mirror; the thing gave off a pungent, sickly, chemical smell so I threw it away. Sitting in the lay-by next to the industrial estate, I'm beginning to wish I hadn't; whoever owned the car before Clive must have been using it as a kennel. It stinks badly of dog and, even though it looks clean, I keep finding long white canine hairs clinging to my suit. Four hours of sitting here, waiting and I've had enough; I'm seriously considering just driving off when our car emerges. I start up and follow at a safe distance. Things are running to plan, just a question of discovering the car's new address then I can pick my time. Through the city traffic into the outskirts, up a few lanes, then I follow it around a bend and grind to a halt feeling as though my world's about to end when I see it disappear beneath a barrier.

George Falkner lives on a gated estate, a bloody gated estate, you can't get in or out without a key fob. Not managing to recover the car won't just scupper our plans to make a quick hundred and fifty thousand pounds, it's far more serious than that. I must get the car back, it's down to me, rented from Marriott in Liverpool. When it comes on top, as it will as soon as Swansea get the snide logbook posted to them, the police will arrive, discover the car's true identity and their next stop will be Marriott who will aim them straight in my direction. It might be just a simple deception charge but with my previous, I'll be straight back inside.

Now I need to rush through town to the hotel and hit Rebecca with the bad news. Unless I come up with a good idea we'll have to sit in that lane for as long as it takes until we can follow the Merc to a suitable location; it might take a week, even longer.

Rutter

After just one night's morphine induced sleep, Rutter stirs; he feels that if he lies there any longer he'll die, he needs to get moving. The first thing on his list is a set of wheels. He selects the most recent free paper from the pile of junk mail on the hall floor next to the front door, then he opens the living room curtains and sits in the armchair. It's late in the morning, the rain has stopped and the daylight seems too bright. He breaks a morphine tablet and washes half down with a strong black coffee. Though he can still feel physical damage the morphine is powerful and his pain is completely dulled.

Flicking through the 'Cars for Sale' section, he stops on a Volvo estate and dials the number. Being overpriced, the car is unsold, still available and, since the owner hasn't received a single enquiry, he's more than willing to deliver the car. Rutter was quick to say that, providing the car is exactly as advertised, he'll pay the full asking price. He gets up and collects a bag of ice from the freezer then returns to the armchair where he spends an hour holding the pack on his swollen face.

Just before the Volvo is due to arrive, he goes into the bathroom, dries his face and stands in front of the mirror. The swelling has definitely reduced but the two black eyes give him a crazed and ugly look. The pair of dark, thick-framed Ray-Ban sunglasses hides most of the blackness and shades out the coldness of his eyes. Satisfied with his appearance, he goes to his cache of emergency supplies and loads a holdall, ski mask, gloves, hunting knife, binoculars, an automatic handgun, box of ammunition then an old snub nosed colt and another box of ammunition. As he opens the wardrobe and finds his black tracksuit, the doorbell rings. He pulls the bedroom curtain aside and looks down at the silver metallic Volvo.

Twenty miles along the coast in Holywell, Wayne was loading his mother's luggage into his BMW boot. Kenny and Janice were almost ready to leave; he had agreed to run them to the airport. Any potential comeback from Rutter was the last thing on his mind; he'd spent the day negotiating with the owner of the car repair garage in the village. It was the only MOT station in Holywell, a thriving business which was on the market because its current owner was ready to retire. As his mother climbs into the back seat, he studies the mountain of luggage, trying to figure a way of stacking the suitcases more efficiently then just gives up and forces the lid down with a click. He gets behind the wheel and grins at his father.

"Do you think you've forgotten anything Mum?"

"Now don't you start", she protests, "I've had it off your father all day."

"How long are you going for Mum?"

"A week, and it's a holiday, I am definitely not doing any bloody ironing."

Kenny joins in. "Yeah, but by the time you've got that lot unpacked, it'll be time to come home."

Janice is beginning to redden with anger.

"I told you Kenny. It's up to you; do you want to look like a bloody tramp? If you do, we can stop right now and I can throw that lot out in the lane."

"Alright um, stop it, we're only joking, don't get all shitty on us."

Janice's holiday mood slowly returns as they drive towards Manchester on the A55.

From his position lying on the hill overlooking the farm, Rutter watches them leave. He places his binoculars back in the leather case and emerges from the brambles, standing painfully, looking down at the smallholding. He decides that, since the Robinson's house is so remote from other dwellings on the lane, he'll use the cover of night; all he needs to do is feed the pack of dogs a handful of morphine pills crushed into some steak, then he'll be able to have his way with the whole family. One by one he will definitely make them pay, they're going to realise that they should have shown him some respect. They're going to realise just exactly who he is.

His route across the fields towards the Volvo brings him to within a hundred yards of the farmyard. The dogs sniff and snap at the air and become instantly agitated, running up and down in a pack, howling. He makes a mental note that on the night he'll approach the farm from downwind. The streetlights are coming on as he drives along the A41 towards Liverpool. This whole bunch of shit started with Pettit and that slag wife of his. They are going to be the first to discover the true order of things, and the last thing they're going to remember is his delighted face as he enjoys their suffering.

Tony The Jogger

There are many different types of gated estates in the UK, from the kind that surround small marinas, to the affluent kind like the one that runs through Wentworth Golf course. George Falkner's estate is the Wentworth kind; long gravel drives leading to pseudo mansions, anonymous behind very tall hedges, all of which are further secured by tall wrought iron gates. Any gated estate makes recovery of your car difficult, however the Wentworth type does offer a consolation or two.

People who live behind very tall hedges don't have a great view of passing traffic and don't usually spend their time minding anyone else's business. There might be an electric gate at the entrance, but such a gate is usually intended to keep people out rather than keep them in. Most gates like these are fitted with an electric eye system. When a car approaches from the inside, they open automatically, unlike the barrier at the entrance to the estate which requires a key fob to lift it. We all know that you can tailgate someone through but, since I intend to take the car while the world is still sleeping, there won't be any other cars to follow in. It was all so complicated, so many angles to work out, that I couldn't settle. About 3 a.m, I gave in and got out of bed. I slipped into my tracksuit and trainers, quietly careful not to disturb Rebecca. If you're out and about in the early pre-dawn, you are really conspicuous walking along a deserted avenue. That's one of the reasons I like to dress as a jogger, "Why are you out so early on this exclusive avenue?" Obvious isn't it, I'm just out for a run and, on the off-chance things go so badly I end up having to flee for my life, then it doesn't seem outlandish when a passer-by sees a jogger racing along the road. Also there's one more advantage to a jogger's outfit, it's a uniform and when you see someone dressed in a uniform, it's almost as good as a disguise, you only remember the uniform.

It took about ten minutes to drive out of the city; I always loved the early morning. Empty streets lead me on to the empty lanes and another ten minutes takes me past the barrier at the entrance to George's estate.

After parking on the forecourt of a closed village petrol station, I begin a gentle jog back down the hill towards the entrance. By the time I reach the barrier, it's no act, I really am out of breath so, as I'm stretching, recovering and catching my breath, I get a chance to inspect the gate. Two heavy wires lead out through a panel to a motor with a 12 volt dc mark on it; so, if I had to, I could hook a car battery to the wires and lift it mechanically. There's a gentle breeze blowing along the avenue as I cross the road to the other end of the barrier, just enough to give the leaves on the tall hedges an occasional gentle rustling, otherwise no movement on the road in front of me. Slipping my fingers beneath the barrier I give it a gentle lift and discover that the only thing keeping it shut is its own weight reduced by the counterbalance, no lock other than gravity holding it down. What a result, now I'm off along the left hand side of the avenue with a smile on my face glancing through the gates

as I pass, no parked Merc's visible on this side, so I cross
back over and jog along the other.

Suddenly there it is, parked next to a Range Rover
and a Porsche; our lovely Merc, all safely corralled behind
a tall gate. I start going through a few stretches and, as I
do, I peer through the gate and see the electric eye mounted
on a white timber post next to the drive just before the gate.

Having seen all I need to, I begin the jog back along
the avenue then up the lane towards the clown car. The
first sign of dawn is beginning to show in the sky as I drive
into Birmingham. Now it's my turn to wake Rebecca up
and tell her I've been for a training session. She's bound to
be impressed.

Rutter

Irene Pettit's anger towards her husband didn't last
long, it never did. As soon as John came to bed and they
moulded together, it was forgotten. They'd been a couple
since schooldays and, contrary to Rutter's low opinion of
her, Irene Pettit had married the only lover she had ever
known. Through the years they'd shared the good times
along with the bad and, even when she spent a seven
stretch with nothing more than a monthly prison visit to
share with him, she had never once even considered taking
up with anyone else. There had been propositions from
several of his so-called friends, one or two coppers and a
prison officer but she had treated them all with pure
contempt. Johnny Pettit was the only man for her and, as
far as she was concerned, that's the way it would always
be. Their small bedroom over the pub was cosy and clean
but hadn't been decorated in years. Not just the bedroom

décor, the whole building was run down and required refurbishment.

Just before midnight, the loose windows vibrate and rattle in their frames as a late bus passes by causing her to stir from a half-remembered dream. John is lying on his back snoring loudly and, as usual, his arm has flopped over her chest, pinning her down. She deals with it in the normal way by wriggling from underneath, then sitting up to lift it across his chest. Then she gets out of bed and stands to roll him on to his side. As he goes over, he mumbles a little, then the snoring stops. Snuggling into his damp sweaty back, she takes a deep breath and feels secure in the safe smell of her man. She can't remember her dream and knows that she must have been enjoying it because she woke up feeling warm and cared for. Next to the bed is a holdall filled with Rutter's cash. They don't really need the contents of that bag, having been paid out for the BMK but, as John said, it is quite a tidy little bonus. She closes her eyes and tries to find her way back into the dream. Thinking about the bag of cash doesn't do it so she imagines the BMK money but that leads nowhere, then as she drifts off it comes to her; it's not about money it's about Michael, their eldest boy's christening.

Everyone from their old school is there, all adults but dressed in their school uniforms. She looks into Michael's crib, shocked to see that he's not a baby but a perfectly proportioned miniature adult, looking exactly as he did when she saw him last week. He climbs out of the cot, jumps down to the floor and asks her for a slice of the christening cake. She turns to cut a piece then, as she hands it down to him, she watches the crib morph into a coffin. Suddenly she snatches herself from the dream, her heart beating fast, trembling and scared. She shakes John's shoulder.

"John! John!"

He stirs. "What's up love?"

"Nightmare love, it was awful."

"Yeah, well you're safe now. I won't let anything happen to you, settle down."

A few minutes pass before John gets back to sleep. Eventually she puts her fear aside and manages to relax, comforted by the rhythm of his light snoring. Just as she's beginning to drift off, she fancies she hears an unusual creak but decides it's nothing. Their building is old and often produces unexplained night-time noises.

Rutter freezes for a moment in the dark cellar, silently cursing the wooden pavement door for creaking as he closed it. A long time has passed since he first gained entry to a pub through the pavement mounted dray doors. Those flaps were always the easiest way into a pub and as a young burglar, he'd lowered himself into more than a few of them. The air in the cellar is a musty mix of sweet alcohol and wet rot.

He remains motionless in total blackness for a full minute before turning the torch on, its halogen beam pans around the whitewashed brick walls until it finds the crazed pale green paintwork on the door to the stairs. Moving as silent as a ghost, he grips the damp, unpolished brass doorknob and turns it. They haven't even bothered to lock it; it opens with another creak so he freezes again waiting, listening, to hear if one creak begets another; but there is only silence, punctuated by the muffled noise of snoring as it filters down through the building. Slowly he begins his stealthy creeping ascent of the stone steps to the hatch in the floor behind the bar. He kills the torchlight before pushing gently on the hatch. It moves freely but, determined not to cause any more noises, he opens it as slowly as a minute finger passing the face of a clock, then he steps out of the cellar on to the worn lino.

The streetlights outside are just bright enough for him to find the stairs to the accommodation; he takes the automatic out of his pocket, the safety catch is off.

Irene's eyes flash open, she doesn't know what it was but something has caused her to wake suddenly, perhaps just John's snoring. She folds her arm around his waist and pulls herself close to him, rests her cheek on his warm back and closes her eyes. Now her eyes open again; she can hear someone behind her breathing. It's been an awful night. It must be her imagination. Uncertain whether this is part of her dream, she turns over slowly and sees Rutter standing next to their bed. Her heart begins pounding in her chest. Her fingernails dig into John's buttock and she screams. John Pettit flies out of bed and stands naked looking directly into the barrel of Rutter's automatic. Rutter grins.

"Now then Pettit, who should I do first, you or the slag?"

"You don't have to do either Jimmy. I've got your cash here and more, I got the BMK money, you can have that too."

"I'm already having the cash, the only choice you're making is who gets it first so, I'll ask one more time. Will it be you or will it be the slag?"

Don't do this Jimmy, please don't do it. At least leave Irene out of it; she didn't do anything to you."

Rutter's grin widens into a smile as he squeezes the trigger. The first bullet smashes into John's kneecap shattering the bone. He falls to the floor, Irene flies at Rutter and before his second bullet crashes through her ribcage into her right lung her fingernails dig in gouging, raking skin from his face. The force of the bullet sends her backwards to where she collapses on the bed. Driven by fury John's body somehow lunges forward towards Rutter.

"You bastard," he screams before Rutter's third shot goes through his skull and penetrates his brain.

"You better believe it", says Rutter as John crumples and he fires his fourth shot into Irene's temple. "You better fucking believe it."

Tony

The afternoon before recovering our Merc, I took Rebecca on a shopping trip but it was a business shop rather than a therapeutic one. The next day's recovery operation required a few odds and ends to make it work; first stop was a B&Q for a large sack of compost and, on the same retail park, a visit to Halfords for a roll of heavy amperage automotive wire, a pair of wire cutters and a pack of hacksaw blades. At 2 a.m. we were on the road headed for George's estate, it was raining and Rebecca was unhappy about driving that stupid clown car. The windows had started misbehaving again, going up and down without warning, letting in the rain.

We're just leaving the outskirts and starting on our trip through the lanes when she says, "Promise me something Tony."

"Promise you what?" I ask pulling the hood on my jogging top up.

"Promise me that when we've got the Mercedes back, we'll get rid of this car."

"Definitely," I reply as the windows close themselves again. Then I run through everything she needs to do if the recovery operation is to be a success.

Approaching the estate, I pull my gloves on, check that she's wearing hers and get her to recite Kenny's telephone number and his address. We had already arranged a local meeting point where I can change the plates or find her if things fell apart for me, so all that's left is to synchronise our watches and I'm off on foot down the lane towards the estate.

Arriving at George's front gates, I slide my carrier bag containing the wire and cutters through the gate railings then, as I climb up, I throw my coat over the spikes at the top before straddling them and lift it off on my way down the other side. Such spikes on the top of gates are so incredibly dangerous; if you don't get impaled by one, you can easily get the leg of your trousers snagged and end up landing on your head on the other side. I'm well prepared in my jogging shorts so spikes are no problem to me. Before I even put a foot on the driveway the garden security lights come on. Always awkward, always a worry when the garden lights up, but they've been around for a long time and the people who have them installed are well used to the fact that they are regularly activated by cats and other night time creatures. Being comforted by that fact doesn't make me any less nervous as I avoid the gravel drive and walk across the grass to the cars. The Porsche and the Range Rover are still there, so I place a length of stripped wire with the cutters on the gravel next to the Porsche and zap the alarm on the Merc.

Moving as quickly as I can, I push the ignition key in then rush back to the Porsche where I slip a hacksaw blade down the driver's window. Just as I expected, its alarm goes off almost instantly. Within a second or two I'm behind the Merc wheel, the engine fires up and I'm stopped at the gates waiting for them to open. It can only be a matter of seconds but it seems like an eternity waiting for those gates to part, then driving through, I glance in the rear view mirror and see the house lights come on but they're too late to see me, I'm off down the road speeding towards the open barrier.

Thank God Rebecca's done her stuff with that large bag of compost, as I pass through I see it perched neatly on the counterbalance holding the barrier up. A couple of miles down the road I pull off into a deserted council salt yard and find Rebecca parked with the lights out. She rushes over to pass me the electric screwdriver and number plates. No more than two minutes to change them and I'm sliding the old ones beneath a pile of road salt thinking, 'It'll be winter by the time you find these.'

Before I get back into the Merc she gives me an unexpected hug, kisses my cheek then runs back to the clown car. No more than ten minutes has passed since I took the car off George's drive. No one could be expected to change a set of number plates that quickly, nevertheless, if the police haven't arrived yet, they're certainly on their way to George's place. I'm praying that our paths don't cross. When they look on the drive, they'll see that someone has been attempting to steal the Porsche; hacksaw blade down the window, a wire link and cutters lying on the driveway should help their thought process along a little. It's blatantly obvious to any cop that a car thief has failed with the Porsche and somehow got lucky with the Merc. It shouldn't dawn on anyone that it's odd that such a recently purchased car should get stolen quite so prematurely.

These next ten minutes are the only dangerous time left. Once I'm on the motorway, our Merc will be just another of the millions of cars driving up and down the country; until then my heart's beating like a drum.

The Bull

At 10 a.m., Irene Pettit's brother, Shaun Murphy walked across Great Howard Street to The Bull. Nothing unusual to find that they weren't up, they often slept late. After collecting and washing last night's glasses, he hosed the gents out and brushed the bar floor. Then he polished the spirit glasses and bar top before jamming the bar door open with a wooden wedge. It was nearly eleven o-clock before he ventured upstairs to ask for the float. He realised something was wrong when he saw the door at the top of the stairs open. Stepping into the bedroom he pulls up, horrified by the scene in front of him; his beautiful baby sister lying naked, lifeless and twisted like a broken doll on the bed and her husband on the floor in a pool of blackening coagulated blood. He sits down on the carpet and begins crying, sobbing. Eventually he stands averting his eyes from the scene and goes downstairs to call the police.

Uniformed police are first on the scene to establish a cordon around the pub and close Dublin Street. Dressed in white paper overalls, scene of crime officers climb the stairs and begin the task of meticulously examining, photographing and recording everything in the bedroom. DI Willis goes back into the incident trailer still feeling angry having just fended off several persistent reporters and banishing them to the public space past the cordon on Great Howard Street. He instructs one of his constables to bring the very red-eyed Shaun Murphy into the trailer and when he arrives, offers him the seat in front of his desk.

"She was your sister, Shaun?"

"Yes she was. And that was her husband."

"Yes Shaun, I knew Johnny Pettit, dealt with him on several occasions in the past."

"It was Jimmy Rutter did it."

"Jimmy Rutter? I haven't heard the name before."

"He was in the nick with Johnny, came to see him the other night and they had a bit of a fall out."

"Quite a serious one by all accounts; what was it all over?"

"Don't know, he didn't tell me, just said that they'd been arguing."

The interview is interrupted by a young Scene-of-Crime Officer coming into the trailer carrying a clear plastic bag with a document and card inside.

"Sorry to just walk in on you Boss, I've got something you'll want to see."

DI Willis acknowledges the officer with a glance then addresses Shaun.

"So that's it for now Shaun, you can go. Will you be going home?"

"Yes I suppose so."

"Good keep yourself available, I'll be around later to take a full statement."

Shaun Murphy walks out of the trailer; the SOCO closes the door behind him, then hands the plastic bag to DI Willis. Willis reads the business card without removing it from the plastic bag.

"DCS Commerford, East Sussex Police.' Interesting, and what's this? A lease for a property on Anglesey. 'The agreement made this day between Mr James Rutter...' Very interesting indeed."

He lifts the phone, reads Commerford's mobile number and dials.

Brighton Pier - Autumn 96 - Fisher

Tony Hurley, Tony The Bumper? Just look at him now, poor bastard. He's a wreck of a man though, don't misunderstand me, I'm not putting the boot in. I genuinely feel sorry for him, that's why I dragged him out of that shelter next to the Penny Lift this morning. Jesus Christ, he must've been cold laying on that bench all night, surrounded by his empty bottles. Yesterday when I drove past, he was roaring drunk, standing there screaming at the seagulls. When I first approached and he threw those few badly aimed punches at me, I thought he might be too far gone to ever find his way back. He seems to be quite lucid now, still shaking but definitely seems to be back in the real world.

So much has changed since I was a young copper. So much, I lose track of it all. I never thought I'd see a time when a man like him would talk to me quite as openly as he has; or for that matter a time when I'd become so completely disillusioned with the force that I'd be sharing such sensitive stuff with anyone, least of all him. Perhaps the things that I know are too much for a man to keep inside, perhaps I might be able to consign it all to the past and get on with my life if I let some of it out; containing it feels as though it's contaminating me, dirtying my soul. The tide's dropped now so there's no spray in the wind and even beneath the grey rain clouds, you can feel a warm, diffused sunlight on your skin.

"So Tony, my boss Superintendent Commerford was in a meeting with the Chief Constable and had left his mobile phone on the desk. When it rang I answered it. I spoke to a DI up in Liverpool, Willis was his name; that was the first time I ever heard of Rutter. I didn't think the boss'd mind me holding a conversation on his behalf. I mean, after all, it was police business. I told Willis that I didn't know anything about any Rutter. Maybe he was a snout. I just didn't know, so took Willis' number down, told him I'd talk to Commerford and get him to call back. As soon as Commerford came in and I told him about the call, he looked nervous. When I mentioned Rutter's name he shut me up, took me into an interview room, slammed the door and said. "Don't ever say that name again. Forget you ever heard it, nothing to do with us." Commerford like many other coppers is a Freemason, so there always was a whole secret side to him."

Then Tony asks, "Aren't you one then?"

"No, I never took to the idea of a secret society. I joined the Force to do the right thing, to make a difference, not to do favours for my fellow members. I would have been promoted to Chief Inspector years ago if I had, that's the way it works. No Tony, I always believed it was one law for everyone not one for them and another for us."

The Major

Patterson breakfasted early and spent his morning wandering around the Chester Arcades looking for a new shirt. Eventually, having found the particular yellow check that complemented his tweed jacket, he walked the city wall on the same route a centurion might have taken a thousand years earlier, then went down the steps to the Dee where he bought a copy of the Times and settled on a bench between the tea stall and the river.

'As British as any London park,' he thinks, watching a pair of swans herding their cygnets on a begging mission towards the tourists who sit along the water's edge. Then, as he begins to unfold the newspaper, his mobile phone rings. It's Commerford, sounding quite anxious.

"Major?"

"Yes, how are you Superintendent?"

"I've been better; I thought you were taking care of things."

"All in due course Superintendent."

"You haven't heard then?"

"Heard what?"

"It looks very much as though he's done another couple, Pettit and his wife."

"When?"

"Found this morning, time of death around 2 a.m. You are being square with me aren't you Major? I mean, whichever angle you see it from; we need to draw a line under this lot."

"Don't worry Superintendent, I'm on the level just as much as you, I simply haven't been able to locate him in the last couple of days"

"They found my card at the scene, along with a lead, a property he's leased on Anglesey."

After writing the address down, Patterson hurries back to The Blossoms, grabs his luggage and collects his Range Rover from the hotel garage. Entering the address into his GPS, he is determined that this time he won't lose his target. His route to Anglesey will take him past the Robinson's farm in Holywell.

Wayne parks his new BMW next to the fisherman's quay in Flint, just a few miles from his father's farm and gets out for a walk. It's a small tidal quay on the Dee Estuary with a few day-fishing boats berthed alongside. He sits on a bollard breathing the seaside smell from the nearby cockle processing plant next to a forty-foot wooden boat, Aderyn Pal, which is David Evans's shrimper.

David is one of the few Welshmen Wayne could call a friend. They were both bullied at school, Wayne because, being from Liverpool, he was an outsider and David because of his thick spectacles and the fact that his parents were in their sixties and kept him wearing shorts until he was nearly fourteen. They even sent him to school with a gabardine mackintosh. Wayne responded well to his father's boxing lessons and when he finally got the courage to stand up and fight back, David threw his glasses down and joined in. They became an unbeatable team and it wasn't long before they were taxing most of the school's dinner money.

Their two-boy protection racket came to an abrupt halt when the police were called to the school. David's parents moved him to the nautical college in Conway and the next time the police were called, Wayne was expelled then later spent a year in youth custody after getting himself into another fight in Holywell. Most of the boys at Conway College went straight into the navy and David was no exception but, soon after, found himself in the Falklands swimming for his life. These days his thick spectacles have been changed for a pair of designer glasses with thin Zeiss lenses, he drags the sandbanks at low water for shrimp and never swims.

Wayne lights a cigarette and looks along the glittering water at the blue sky, wondering where his old friend is. He arranged to meet Angie here at three o'clock and came down an hour early hoping to see him. David is always short of cash and, for once in his life, he's in a position to help. Last time they met up, he was trying to get enough together to buy a new engine for the boat. Finishing his cigarette, Wayne looks up towards the cockle plant and sees David lumbering down the hill towards him, dragging a heavy chain along the road. David is a tall, strongly built, dark haired man; Wayne shakes his big hand, David smiles and glances at the rusty chain.

"Just been to the welding shop to borrow their angle grinder and cut a seized shackle off my old tickle chain. Been here long?"

"Couple of minutes."

Then, seeing Wayne's new BMW. "That yours?"

"Yeah"

"Wow, whopper isn't it."

They step aboard the boat and both sit on the gunwales, Wayne lights another cigarette and asks, "Did you manage to get that new engine?"

"Yeah look," he replies proudly, getting up to raise the engine cover, "brand new Yanmar. Got it for two grand."

"So you're alright now, I mean for cash?"

"Of course; haven't seen you for a while what are you up to?"

"I'm meeting Angie down here at three."

"You'll have to be careful; your Tracy'll kill you if she finds out."

"She isn't going to find out; my dad's gone abroad for a few days I'm looking after the farm."

"She as horny as she looks?"

"Hornier, she can't get enough of it."

Angie Thomas was nineteen years old and had lived in Holywell all of her life. She was a very fiery, passionate redhead and always came out with what was on her mind. One thing about living in Holywell that really annoyed her, was the way they all gossiped. She hated the way a young woman doing what she fancied ended up with a dirty name while a young man behaving in a similar way ended up being thought of as a star performer. Even though she hated the gossip, she did pay attention when other girls were describing Wayne's sexual prowess and physical attributes. Such gossip served to fuel her desire and that desire instantly converted to lust when she realised that every remark made about Wayne was an understatement.

A year had passed since they got together for the first time, since then she's never had sex with anyone else. Wayne was the best in the village, the fittest; she'd found everything she wanted in one man. A day spent in bed with Wayne was a series of endless orgasms; he was perfect and never ever seemed to run out of energy.

She concentrates on her image reflected in the bedroom mirror as she paints on the lip gloss, her green eyes sparkle as she pouts then she smiles, now she's ready for him.

David sees Angie tottering down the hill in her new high heels then looks at his watch grinning. "Here she comes Wayne, she's fifteen minutes early, you're a lucky bastard."

Wayne glances in her direction and waves.

"Are you taking the boat out tonight Dave?"

"No, there's bad weather coming."

"Bad weather? The sky's blue, hardly a cloud up there."

"Take a look at those clouds over there," he says pointing at some high cloud over the sea." See the way they look like mackerel skin? That's what you call a mackerel sky, it means that there's strong winds coming, very strong winds."

"Yeah well I suppose if anyone knows, you'd be the one Dave. Anyway I'm off," he says, getting up to meet Angie.

Dave watches them get into the BMW and drive off, then he goes into the wheelhouse to take a beer from the fridge. Settling on the anchor winch, he takes a sip of his beer and looks downstream towards the sea. The tide is beginning to turn. One by one the boats moored in the estuary begin to spin on their moorings, presenting their bows to the incoming current and, as they do, he feels the wind starting to pick up and tug at his shirt.

"Big wind, maybe a storm," he thinks, taking another mouthful of beer.

Rebecca and Tony arrived in Peterborough before the morning rush hour and booked into The Marriott Hotel. When they stopped outside the hotel, steam was hissing from the bonnet of the clown car so she parked it quickly and stopped the engine. After a breakfast followed by a few hours' sleep, they got up in time for a late lunch. Rebecca phoned up and arranged a 5 p.m. viewing with the next punter then they went out to look at the old car.

Tony

Taking the cap off the cooling water reservoir, I find that, apart from a coating of buttery, emulsified oil, it's completely empty. Then dipping the oil, I see the top half of the stick wet with coolant and the bottom covered in white emulsion.

"Does it need water?" she asks.

"Too late for that," I reply, shaking my head. "It's knackered, looks as though we're on foot until we get another."

"What do we do now Tony?"

"Just go with the flow. You did make me promise to get rid of the car so I'll call a scrap dealer to collect it. If your punter buys the Merc and won't give you a lift back to the hotel, you'll have to call a cab. Then we'll hire a car to recapture it."

Now she looks worried. "But what if something awful happens and I'm there on my own? What will I do?"

I close the car door and give her a hug.

"You don't really think I was going to leave you on your own. You'll drop me off on the corner, program your phone first with a text telling me there's a problem and I'll be there in a flash if you send it. We're a team right?"

Just as well I came along with her because the address that she's arranged to show the Merc is a rough one. We're driving along Burghley Road looking for Park Road and almost everywhere we look, we see business girls showing out to the passing motorists. The actual address on Lincoln Road turns out to be a run down, dirty looking Pizza takeaway/delivery business. We cruise past and she pulls over to stop a few streets along. I'm beginning to have serious misgivings about this one.

"Probably a drug dealer cleaning his money through the shop, what did you say his name was?"

"Vladimir Buchak, didn't recognise his accent but with a name like that he's got to be a Russian"

"Maybe I should do this one, he's probably escaped from the Gulag, might be rough bastard."

"Don't worry, we're a team aren't we and I'm certainly not scared of any stupid Russian. You just stay close and come running if you get the text."

Before getting out of the car, I leaned over to kiss her cheek and she smelled so good. Then watching her drive off I thought, "You might be total wind up of a prick teaser but you're a plucky little bitch."

She looked so tiny behind the wheel of that big car, so vulnerable.

The Major

Patterson arrived at Amlwch Harbour about two hours before sunset and spent those last hours of daylight moving around on foot observing the cottage from different locations. His suspicion that the cottage was deserted was confirmed as night fell and the house remained unlit. He usually favoured entering houses via the front door, especially those like this cottage without a deadbolt fitted.

He had a particular knack with that neat telescopic crow bar and could open most such doors without even slowing down. Nosey neighbours never even caught sight of the tool beneath his jacket and, from a distance, he appeared to be opening the door with a key.

Having breached the door with his usual ease, the heel of his gloved hand pushes the Yale keep back into position and he shuts the door. If Rutter returns unexpectedly, the door will have the appearance of being locked and, as long as he doesn't push it too hard, the keep should remain in place.

The wind howls, rattling the window frames and trees at the rear of the cottage which cast nervous shadows on the white walls as he begins his search of the kitchen. His torch beam illuminates a few dirty dishes in the sink, then a black plastic bin liner. Inside the bin liner is some blood stained cotton wool. Nothing else of particular interest in the kitchen, other than a shovel wedged against the broken back door lock, which he gives a push and decides it's tight enough to hold against the wind. If it blew open, the through draught might be strong enough to pull the loose keep off the front door. A check of all the downstairs rooms draws a blank, so he moves up creaking stairs into the front bedroom.

His torch beam discloses an empty plastic bag labelled 'morphine'. Nothing under the mattress, then his fingers find the loose floorboards beneath the bed and he discovers the plastic bags. Tipping the contents of the first bag on to the bed, he sees several smaller red bags, bank bags containing teller counted cash, several thousands, and a large quantity of assorted drugs in others.

He could never get his head around the idea that so many people value narcotics as highly as they do. It never made sense when in his life, drugs had only ever been administered by medical staff and never prescribed without an ailment to cure. Surely people who depend upon drugs, simply to make themselves feel good, must have a degree of mental illness, at least some kind of deficiency. Hitler had the perfect solution for such deviants. The whole drug-fuelled criminal world could disappear very quickly if the politicians were willing to let the authorities actually mount some kind of attack on the perpetrators. Then he tips the contents of the second plastic bag on the bed and sees several boxes of different calibre ammunition, .22, .38, .45 shells, along with a few boxes of shotgun cartridges.

The fact that there are no actual weapons in the cache indicates that, wherever Rutter is, he's almost certainly armed to the teeth. He decides to accelerate the level of this operation. Little wonder Commerford was so nervous, Rutter has already killed several times and needs stopping. Replacing the plastic bags, complete with drugs, cash and ammunition, exactly as he found them and realising his target must return, if only to collect those drugs and cash, he decides to bring two of his trusted associates into the operation. One can plot up close to the cottage, which will leave him free to hunt for Rutter and, hopefully, stop him before he kills again. After using his mobile phone to make the necessary arrangements, he exits the house and walks back through the storm to his Range Rover parked at a vantage point from where he can observe the cottage.

Sitting waiting for his men to arrive, he crunches the facts and begins to make sense of Rutter's actions. His last operation took him to the Robinson farm. It's obvious that they've tippled to the real purpose of his visit and beaten him up. Rutter is simply exacting his revenge. First the Pettits, next will be either the Robinsons, it would have to be both father and son, or it will be Jones. It would be a much better solution to just let him get on with it, they're all scum and would be getting their just desserts but unfortunately, when Pettit was running off at the mouth, he neglected to mention who had commissioned the BMK robbery, besides which, some innocent bystander might get in Rutter's way and he had given his word to Commerford.

The Robinson Farm

Drive towards the Robinson farm by daylight and permanently tilted patches of gorse clearly indicate the prevailing wind direction. They also disclose the fact that, when the wind blows uphill, it does so with regular and considerable force. Drive up on a night like this, when the gale is capable of felling trees, you can understand why such hardy scrub evolved that way.

Rutter drives up the hill past the farm and parks in the disused slate quarry. He spends a few moments using a Stanley knife to cut slits into the lumps of rump steak. There isn't very much blood spilled in the process because he took the precaution of having the butcher freeze the meat for a couple of hours before he collected it and it has only just started to soften.

After pushing around twenty morphine tablets into the slits, he re-bags the chunks of meat then cleans the greasy blood from his hands with a tissue. After a final weapon check, he pushes the snub nosed revolver into his shoulder holster and the automatic into the back of his waistband.

He checks that the zips on the pockets of his black hooded jacket are closed and pats them. In his right pocket are twenty extra .38 calibre bullets and his left another twenty of the .45. Stepping from the Volvo into the gale, he peers downhill through horizontal driving rain and sees a single light shining into the darkness. Leaning into the wind, he begins his descent through brambles and gorse towards the farm.

11 p.m. Wayne is naked and alone in the living room, sitting in the leather armchair waiting for the phone to ring. His father gave him a quick call earlier and said he'll call back at midnight, Portuguese time, which is when they plan to return to the hotel.

Sitting on a towel to prevent his buttocks from sticking to and spoiling the leather, his whole body is wet with sweat. Angie has been working him harder than usual and, even though she is the horniest and most wonderful thing that has ever happened to him, he is grateful for the opportunity to take a breather. He vacuums another line of coke from the coffee table and shivers as he rests his back on the cold leather. Angie is so passionate about and good at sex, if it wasn't for the fact that every one of his friends has been there before him, he'd happily desert his wife and children for her.

Since the age of fourteen Wayne has never been short of women, in fact he's been inundated with willing females and gave up trying to recall all of their names and faces years ago. Most of them exaggerated the joy and the wonder of it all; some of them were actresses blatantly faking it all for his gratification, what a turn off they were. But, every now and then, he found a woman without inhibitions who loved sex. Angie is one of those but in a whole different league to the others, in fact she's one of a kind. She breathes, eats, sleeps, dreams and worships sex; calling her a nymphomaniac infuriates her since she believes that her volcanic sex drive might be slightly high but that it's basically normal. Angie can sit alone and conjure an orgasm for herself without any physical contact. She loves to be fucked hard, she loves it gentle and she loves to be the meat on a spit roast though, invariably, she feels let down by the male participants of such threesome adventures. Many of them are too taken with each other and she ends up feeling left out. Some of them fail to get hard, being upstaged by the better performer, and some of them even get jealous, believing they can own her. Angie would never agree to be owned by anyone unless that particular 'anyone' happened to be the very thick, hard and energetic Wayne Robinson; he could be her master, she could kneel in front of him to worship for eternity and would always be willing to point in either direction.

He hears her calling from the bedroom, "God I love you Wayne Robinson."

"You mean you love cock," he calls back laughing.

"I mean love your cock, bring it back in here, I need to eat it, I need to ride it until it breaks."

Before he can reply the phone starts ringing.

"Keep quiet now Angie for fuck sake, this is my dad."

He delays a moment before answering in case she does reply, then he picks the phone up. "Hello Dad, sounded like you were having a good time when you phoned earlier. I could hardly hear you, were you in a bar?"

Angie listens to the muffled sound of the phone conversation and gets up from the bed naked and mischievous; she walks out of the bedroom past Wayne into the kitchen grinning seductively as he continues with the call.

Kenny replies, "Yeah we were in Little Austin's bar, had a laugh, he's having it bang off on the Algarve. Got the local plod straightened right out; says you can do what you like as long as you throw a few euros in their direction, it'll definitely be cool to bring the caravans over. Is everything all right on the farm?"

"Sound. There's a bit of a gale blowing and the dogs were a bit lively earlier. Must've been a fox or something. They're quiet now though."

Outside in the farmyard, each member of the pack of dogs has separated chewing on its own chunk of semi frozen rump steak.

Back inside the cottage Angie floats in from the kitchen. It's difficult enough for Wayne to hold a serious telephone conversation with her in the same room so beautifully naked but when, with her hands behind her back, she lifts one of her feet on to the arm of his chair and he finds himself at eye level with her lusciously shaved wet and pouting vagina, it becomes just about impossible.

"Well then Dad that's it, nothing to report, everything's alright here. I'm about ready for bed now."

"Are you sure everything's alright there Son? You sound a bit odd, nervous. You are alone aren't you?"

She brings one of her hands from behind her back, raises the long bent cucumber to her mouth and licks it in the most provocative way imaginable, then lowers it to eye level and enters the tip.

"Yes Dad, completely alone, off to bed now I'll call you first thing in the morning."

Inch by inch, she slides the cold cucumber deeper into her body until only three of its twelve inches are still visible. Then she releases it from her hand, holding it in position with her famous grip and flexes her muscles spasmodically, causing it to wobble.

"Right then, good night Son."

"Yeah goodnight Dad."

He quickly slams the phone down, withdraws the cucumber causing her to gasp and drops it on the floor. Then he springs, almost leaps to his feet, spinning her around and bending her over the arm of the chair to replace her vegetarian meal with a lump of thick fresh meat. Then, as he thrusts slowly in and out of her he says, "You filthy dirty little girl, remind me to never eat any salad at your house."

Matilda, the oldest Ridgeback bitch and the mother of the other two bitches, struggles to her nightly resting place just inside the barn; one by one the other three Ridgebacks join her and lay down to sleep. Though bred in the UK, Rhodesian Ridgebacks are creatures evolved to suit life in higher temperatures so it was never unusual to see the pack laying snuggled together in order to maintain body heat. The only unusual thing about this grouping is the fact that they have lain down for the last time; sleep sinks to unconsciousness and within a few minutes death. Rutter's boot nudges them one by one and, when they fail to react, he re-sheathes his sharp hunting knife and creeps slowly towards the curtainless window. He lingers a few minutes watching Wayne's live sex show, realising that Kenny can't possibly be on the farm as he'd never stand for such antics in his living room. A moment passes as he considers postponing his revenge but killing the dogs has taken him past the point of no return so, for the time being, he'll just have to be content with Wayne. He moves deliberately quietly to the kitchen door and, just as he expects, he finds it unlocked.

The flames in the log fire roar momentarily as the kitchen door opens. Angie pulls herself free from their coupling, sensing that they are not alone. There's a terrified look on her face.

"Shush" whispers Wayne as he grabs a poker from the hearth, but he's too late. Rutter stands in the doorway aiming the revolver at his face.

"Drop it," hisses Rutter lowering the revolver to aim at his genitals. "Drop it or I'll blow your fucking balls off."

Wayne doesn't even consider the possibility of rolling over for anyone, least of all a grass. Instead, he hurls the poker at Rutter and, before the poker glances off Rutter's forehead, the bullet smashes into his testicles, then a second shatters through his metatarsus and flattens on the sandstone flag beneath. His powerfully built naked body crumples in agony and he lies helpless at Rutter's feet. Angie screams and Rutter silences her with a single merciful bullet to the head.

"Remember what you did to me the other night Robinson? Now's your chance to tell me how sorry you are."

"Fuck you, you fucking lunatic."

"Fuck me? Correct me if I'm wrong but you're the one laying on the floor with no bollocks. You got nothing to fuck anyone with."

"Well go and fuck yourself then!"

Half admiring his resolve, Rutter lets him have a final bullet in the temple and, after a quick and fruitless search for anything of value, leaves the farmhouse and makes his way back up the hill to his Volvo.

Peterborough

Vladimir Buchak, born one cold December 25th in Ukraine, was no baby Jesus; he was just another unwanted infant. Being the offspring of an alcoholic prostitute meant that he never experienced anything like a family life and spent his first three years confined in a stinking mildewed cot. His next three years passed with him tied to a metal cage that some decent-minded people might regard as a playpen. By the age of six when he was set free from the cage to lie on an equally filthy bed, he'd learned that crying only caused a sore throat and delivered pain since it caused slaps, punches, and kicks to be administered. Aged eleven, as the hardcore abuse started, he realised that all the adults he came into contact with were either sadists or perverts.

On his thirteenth birthday he made his first escape from the institution but was recaptured soon after suffering from hypothermia. His second escape was more successful and he remained on the streets for five years until he was twenty. In those early days of freedom, he teamed up with two other boys who made a living working the streets of Moscow's Kitia-Gorod red light district and spent their nights in a chamber off a service tunnel close to Belorussky station on the Koltsevaya Metro line. The station closed its doors to the bitterly cold Moscow mornings at 1 a.m. but he knew the chief security guard who, in return for a small favour, never failed to let them in.

Eventually, when he met and moved into a government flat with a young woman, he found that she could earn much more on the streets than he could. When he enlisted one of her friends, then another, the roubles started rolling in and the young woman's flat became a fully-fledged brothel, which he ruled with an iron fist. Jailed at twenty, then again at thirty he bribed his way out and crossed the border to Finnmark in Norway. From there, he thieved his way through Denmark, The Netherlands, Belgium and France, where he paid a truck driver to ferry him across the English Channel.

Since arriving in the Promised Land he has amassed quite a fortune. The British are a flabby, soft, lazy race with such an ineffective police force. Their welfare state is wonderful and, since he began importing his own labour four years ago, he has been running multiple benefits claims. For every one of the hopeless trafficked girls serving his five brothels, there is a national insurance number, a bank account and a claim. He controls twenty-seven bank accounts in female names, emptying each one weekly with its debit card; a perfect bonus. Over eighteen hundred a week coming in before he even puts them to work, and all with no crime committed because a woman is only trafficked if she has the courage to escape and complain to the police.

To say that Buchak is a violent man would be like saying that Adolph Hitler wasn't always kind to Jews. Peterborough never had much of a criminal underworld until he arrived but it did have a few run down council estates that produced a large number of addicted prostitutes. All they needed was a good manager, so he enlisted them and kept them apart from his Eastern

Europeans. They also needed a reliable regular supplier as the others were strictly small time, barely earning enough to feed their own habits. Having pushed their snouts well away from the trough, it was all his. Mr Buck, as he was known to the locals, was Mister Big in prostitution and Mister Big in smack; regular shipments from Afghanistan via Ukraine took care of that.

Buchak gets behind the wheel of the Mercedes and Rebecca gets nervously into the passenger seat, almost trembling as she passes him the keys. The previous five minutes spent with him in the office behind the pizza shop were extremely uncomfortable. The stink coming from the collection of overstuffed bin bags in the doorway made her feel quite nauseous.

Now sitting next to him in the car, the stink of rotting food waste has been replaced by an unwashed sweaty smell drifting into her nostrils every time he moves. As he selects 'drive' his stained open-collared black silk shirt pops a button, disclosing an unnatural amount of thick black hair covering his fat stomach; now there's a cheesy smell, far more repugnant than plain sweat. They drive past Tony who is standing waiting on the corner of Park Street, then around the block and stop outside the shop. Rebecca was always repulsed by hairy men but it's not just the hair or the smell, it's his whole attitude; he's sitting looking at her lustfully, almost daring her to complain. She can feel his eyes wandering over her breasts then down to her legs; she adjusts the skirt of her business suit as far down her knees as it will go.

"Do you have a man, Miss Jones?"

"I'm a busy woman Mr Buchak, do you want this car or not?"

"I might want the car. What will you let me have to help me make my decision?"

"I might let you have a five hundred pounds discount."

He begins laughing but his eyes are cold and emotionless when he lays a hand on her shoulder. Her skin crawls as she lifts it off and pushes it back towards him.

"I don't know how long you've been in England Mr Buchak but no one ever puts their hands on a stranger here, especially on a woman."

"Ha you English. The great capitalist master race; think you're better than anyone else. The days of your great empire are finished."

"That's all beside the point Mr Buchak. Do you want this car or not?"

His hand starts to move in her direction again, she raises her hers.

"I've told you; do not put your hands anywhere near me"

Like all bullies, Buchak swims in a small pond and knows that straying outside it can be dangerous. He concentrates his efforts on the weak and the not very bright, the fact that this woman won't bend to his aggression and that she owns a thirty thousand pound vehicle, puts her out of his reach. If one of his own women spoke to him in such a way he'd be quick to show her the error of her ways but she isn't one of his women and he does so much want to own the Mercedes.

"Not fifteen, I'll give you twelve thousand."

She smiles and shakes her head.

"No Mr Buchak, it's advertised for fifteen."

"Take it or leave it, this is my offer."

"I'll leave it then, other customers to visit, please shut the door gently when you get out."

He opens the door, half gets out, then leans back and turns to face her.

"Twelve thousand five hundred then."

She replies very quickly. "Fourteen so make your mind up now; I haven't really got time for all this."

Buchak has been planning a recruitment trip to Lithuania and a shiny new Mercedes would be just the car to impress the locals, especially since, at fifteen thousand, it's less than half price.

"I take it for thirteen right now."

"You're nearly there Mr Buchak, thirteen and a half and it's yours."

"I take it. Come inside and I pay you the cash."

"No, I'll wait here; you can bring the cash out to the car."

He sighs getting out and, as he does, she slides behind the wheel and opens the windows then her phone but, instead of texting Tony, she calls him. He answers straight away asking, "Are you alright?"

"Yes but only just, he's gone in for the cash. Are you still on the same corner?"

"No I'm in a blue minicab next to where you just turned left in the Merc."

"Good, I'll be on foot."

Then seeing Buchak coming out, she hangs up. He gets into the car next to her, in his hand a plastic carrier bag full of cash. She hands him the forged paperwork and a pen, then takes the carrier bag and starts counting. The cash seems to be about a hundred short but instead of querying the amount, she hands him the key and steps out of the car. He gets out of the other side and gives her a menacing look across the roof.

"Don't you want a lift? This can be a dangerous area; it's a lot of cash for a woman to carry."

She doesn't reply, instead she begins walking away quickly and, as she does, a young thin man wearing a hooded top and tracksuit steps out of the shadows next to the pizza place, Buchak looks in his direction and gives him an encouraging nod and she hears footsteps behind her beginning to speed up, gaining ground.

Buchak stands watching and whispers, "You were warned."

She breaks into a run, rounds the corner and finds Tony's minicab with the closest door open; she throws the bag of cash to Tony and turns to face the young addict shouting.

"You want something from me you bastard?"

He backs up then turns and walks away empty-handed.

Tony

We'd travelled about a mile before she was calm enough to speak. Even then she didn't say much in front of the minicab driver who was quite a friendly man. In the ten minutes that we waited for her to conclude the business, he put me in the picture about Buchak. Any way you look at it, she'd been lucky to walk away from that place with any cash at all though, to be fair, she wasn't exactly walking, she'd been running for her life. I paid the minicab and gave him a good tip, then followed her into the hotel bar for a quick drink or two before turning in.

Sitting like a princess on a throne in that red bucket chair opposite me you can't help but admire her. She's such a feisty girl and, even though I'm beginning to believe that I might never get her to give herself the way she should, it's starting to matter less; we've definitely developed a special kind of closeness. I've grafted with a few partners in the past but none as plucky as her, it's like she's determined to pull her weight, no matter what it might entail. Even when I offered to take over on this one, she refused to let me.

She takes a sip of her drink and says "We'll have to fumigate the Merc when we get it back. He's a stinking bastard. Even the cash has got a bad smell to it."

Then she goes on to tell me the way he was trying to intimidate her out of a few grand and the way he told her that she wasn't going to be safe with the cash before he sent that smack head after her.

"So you don't feel guilty about this one then?"

"No Tony he's an animal, deserves everything he gets and the sooner he gets it the better."

"You want me to take it back tonight then?"

"I thought you said we should always leave it with them for at least two days?"

"I did but then I was talking about an ordinary punter, this one's different. If half of the things the cab driver said about him are true, he won't be complaining to the police, he'll have to just swallow and get over it. And another thing, if I take it back tonight he'll be certain you've fucked him over and you'll have the satisfaction of knowing that."

"But what if he finds us?"

"Sixty three million people in the UK, Rebecca, where's one smelly little Russian going to look for us?"

"I don't know."

"Well don't worry then because neither does he."

Getting up and walking to the hotel desk for a local car hire number I was already beginning to regret offering to do it straight away. When I make rules for myself they're always for a reason and I never break them. There I was, about to antagonise a potentially very dangerous bastard for no other reason than to make her feel as though he knew he'd lost his little game with her. Or was I doing it to prove what a hero I was to show her how much she meant to me? God knows, all I knew was that I was about to do something crazy and I was too much of a bighead to change my mind.

Rutter

It's just after midnight. The storm has blown itself out and there's hardly any traffic about when Rutter's Volvo crosses the Britannia Bridge. He passes over the Menai Strait hardly noticing the beautiful moonlit view beneath; what does catch his attention as he drives through the pool of highway light at the end of the bridge, is an almost new, khaki coloured Range Rover crossing in the opposite direction. The hairs on the back of his neck prickle; he's definitely seen that car at least twice before, close to Pettit's pub. He's certain it's the same one because he remembers noticing the Southern Counties suffix of its registration number and thinking what an awful colour it was for such a new and expensive vehicle. Could they have found his Audi? He certainly couldn't. The lease to his cottage was in the glove compartment. If the police or MI5 have got that car, then they've got his bolthole as well.

Instead of driving past the harbour to his cottage, he turns up the steep farm track just before Almwch and follows it to the brow of the hill overlooking the front. Panning slowly around the area, his binoculars focus on another Range Rover parked with just its sidelights on in a position where it would be unseen by anyone approaching his cottage from the usual direction. Silhouetted against the moonlit sea is the shape of a man sitting motionless in the driver's seat. Operating the zoom lever, he pans slowly down, rests his elbows on the Volvo roof to steady the image and reads the southern suffix of its registration plate. Another new Range Rover with a southern plate is too much of a coincidence. The arrival of either an unknown copper or a faceless MI5 agent presents him with two choices. He can just drive off leaving his cash, ammunition and cocaine behind, or he can go down the hill and confront the prick.

Patterson - The Major

Patterson's decision to bring two colleagues into the operation means that it is no longer necessary for him to drive. He would rather be chauffeured, since it allows him to concentrate more intently on the operation. He chose the two men from that very select group of operatives he brought over from the armed forces. Both have served in numerous conflicts and know how to follow orders without asking awkward questions.

While Patterson dislikes times like this, when it becomes necessary for him to step out of the shadows, and

1 a.m. is not be the ideal time to knock on anyone's door, he does have a police warrant card in the name of Detective Inspector Phillips and the Robinson family will be no strangers to a nocturnal police visit. His driver turns off the lane and stops in the Robinson's yard and they both get out. The cobbled path to the front door takes them past the curtainless window of a room with the lights on where they're pulled up by the macabre scene. It's like a shop window that might be designed to draw customers in to a Madame Tussauds exhibition. The two bodies have a pale, waxed tone to them and that paleness is highlighted by sharp streaks and pools of bright red blood, shining in the stark electric light. Finding the front door locked, they gain access via the kitchen. Patterson sends Jameson to check the other rooms of the single story building and kneels studying the scene but doesn't disturb anything. After removing his leather glove he lays the back of his hand on Wayne's face and looks up at Jameson who has now returned and is standing next to him.

"Any more?"

"No Sir, just these two. Place has been spun though. You think it's our man?"

"Definitely and, by the feel of this poor fellow, we can't be more than a couple of hours behind him."

Then as they walk back into the yard, Patterson sees the sad pack of dogs lying dead in the barn doorway.

"Poisoned," he says looking down at them. "Spent a little thought on this, didn't he? Must have approached from downwind, probably came down that hill to administer the poison."

"What next Sir?"

"First I'll call this lot in to the North Wales police and then we'll visit Jones, with any luck before our man visits to him. Hopefully he'll return to Almwch first, in which case Spud will conclude the operation then we can all go for a well-earned breakfast."

Rutter

It took Rutter three quarters of an hour to circumnavigate the Range Rover parked along the lane from his cottage. First he went south to the sea, then he picked his way along the boulder-strewn beach to a steep path leading up between the cliffs to a grassy level where he rested for a few minutes, before continuing up through the bushes. The Range Rover is parked between two bushes with its tailgate above the start of a slope down towards the beach.

Approaching from the rear of the vehicle he has a view of the chassis, wheels and exhaust. Lying out of sight of the mirrors, he reloads his revolver and rests, listening the sound of a world service report coming from the car radio, muffled against the engine ticking over and the car heater blowing.

Inside the vehicle, Michael Spud Murphy is beginning to feel uncomfortable, having sat in the same position for two hours. He adjusts the leather seat to a new and more comfortable angle; then he laughs at his own recently developed softness, as his mind wanders back to the time he spent secreted in a wet Irish ditch for two days, waiting for a clear shot at an IRA man. That had been his first operation with Major Patterson twenty years earlier. These days he's forty-three pounds heavier, far less patient and beginning to develop an arthritic hip. He sometimes feels as though he's turning into a grumpy old man, his tolerance to change is wearing thin. So many things annoy him these days, like modern cars, this new Range Rover might be the height of motoring luxury but why must the sidelights come on automatically every time the engine starts? Then there's the fact that he doesn't seem to be able to go for more than an hour without needing to piss.

He stops the engine removes the key, steps out into the cold night air and unzips his fly. The first drops of urine haven't even reached the bushes when Rutter's bullet punches a hole in the back of his skull. His body remains upright for a few seconds then falls forwards into the brambles. Rutter rolls it over to search the pockets. He finds several police warrant cards in different names, a driving licence in another name and, beneath his jacket, a holstered automatic weapon which he removes and pockets. Then he rolls and pushes the body back into the brambles and quickly retrieves his cash and drugs from the cottage. Within ten minutes, he's driving back over the Britannia Bridge to the Welsh mainland. Now there's no doubt in his mind that MI5 are on his case and he needs to put some distance behind him. His shop and flat on Guildford High Street are definitely not known to the authorities, since he bought them in his dead mother's name. He decides to make his new base there. If he can just get it sold and perhaps get his hands on that BMK cash he'll leave the UK and set up home somewhere in Europe, maybe Spain.

Tony

The hotel managed to locate a Ford Focus for us to hire and, instead of turning in we paid the bill, checked out, then went looking for a good place to swap the Merc plates. About five miles out of the city centre we found the ideal place in Castor Village. Station Road is long and deserted, running through sugar beet fields with no houses on either side. It comes to an end just after a level crossing over a single-track railway line with a disused signal box next to it. Past the level crossing, there's just a track to the River Nene, which is used by anglers.

It was about 2 a.m. when we took a quick drive past the pizza place. Parked outside, half on the pavement, we saw our lovely shiny Mercedes just dying to be set free. At that point, I had no idea that Kenny was in Portugal or that Wayne had been murdered so, as usual, I got her to recite Kenny's address and telephone number before getting out and sending her back to Castor Village.

There were only a few girls out on the street. The lights of the pizza place were the only ones that lit the street and its front door was open. After giving her about five minutes to get clear, I walked towards the Mercedes with the key in my hand all ready to go, when Buchak came out of the shop carrying a suitcase and a hold-all. Not wanting to give the game away, I kept walking and, as I passed him, he opened the boot and turned to look at me. If looks could kill I'd have been dead, it was as though he owned the street and resented anyone else walking along it. Safely around the corner, I watched his reflection in the shop window across the road as he loaded the two bags into the boot and closed it. Then he zapped the alarm and, the very moment he walked back into the shop, I began stepping fast towards the car, key in my hand and ready, hoping it wasn't a suicide mission. Almost up to the car I zapped the alarm, then I threw the door open, flew into the driver's seat and hit the central locking button.

In a second he's there right next to the window zapping the alarm with his key. His face is right next to the window but the thumb of my left hand remains on the button holding it down, keeping it depressed. I've got my key in the ignition and he's zapping away madly trying to unlock the door. His hairy fist slams right next to my face but the glass fails to break. The engine fires first time and the wheels screech as I roar away and he's behind me running along the road for all he's worth, which isn't a lot because after about 200 yards, he pulls up with his chest heaving, trying to catch his breath. I just can't resist it so I have to pull up and see how far I can keep him running. When he's almost on top of me, I pull away another couple of hundred yards and stop. Now he's really struggling for breath, he's got no chance of catching me, so I open the door and step out for a moment to shout, "Miss Jones sends her regards you smelly bastard."

I don't know what compelled me to behave in such an unprofessional way, lingering to taunt him for no other reason than he'd intimidated Rebecca. It was like I'd lost my common sense, thrown away caution over a woman who I hadn't even screwed. As I drove away I opened the window and listened to his voice fading into the distance. I couldn't understand what he was shouting, it must've been Russian, but I'm pretty certain he wasn't wishing me luck.

Rebecca Mosley, a.k.a Miss Jones, made a U-turn and parked her hired Ford close to the level crossing where she sits, peering through the windscreen, willing the Mercedes to appear. Five minutes can seem like five hours when you're as worried as she is. She never intended to begin caring for anyone, least of all a short balding forty-year old Irishman but she does and there's no way of changing it. What if the Russian caught him? He might be laying on a dark street somewhere, bleeding to death. It's all her fault she should never have agreed to him taking it back straight away. She starts the car. She'll have to go and find him. Then she stops the engine and sighs with relief as she sees the familiar blue glare of the Mercedes headlights turning on to Station Road. He kills the lights as he rolls to a stop and parks, then he steps out laughing.

"I really enjoyed that."

"What?"

"I'll tell you as I change the plates. Where are they?"

She gives him a scornful look then takes them out of the Ford and passes them to him. He touches her hand affectionately.

"What's up? You look angry"

"No, nothing. No, I'm not angry."

He kneels quickly at the front of the Mercedes, zipping the screws out of the plate with his re-chargeable screwdriver, then looks up at her with a grin.

"I know what it is. You were worried about me."

She feels herself reddening and doesn't reply straight away.

"You were weren't you?"

"No really, well slightly, I just didn't feel much like driving around Peterborough looking for your body."

Tony is about to reply when his face suddenly fills with alarm and he whispers urgently, "Police, don't move, don't look around keep still."

From his position kneeling in front of the car he can see past her to a police patrol car creeping along the road towards them. She hears the engine and the tyres crunching gravel as they get closer. He quickly slides the three number plates beneath the front of the Mercedes and stands whispering, "Now kiss me and look as though you mean it!" She complies quickly.

There we were, locked in our reluctant embrace, standing next to a nearly new Mercedes with no front number plate but three underneath it and me with a rechargeable screwdriver hanging out of my pocket, uncertain whether the Russian had reported the stolen Merc. As you can imagine, with two coppers in a patrol car closing in, I was more than slightly worried.

The Major

On reporting the murders to Heddlu Gogledd Cymru, the North Welsh police authority, Patterson agreed to secure the scene until the local police arrived. There would be no questions to answer, instead, he would furnish them a simple statement informing them that the crime scene has remained undisturbed and is exactly as he came upon it. Why he was there and any details of his operation are definitely classified pieces of information and will remain so. Sitting waiting for them to arrive, he realises that Spud is late checking in so calls his number.

Twenty miles away on Anglesey, Spud's mobile which has been set on silent mode, vibrates, moving in the grass where Rutter dropped it. Spud's body, resting face down in the brambles next to it, is as still as a gravestone and getting colder by the minute. Soon it will be as cold as Rutter's trail.

Patterson gives Jameson a concerned look.

Jameson asks "Spud?"

Patterson nods solemnly.

"You want me to get back there, Sir?"

"No, we'll give him another ten minutes. He might be busy with our man. I'll try again before we assume the worst."

They are interrupted by the sound of a police siren screaming up the lane towards the farm; the car turns in and skids to a halt, followed by another. Patterson opens the Range Rover door and as he steps out, says beneath his breath, "Bloody Keystone Cops."

The uniformed police sergeant gets out and approaches him.

"Major Patterson?"

Patterson nods.

"Any identity Sir?"

He flashes his identity card and says, "Everything is exactly as it was when we came upon the scene. Now that you're here Sergeant, we'll be on our way."

The sergeant raises his hand. "Just hold on a moment Major. What was happening? What was going on? Why were you here?"

Patterson replies as he turns back towards the Range Rover. "We weren't here Sergeant and we didn't even come upon the scene. You do understand don't you?"

The police sergeant reddens with embarrassment in front of the young uniformed constable now standing next to him.

"Yes Sir, sorry, I do understand but..."

Patterson interrupts through the open Range Rover window, "... but, Sergeant? No buts about it man; you've got a double murder to investigate. Don't you think you'd better get on with it?"

The police sergeant almost salutes before he turns to walk away.

As the Range Rover glides back through the gate, Patterson taps Spud's number into his phone, listens to it ringing out for some time then ends the call. Jameson stops at the end of the lane where he would turn left for Anglesey or right for Liverpool and glances at Patterson for instruction.

"Back to Anglesey Jameson, I've got the feeling that getting there sooner isn't going to make any difference to poor old Spud but step on it anyway."

Tony

When you've put yourself in danger and you've got nothing left to rely on but lady luck, then there's no one else to blame when things go wrong. If ignoring you own best advice gets you clipped by a pair of handcuffs, it's definitely your own fault. One of the two cops was a young male; the other was a female so, on reflection, they were probably driving down that deserted dead end for a little semi-uniformed fun over the bonnet of their patrol car. As our awkward kiss ended, I pulled away from Rebecca; they were doing a three-point turn and I looked straight into their faces through their windscreen. Lady luck was with us. He looked disappointed that we were there; she looked embarrassed. As soon as they went out of the road I changed the back number plate. As I was working away, I promised myself I'd try to start thinking of her as a friend. Thinking of her as a lover, which is something she definitely wasn't, could end up with me back in jail. I decided not to tell her about goading the Russian, which was a pathetically stupid and juvenile thing to do.

Within a few minutes we were ready to leave for Dover. I was in the Merc; she was about to get into the Ford. She turned and asked me not to drive too far ahead of her. Then all ideas of changing the way I thought of her were sent to Hell; she came over to the car window, leaned in to kiss me and said, "Be careful love I'd hate to lose you". I was just sitting there with the taste of her still on my lips, being kissed again, this time willingly and called "love". I suppose you can't help the way you feel about a woman, it was definitely way beyond my control.

The Major

Kneeling on the grass next to Spud's body, Patterson's cavalry twill trousers are wet and the front crease of one leg has flattened. With the dawn sun rising behind him, he stands and remains motionless for some time before speaking.

"Well at least it was quick."

"Yes Sir" replies Jameson, "Quite a little professional this one."

"I wouldn't call him a professional but he was certainly lucky to get behind Spud, looks as though he's approached from the beach and hidden waiting for poor old Spud to get out."

Jameson follows him into the cottage where they discover that Rutter's cache has been emptied. On an armchair in the living room they find a copy of Auto Trader. Patterson already knows that Rutter left the hospital by taxi and realises that, by now, he's mobile. Somewhere within the pages of this Auto Trader is the phone number of the person who sold him the car and, identifying what vehicle he's driving will make him very much easier to find. Sadly he hasn't marked any of the adverts and there are over a thousand.

Patterson begins examining the publication. Closing it and laying it on the table in front of him, he can see a few pages which seem to be slightly misaligned. His best guess is that somewhere in pages 27, 28 and 29 is the car he bought, since this indicates that the magazine has been open long enough on those pages to crease the edges closest to the spine and cause them to lie differently. Fifty ads on each page means potentially calling a hundred and fifty numbers before identifying the car the subject is driving. He checks his watch. It's way too early to be calling people asking who bought their car at just a little before 04:30; he decides to wait until eight before phoning the advertisers. In the meantime, there's Spud's body to remove and his Range Rover to get back to HQ. Jameson stoops next to Spud's body in order to pinch closed his eyes which have been staring straight ahead since the bullet entered his brain. Patterson rolls the body bag out on the grass next to him, unzips it, then takes the legs with Jameson taking the arms, to lift the dead weight into the black receptacle.

Patterson pauses a moment. "Goodbye Spud," then he pulls the zip closed and they lift him over his Range Rover tailgate into the boot.

"It'll be nice to let this Rutter bastard have a little suffering when we catch up to him."

"Yes," replies Patterson. "If the situation permits, we'll make it hurt. A good man, Murphy. A very good man."

Jameson follows Patterson's Range Rover to the Royal Welsh Dale barracks in Chester where they deposit Murphy's body with the camp's medical officer and leave his Range Rover. It's 8 a.m. when they exit the camp and, taking a page each, they begin the arduous task of phoning every advert, trying to discover the identity of Rutter's new vehicle.

Kenny

Sitting on the front balcony of their villa, Kenny is relaxing, drinking a glass of freshly squeezed orange juice. He loves the Algarve, the warm morning breeze on his face, everything about the place is special, even the local eggs are wonderful. Janice fried a couple for his breakfast and they both had double yokes. They rented the villa for a fortnight and everything is going well with the farm deal, in fact he has an appointment with a Notary this afternoon to sign the agreement.

The villa is situated on the coast road just outside Quarteira overlooking the Atlantic; it's a wonderful view to be greeted by every morning. He has decided that Portugal will definitely be his future, that, however long he has left, however many years before him, he will spend them all here in the comfortable warm sunshine. This is one of the few moments in his life when he can say he feels at peace. He hears his phone ringing and getting louder as Janice comes out on to the balcony to hand it to him. He answers and, as he does, his whole world changes. All serenity is replaced instantly by grief and confusion.

He doesn't reply, instead ends the call then with sad eyes and very grey-faced he says, "Pack the bags, we're going home" and swallows before continuing, "It's our Wayne love. He's been murdered."

Janice breaks down instantly then, with tears streaming down her face she screams. Her scream carries over the road on to the sea; it's the same shriek of grief made by any mother discovering her child has been taken away forever. Kenny wraps his arms around her in an attempt to contain her sadness; she breaks free to look into his face and struggles to utter the one word.

"Rutter" which he repeats.

Then she begins packing the suitcases. There's nothing she can do to change things when she gets there but she's going home. Perhaps it might not have happened if they hadn't come to Portugal. Kenny's feelings about Portugal have now turned upside down. A minute ago he was floating on the joy of just being there, now he's glad he hasn't handed the cash over and signed those farm papers. He won't bother calling the Notary to cancel their meeting; he'll simply fail to turn up. Within half an hour, the luggage is piled into their hire car and they're driving along the coast towards Faro airport. When the road takes them across the sandy delta where Kenny had planned to buy the farm, they remain silent and, even driving past the turn off to the farm entrance, he fails to even mention it.

Now there's just one purpose left for him, one direction to take; the vengeful one. In his whole sixty years he never even considered killing anyone, now suddenly he's committed to find and kill Rutter. Wayne didn't have an enemy in the world; Even the McGregor brothers didn't have a motive since they'd paid in full for their goods.

"Definitely Rutter did this," he thinks, getting out of the hire car. Then, as he loads their suitcases on to the luggage trolley, he vows silently, "and I'll kill the bastard."

Tony

Our visit to Dover was short and sharp we were there to show the car to one punter. I never liked Dover much, too many travellers passing through and there aren't any decent hotels. We had a pleasant surprise when we opened the boot as a search of the Russian's suitcase and hold-all came up with a couple of grand in euros, a couple of Bulgarian passports and an assortment of un-ironed men's clothes, which we quickly dumped in a layby.

Our next punter was an I.T. man working from home; he must have been doing a lot of cash work because she parted him from fourteen thousand five hundred with the greatest of ease. She was definitely better than me when it came to getting a good price. We were up to just over forty grand already and she'd only sold it three times. Three sales from each advert and three from one phone that was my rule and I would never break it. The next advert was due to appear in the South Coast Friday-Ad so the first phone was ready to be turned off; it was just a throwaway and had become polluted with endless threats from the Russian.

She drove the Ford Focus along the coast to Brighton where we intended to stay for a couple of days before recapturing the Merc, which made good sense since she'd suggested we use her flat instead of booking into a hotel. I liked Marine Square, especially when the sun was shining. I liked the tall hedges around its private gardens, the white stone buildings with their enormous front doors and the steep narrow winding staircase to her flat door on the fifth floor. Her front windows looked out over the gardens to the English Channel, which always had a kind of milky colour, I suppose because of the white chalky cliffs slowly dissolving into it. She makes me a coffee and, drinking it sitting next to an open front window, I look out over Madeira Drive at the strange small, square building close to the railings, it seems to have a globe and some other sculptures on top of it.

"What's that building?"

"That's the Penny Lift," she replies. "They used to charge a penny to take you down to the beach. It's free now though and it's got dragons on the top and a globe. I often sit over there watching the boats go by. There's always a cool breeze there on days like this. If you like, we can go over there when you've finished your coffee."

A few minutes later we were there beneath the dragons, sitting on the bench around the back, looking out to sea.

"I'd like to live here one day, maybe buy myself a little flat like yours and settle down."

"It's a great place Brighton," she replies, "a little bit like London the way people mind their own business, sort of more grown up than the rest of England."

Then, as a middle aged transvestite totters by on dangerously high heels I reply, "Well it's certainly different I'll give you that." Then I continue, "I wonder what made you get into bed with me that first night we met. I woke up feeling as though I was the luckiest man in the world, you looked beautiful naked."

She reddens. "I don't know, I must've been ever so drunk to take my clothes off."

"I wish you'd do it again. "She reddens even more. "You know you want to, you might as well just admit it. You do want me don't you?"

She gets up stuffs her hands deep into her pockets as if closing me out and says, "Put words into someone's mouth Tony and all you end up with is a parrot or a puppet. No one pulls my strings. I dance to my own tune. It's about time you realised that females weren't put on this world to make Tony feel good by letting him screw them."

"Well forgive me for being attracted to you."

A few moments pass in awkward silence, then I ask "I wonder, it is OK these days you know, perfectly acceptable, but are you a lesbian?"

"Tony, just fuck off will you. How dare you make me into a lesbian just because I haven't screwed you?"

"I thought it was a perfectly reasonable question. I didn't mean to offend."

"Look Tony, we've got what we've got and that's it. That's all there is to it, we are just working partners. That's the way it is."

"That's me put in my place then hasn't it? I'll never mention the subject again."

She takes her hands back out of her pockets, sits down next to me and pats my thigh as she speaks.

"Good, now you said you were going to fix the lock on my front door, shall we go and buy some tools?"

There she goes again, in one breath she doesn't ever want it to go any further, in the next she's patting my thigh.

"OK then where's the shop?"

We quickly went for a screwdriver, a pack of long screws and, after fixing her front door without talking to each other, I gave in eventually and broke the silence.

"Right then, I'll just call Kenny and give him the new number, then we can dump this phone."

Kenny took a long time to answer. When he did there was a strange, businesslike tone in his voice and he talked fast. I had never heard him speak that way before.

"Our Wayne's been murdered, you'd better come up and stay for a few days, funeral's on Thursday. OK, we'll talk when you get here."

That's all he said, didn't even wait for me to reply, he just hung up. So we filled up with diesel and got on the road straight away; what had happened to Wayne hardly registered until I was sitting in the passenger seat with nothing to do but remember. My mind wandered back to the time I took him to the fair for his eighth birthday. He was a cocky little fella with that baseball cap and his tiny designer trainers moving so fast they were just a blur; used to call me Uncle Tony. Then when he was eleven I went to watch one of his first boxing matches, they were paired to fight by age rather than weight and the other kid was twice as big but he gave as good as he got. Well he didn't really, he got hammered but he took it well.

I felt a tear creeping down my cheek and she asked me if I was all right. I told her I'd be OK. I just turned on to my side and pretended to be asleep all the way to Wales.

Kenny Robinson's spade sparks as he drives it into the stony ground in front of the barn. His whole body is wet with sweat as he digs deeper and deeper. The pile of stone laden earth next to the excavation is a couple of feet high when he steps down. The simple act of making such a large deep hole empties his mind and stops him thinking about the cruel tragedy of Wayne and Angie's murders.

After a couple of hours of digging, the blisters on his hands burst and sting but, with his back and shoulders aching, he keeps on digging. The hole is about ten feet long and five feet deep when he finally throws his spade on to the pile of excavated soil next to it and climbs out. One by one he drags the three heavy dogs to the edge of the grave and pushes them in. Now as he shovels soil into the hole covering his dogs he imagines that Rutter is lying at the bottom of that hole with his arms and legs bound and that he is in the act of burying the bastard alive. Perhaps this is a practice run because, if he ever gets the opportunity, he will certainly do it. Eventually, when the hole is backfilled level, he finds that he is still left with quite a large pile of soil next to it and supposes that it must be equal to the volume of space taken up by their bodies. The light is fading as he wheels the last barrow of surplus soil on to the field and loses it by spreading it. When he's finished, he rests his shovel on the barn door and looks at the gate to see a Ford turning into the yard. It's Tony and Rebecca.

I thought it was odd not to be greeted by the pack of Ridgebacks and to see Kenny standing in front of the barn. He was very dirty and looked tired as we approached. Unable to come up with anything meaningful or sympathetic enough to say about the loss of his son I just said, "You're dirty. What have you been up to?"

Perhaps I should have just kept my mouth shut. He replied, "The dogs, I've been burying the dogs. The bastard poisoned them."

Then he did something I've never seen him do before, he broke down and cried. I sent Rebecca in to Janice and gave his heaving shoulders a hug.

The Funeral

The hearse left the Black Bull in Walton and moved slowly along the main road towards Norris Green Cemetery. The words "Goodbye Son" were written in lilies leaning on the coffin. All occupants of the first three cars were family members, some of whom had never spoken to each other in years but had been drawn together by the tragedy. All the words said in those mourner's cars only served to fuel the sadness; sayings like "only the good die young" were being uttered by the older family members. Kenny felt like telling them all to shut up but he was choking with his own grief and unable to speak. The procession of mourners' cars following the hearse was so long that it caused a traffic jam from Norris Green to the city centre but no one overtook.

High above the sad procession, Patterson's helicopter hovered. Unlike the usual police helicopter often seen in the skies above Liverpool, it was unmarked. With nothing more than a civil aviation number on its tail, it could be just another anonymous press flight. Patterson having made dozens of phone calls to identify Rutter's vehicle, was looking for a five year old silver metallic Volvo. There was no such vehicle in either the procession or any of the side streets coming near to the route. The chopper descended into Norris Green Park where Jameson met him with the Range Rover.

As the hearse passes between the sandstone gate pillars into the cemetery, it moves close to an unmarked van parked next to a mini digger that looks as though it has just finished cutting a new grave. Riding in the first limousine, Kenny sees the van and doesn't give it a second thought as, one by one, the mourners alight and gather near to the grave, waiting for the crowds who are parking cars in the local side streets and abandoning others close to the cemetery. Billy Jones and Little Austin rush through the gates, determined not to be late paying their last respects but Billy Jones, paranoid by nature, stops next to the unmarked van and gives Little Austin a concerned glance.

"Leave it for fuck sake Jonesy" says Little Austin but Billy Jones can't resist temptation and opens one of the rear doors. Inside the van, two startled plain clothed police officers cower; one drops his camera in panic, the other shouts into his radio for back up. Billy Jones roars at the top of his voice "There's a van full of fucking coppers here."

By now there are a few hundred people in the cemetery, most of whom are criminals and all are appalled by the idea that the police would choose such an indiscreet time to update their photo records. It was bang out of order, an absolutely blatant act of disrespect. The two plain clothed police make a run for it through the gravestones towards Lower House Lane, hotly pursued by a crowd of young outraged criminals. A weak smile breaks though the grief on Kenny's face. It made a pleasant change to see a couple of them at the receiving end.

Tony

Since everyone wanted to give Wayne a good send-off, there was an almighty piss up in the Western Approaches after the funeral. I've always thought it disgusting the way such sad occasions can descend into orgies of drunken violence but it often happens. A few old disputes were settled in the car park and Billy Jones was sitting on a chair near the pool table, having some shards of glass removed from the back of his head by Little Austin's wife. Rebecca was already uncomfortable but when Joey McGregor walked across to offer his respects to Wayne's family, she went pale and began trembling; I held her hand.

"Bad news all this," he says to Kenny as Billy joins us. Then Billy gives Rebecca a lecherous look and says, "Have you got our fucking money yet?"

Kenny stiffens and glares at him, it looks as though he's a second away from lashing out when Joey McGregor raises his hand and defuses the situation.

"Shut your mouth Billy, this is neither the time nor the place. Sorry Kenny, he was a good lad your Wayne. He'll be missed."

Before leaving, Billy gives me one of those "You'd better give us our money back" looks of his and about half an hour later we were on our way to North Wales driving Kenny and Janice home. We didn't do much talking on that journey to the farm, perhaps I should've been thinking about Wayne but I found myself reflecting on the way time is such a great healer. That was the first time we'd run into the dimwit brothers since Rebecca's flat but hardly more than a week had passed and already what had been the threat of imminent death, had paled into a couple of dangerous looks. There were two reasons I was trying get a hundred and fifty grand together and neither was to benefit the McGregors. One, I loved having cash to spend and two, it was the only way I could get her to stay with me and being trapped on a mission to recover their cash certainly did that. I knew that eventually we'd reach a time when I would have to convince her that we were going to bump them and hold on to their money but, hard as I tried, I couldn't imagine a way to make her lose all of that fear. We left early next morning and headed south to recover the Mercedes and get it sold again.

Kenny

It's strangely quiet on the farm with no dogs running around and with no children playing. Since Wayne had been on the farm with Angie when they were murdered, his wife believed that his infidelity had been in some way condoned or at least accepted by his parents. It was for that reason that she hadn't attended the funeral and refused to let her children visit their grandparents.

Kenny carries a bundle of recycled floorboards across the yard and into the barn, where he lays them on the workbench and begins chopping them into six-inch lengths with a circular saw. This morning, just after Tony left, he walked up the lane to the old slate quarry where Rutter had parked before and during the murder. It would have been impossible for him to leave a vehicle anywhere on that cut out single track, so the quarry would be the logical place to have left his vehicle. Standing next to the abandoned workings, looking down at the farm had made Kenny realise just how vulnerable they would be in the night.

The sawing now finished, he has thirty small, square pieces of board into which he begins hammering four inch nails. He drives three of the bright sharp nails through every board and when the boards are all fully spiked, he opens the tin of green paint, dips the brush and paints until the bright nails protruding and the face of each board is green. Then he turns the barn heating to full in order to speed the paint's drying process and goes across the yard to the cottage.

The place is so quiet, it's like someone else's home. Janice is asleep, the television is off and even the kitchen clock has stopped since he ignored the fact that it needed winding. He fills the kettle, then dumps it on top of the sink-load of dirty dishes, having changed his mind in favour of whisky. Settling into his armchair in front of the television, he aims his remote control and, when the screen lights up he selects the security camera, then pours himself a drink. Everything is working as it should. He checked it earlier but he just needs to re-check the view now that his camera and security light is pointing up the hill, instead of down the lane. A perfect monochrome image of the gorse-covered hill appears; Rutter will need to descend that hill before launching another attack.

He takes a sip of his whisky, wondering how Wayne missed Rutter coming up the lane. Perhaps he didn't even have the camera turned on, then he smiles weakly, remembering his own youth and realising that if he had been with a beautiful young girl, perhaps he might have neglected to pay attention to the security camera.

He spends an hour cleaning and oiling the only firearm in the house, a single barrel shot gun worth more as an antique than a weapon. That's all he has, a single shot duck gun and a machete which he spends an hour honing on an oil stone until it's sharp enough to slice a sheet of paper. He's never killed anyone before and wonders if it will make him feel guilty. He's pointed sawn off shotguns at people over the years as the route of his life led him into armed robbery, but those shot guns were never intended to kill anyone. They were just a prop; only ever used to shower victims in plaster as he blasted holes in ceilings to convince them of his serious intent. This time, there's no doubt in his mind that he'll carry it through. If Rutter doesn't show up over the next couple of nights, he'll pack Janice off to the safety of her sister's house and take the initiative by hunting the bastard down.

It's late afternoon when he gets up from the chair, searching the kitchen cupboard for Janice's Marigolds. One of them tears as he forces his big hand into it but he leaves it on. Torn or not, it should keep some of the green paint off his hand. Even with the heating on it can't be fully dried out yet.

Outside the barn, he finds a couple of old plastic fertiliser sacks and goes inside to load them with his homemade green porcupines. Then, almost as an afterthought, he reaches for the can of rat poison and drops it into one of the sacks. Slowly, he makes his way up the gorse hill, placing a porcupine every few feet, being careful to cover every possible way down from the quarry but only on the closest half of the hill which should be well in range. Each time he lays one of his green porcupines in the grass, he pulls up the stems and blades around it, then sprinkles a few crystals of the rat poison on every one. The brown crystals could pass for soil and the green spiked boards blend in so perfectly that, after laying the last one in the fading light, he is unsure about going back down. Instead he continues up the second half of the hill to the quarry and makes his way back to the farm along the road. His plan is a simple one, when Rutter arrives, he'll come half way down the hill before he impales his foot on one of the porcupines. When that happens, he'll turn on the spotlight and should see Rutter wounded and on the retreat. Being blinded by the bright light, Rutter will almost certainly impale himself again, which should slow him down enough to allow time for Kenny to race up the lane and get between him and his vehicle. That will be the end of Rutter. The only thing that causes Kenny to doubt the final outcome is his own lack of firepower. With one shot at a time, he'll have to be lucky; it takes about ten seconds to load another cartridge and Rutter has probably got a whole modern arsenal to draw upon. Arriving back at the farm, he goes in and, after cleaning the green paint from his hands and clothes, picks up the phone and calls Little Austin. Perhaps he knows who might be selling some more serviceable modern weapons.

At 2 p.m. James Rutter exits the accommodation over his vacant shop on Guildford High Street and walks down the concrete steps into the yard then through the gate, padlocking it before continuing out of the cobbled entry. There's almost nowhere to park in central Guildford so he starts on his long walk, crossing the bridge then past the Yvonne Arnaud Theatre and along the grassy riverbank towards the side street where he left his car. Warm weather always brings groups of children and their mothers to the riverside and today is no exception. Resting on a wooden bench, he smokes a cigarette as he watches them paddle and play, studying them, wondering how they can find such happiness in something as simple as playing in water.

Life was never like that for Rutter. When he was a boy he only smiled when he got the better of other children, and never truly let go and laughed honestly until he discovered cocaine. Many years have passed since he grew the nail on the little finger of his left hand until it became the perfect coke scoop. At times like this, sitting in a public space, he can feed his nose with white powder very discreetly and, as he does, his mind sharpens. Pinprick clear images of Kenny Robinson come to him as he remembers the other cons gathering around him on H Wing, listening to his stories. Who the fuck does Kenny Robinson think he is, some kind of criminal fucking guru? Kenny Robinson's fuck all, a family man, a fucking insect. Then standing to continue his journey, he gives the gathering at the river resentful looks thinking, "Just like this lot Robinson, another fucking insect."

One of the mothers quickly draws her children close to her when she sees that hateful expression on his thin lips. She can tell, anyone could tell, even a blind man would see, that Rutter hasn't got any decency to him, any humanity. She sighs with relief as he walks away along the riverbank but doesn't release her children until he is completely out of sight.

Walking the final few hundred yards to his car, he crunches the possibilities. All it took was a few discreet telephone calls to discover that Wayne Robinson had stolen the BMK for the McGregor brothers and had been paid in full. With Wayne gone, his father would almost certainly be holding the proceeds. Billy Jones is no longer an important target, Rutter's primary purpose is to get hold of enough cash and disappear into Europe. Robinson definitely won't be expecting another attack so soon and, being a family man, he'll probably be so cut up over the loss of his precious fucking son, it should be easy to get the better of him. If Kenny Robinson doesn't have the cash, then he'll just have to tax the McGregor brothers. Smiling as he gets in and starts the car, he decides to hit the McGregors anyway; the more money he can get hold of the better.

The Major

Patterson kept the details of Spud's demise a complete secret; no report was made to the local police therefore no investigation other than his own would ever take place; it was better that way, playing it close to his chest.

He assumes that Rutter will be scanning the media for reports of the murder and, the fact that there are none, will indicate that an organisation, other than and far more lethal than the police, are on his case though if he hasn't realised that fact already he must be very slow on the uptake. Patterson takes a sip of his tea and smiles at Jameson; they are finishing lunch at the Holywell Little Chef where they spent the night. Being situated just five miles from the Robinson farm, it was the obvious choice but he was never comfortable staying in such down-market accommodation, an inch away from being a knocking shop with most of its rooms used by couples having extra marital affairs. Last night was no exception; the lovers in the room next door were extremely loud.

Still smiling, he asks "Were you disturbed at all last night?"

"Disturbed?" replies Jameson "He was nearly driving her through the wall. At it for hours weren't they?"

"Perhaps you should have knocked on the door and offered him a little assistance."

"I don't think so Sir, sounded like torture to me, must've been using the whip on the poor bastard the way he was going. I wonder if he survived, it went very quiet very suddenly" he replies, grinning.

Patterson genuinely likes Jameson even if, since leaving the army, his dress sense has plummeted and he seems always to be wearing jeans and trainers. He gives his own tan leather brogues an admiring glance and is about to offer a gentle fashion hint but Jameson pre-empts it. "Nice shoes those, Sir."

"You know better than to call me 'Sir' in pubic Jameson. Yes they are rather good ones, not very expensive at all when you take into consideration that they last for years. I could show you where I get them if you like."

"No not for me, I love my Nikes, non-slip sole, heel cushioning, protects my joints and I can corner at high speed without losing my footing."

"Well so be it; but if you ever decide to upgrade to British shoes fashioned from genuine leather by British craftsmen, away from those synthetic things put together by Chinese prisoners, I'll happily introduce you to a good Loakes supplier."

Knowing that characters such as Rutter mount their assaults under cover of darkness they spend the afternoon on such small talk, just waiting. By now Patterson has discovered that Wayne stole the BMK for the McGregor brothers, also that he has probably been paid. Since Rutter seems to be motivated by a ruthless blend of greed and revenge, Patterson's logic tells him that, since Robinson offers a combination of both rewards, Rutter's next target will almost certainly be him. Patterson had been passed the statements collected during the Pettit murder investigation and knows the identity of everyone who was at the farm when Rutter received his beating. He knows that Billy Jones took part and will be another potential target for Rutter, but he also knows that Billy Jones is on a family trip to Disneyland and has in fact flown to the U.S this morning.

He calls his contact in the local police headquarters to ascertain whether the Wayne Robinson investigation has left the crime scene. On receiving confirmation that they released the scene on Friday, he smiles at Jameson.

"The hunting season's fully open."

Jameson replies with enthusiasm, "Good, we won't feed the hounds then."

"No let's locate this animal, get ourselves blooded and back to civilization."

It was about 8 p.m. when Kenny finally decided that Janice should disappear to her sister's sooner rather than later. Despite her protests, he loaded her suitcase into their little estate car and sent her on her way. It was more than a premonition. Rutter had unfinished business with Kenny and he could feel disaster hovering somewhere close, a cloud of black misery waiting to engulf him and no way of knowing exactly when.

He shared his worries with Little Austin when he was enquiring about a more capable weapon. Austin who definitely owed him more than one favour, not only said that he had a couple of .38 automatics with over a hundred rounds, but that he would deliver them tonight then stick around until the finish. If Rutter doesn't show his face in the next couple of days, he'll tag along on the hunt for him. That was three long hours ago when it was still daylight. He'd been sitting in front of the television studying the hill for any movement but now that night has fallen and there's no moon, just blackness, he switches the monitor off and turns the cottage lights out.

Moving silently through the darkened rooms he makes his way to the kitchen door and goes out into the yard. Quiet as a grave around the farm, not a single vehicle has moved in either direction on the lane in three hours. Earlier he wired the security light to a switched extension lead now he flicks the switch and the whole hillside lights up.

"Good," he whispers to himself, then flicks the switch back to darkness thinking, "Come on Austin, you should be here by now."

Another hour passes and now he's beginning to accept that Austin isn't going to show. Sitting alone on a tree stump in the darkened yard, he cocks the single shotgun hammer and gains comfort by touching the cartridges in his pocket. Then, resting the long gun across his knees, he grips the machete handle tight and slides the leather loop attached to it over his wrist.

"Come on you bastard I'm ready for you now. Where the fuck are you?"

Rutter's blacked out Volvo creeps along the lane barely ticking over. It's difficult to navigate the narrow, winding lane in complete darkness; the front wings brush

244

on grass sprouting from the high clay banks on either side. Passing the tall chain link gate, he peers into the farmyard but fails to see Kenny crouching in the darkness.

Kenny's eyes narrow and, as they follow the sound of the engine ticking slowly past, he can't see the Volvo but, when Rutter brakes before turning into the quarry, the surrounding area glows red in the tail lights, then the hills go to red again as he brakes turning the car around. It might be a courting couple but he knows it isn't. This is definitely Rutter, he doesn't know how he knows but he's certain; his heart begins pounding so loudly that he can hear it.

Rutter sets the handbrake; he doesn't drag the ratchet, instead he keeps the button depressed pulling the handle hard, then releases it very slowly without producing a single click. The quarry is dark but remembering the geography, he picks his way through the boulders then feels his way through gorse to the crest of the hill. Unlike his last visit the farm, it is blacked out. This might mean that there's no one there, it might mean that they're all sleeping or it might mean that Robinson is lying in wait for him. What if Robinson has recruited some help? What if he's walking straight into a trap? He unclips the fastening on his shoulder holster, freeing the automatic for a fast withdrawal and, with his revolver in his left hand, he lowers himself to the ground and snakes forwards on his belly.

Moving though the short grass, his revolver butt clicks on something metallic. He investigates, feeling with his free hand and finds the first porcupine. This is no mistake; the paint is still tacky and the fact that Robinson has taken the time to booby trap the hill indicates that he's probably alone, he grins thinking, "Slippery bastard."

Then, instead of descending the hill in a straight line to the farm he decides to crawl east along the crest before going down to approach the farm from its eastern perimeter. This cautious decision takes him clear of Kenny's homemade minefield.

Jameson turns the Range Rover off the A55 and drives up the lane towards the Robinson farm. Patterson's finger presses the button and lowers the passenger window. Unlike the Volvo, the Range Rover roars up the lane past the farm with its headlights on main beam. Passing the farm, Patterson sees Kenny's crouching form illuminated by the peripheral light.

"One in the yard," he declares un-holstering his weapon. Then, turning into the quarry, they see Rutter's unoccupied Volvo.

"Stay with the vehicle Jameson."

Jameson stops the engine and looks at Patterson imploringly virtually begging to be allowed a part in the kill.

"But, Sir?"

"Right you are then but stay close and no mistakes, no accidents."

They both alight quickly with weapons drawn and move on to the hill.

From his position, now east of the farm, Rutter sees their headlights and believes that he has just slipped clear of a trap. He assumes that whoever has just pulled up in the quarry is one of Kenny's associates.

Kenny crouches with his finger poised on the extension switch ready to illuminate the gorse hill. If only

246

those headlights were Austin's but he knows they're not. Austin doesn't own a Range Rover.

Jameson and Patterson begin moving quickly towards the farm. Being eager for the kill, the athletic Jameson's foot striding forwards finds the first porcupine. He screams with agony as two of the spikes punch through the sole of his Nike, not stopping at his foot but entering beneath his arch and grating on the metatarsals before bursting through the top of his foot just beneath the Nike laces. Patterson freezes.

Hearing Jameson's agonised scream echoing around the valley, Kenny throws the switch and floods the hillside with bright light. Then, before even attempting to identify who it is, he lets fly with the duck gun.

Patterson raises his weapon and fires three shots in rapid succession. Shards of shattered glass and metal shower the yard around Kenny as Patterson's bullet finds the spotlight plunging the field is back into darkness.

Seeing the flash produced by Kenny's single barrel shot gun, both Patterson and Jameson dropped defensively to the ground and, as they did, Jameson took a second porcupine in the hand. Still on their bellies Jameson pulls his hand off the nail board and groans.

"What now Sir?"

"We'll fall back to the vehicle and wait for him to return for his."

Rutter retreats quickly, still believing that he has slipped Kenny's carefully laid trap and that his best move is to escape and postpone his revenge. Stepping out of the gorse on to the hard, level quarry ground he moves towards his Volvo then, seeing the Range Rover, he realises that the two men on the hill are certainly not Kenny's friends and definitely not his.

"MI5", he whispers in a trembling tone. Then he opens the window, starts the Volvo and, as he drives past, shoots the two Front Range Rover tyres out before screeching down the lane. Passing the farm gate, he sees the flash of Kenny's single barrel firing. It peppers the driver's door but none of the shot penetrates even the outer door skin and Rutter is safely away.

With Jameson's arm around his shoulder, Patterson approaches their Range Rover. He helps the wounded man on to the passenger seat, closes the door and starts up.

"I should have stayed with the vehicle," says Jameson apologetically.

"Yes, you would have had the bastard when he came back for his car. But then I'd have been sitting there with a badly damaged foot. We're not too far behind we may still catch him."

He starts up and drives out of the quarry then pulls up.

"Those two shots we heard. The bastard's taken the two front tyres out."

Then he selects four-wheel drive, slams the gear stick into first and continues rumbling down the lane on the pair of flat tyres. Kenny sees them passing the farm entrance but stays well back in the shadows, realising that these two in the new Range Rover are probably police on the hunt for Rutter, also that they are better armed than him. A few minutes pass before Little Austin walks up the lane and arrives at the farm. He's carrying a gym bag with a change of clothes and the weapons inside.

"Sorry I'm late Kenny, the car broke down in Flint and I've had to walk."

"You just missed him"

"Yeah I know, tore past me coming out of the lane, nearly run me down, the prick. Who were the other two with the flat tyres?"

"I don't know Austie, maybe police."

Tony

During the next few days we recovered the Mercedes and sold it again; this time it went for the giveaway price of thirteen grand to a punter in Eastbourne. It was an easy one to recover, no gated estates or Russian pimps, he was just a builder who I guess had been doing cash jobs to avoid paying VAT. It was nothing but business as usual to me but Eastbourne was a little too close for comfort as far as Rebecca was concerned. I had to convince her that there was nothing to worry about. OK, Eastbourne might only be twenty-five miles from Brighton but, in all the time she's lived in Brighton, has she ever met this builder before? No, of course she hasn't, so why should she ever meet him again? If she does, then all she's done is sold him a beautiful car for a knockdown price. Absolutely nothing to lose any sleep over. She was far happier when we'd serviced the last of the three punters that the Friday-Ad produced and travelled north to begin servicing the NW Coast Loot adverts. The circulation of that free paper covers the Fylde and Wyre Coast, Lancaster, Morecambe, Southport and Blackpool. There's always a few quid to be had out of their local entrepreneurs. So, after a long lonely drive following her up the motorway, we pulled into Morecambe and booked into the Midland Hotel on the seafront and were lucky enough to get a room with sea views and a balcony. I always loved that place and was careful not to do anything likely to sully my reputation. As far as they were concerned, I was a quiet respectable man who kept his business to himself.

Morecambe

The Midland Hotel Morecambe was built on the site of an earlier hotel, also known as the Midland. When the original hotel was built back in 1840, Morecambe, as we know it today, hardly existed. It was just a sleepy village of fishermen's cottages known as Poulton-Le-Sands. By 1933, when the original Midland was demolished and Morecambe was developing into a bustling seaside resort, the modern Midland was built. The 1933 version is an art deco classic, built in a blunt-ended crescent shape with forty pristine rooms, many of which look out across Morecambe Bay. Over recent years, since people have begun to celebrate such neat, modern architecture, it is visited not just by tourists but by art deco enthusiasts. Tony is sitting alone on the balcony studying a very large Collins Road Atlas. The first enquiry has come from the Loot advert and Rebecca has arranged to take the car to be viewed, but he's having second thoughts about letting her sell the car. Rebecca walks out on to the balcony, passes him a glass of whisky and sits in the deckchair next to his.

"Well what do you think?" she asks.

"I just don't know. Here, look at the map, that's Lake Windermere, the Swan Hotel is at one end of the lake just here. The only way out of there when I nick it back is along this road here, no bigger than a lane; it's about ten miles to the nearest proper road, then another five or so to the motorway. If they see it go it'll be awkward."

"So we're not going to let him have it then?"

"I don't know" he replies" Why don't we take a ride up there this afternoon give the whole area a look. I know the place, been there before but it was a while ago. Let's just go and see how we feel when we see it"

Tony

Three-quarters of an hour later we were there, testing the route out. There was quite heavy traffic in the afternoon but we would almost certainly take it back in the middle of the night so the roads would be empty. OK, that meant we could move along them faster, but it also meant that we'd be very easy to find if it came on top. I parked the Ford next to the lake opposite the timber pier which goes out over the water to enable passengers to board The Swan, a converted lake steamer. The crowds of Japanese tourists, parties of schoolchildren and ancient, white-legged anorak-wearing hikers ambling along the lakeside, were not very different than the last time I visited the place. It was uncomfortably hot in the car so we got out and went to sit down in a hut, the kind of timber building where tourists sit to feed the swans and ducks.

As we sat on the wooden bench, I looked up at the flaking cream-paned board ceiling and saw the trap door, now with a huge padlock keeping it closed. She caught on to my amusement and asked me what it was all about but I told her it was nothing worth mentioning.

My mind dragged me back to when I was fourteen and my mother brought me over from Dublin so we could live with my father. I hated Liverpool, missed all my mates and it wasn't long before I was in trouble and got myself locked up. When the bombs went off in Guildford, Birmingham and Warrington, it wasn't the greatest time to be Irish and I was always getting into a fight on account of being a 'Mick' or a 'Paddy'. Eventually, sick of all the shite I was getting, I escaped from approved school with a Scottish kid and we hitchhiked north towards Edinburgh but only got as far as the Lake District. Now here I am about twenty-five years older, sitting in the same lakeside hut beneath the trap door that we used to open every night to climb up and sleep in the rafters. Across the road is the same wishing well with its metal frame carrying bells for benefactors to ring by throwing pennies that dropped and splashed into the small stone well beneath. Every evening, just before sunset, a council worker used to come with his net to fish the donations out of the shallow water. Needless to say, donations plummeted over the summer we spent sleeping above the hut, since we used to help him out by almost, but never quite, emptying it just before he arrived. So it's not just the tourists that haven't changed, it's me as well, still more or less homeless and stealing other people's wishes on a regular basis.

"Come on, tell me," she says. "What's so amusing?"

So I did but left out the pathetic stuff about being bullied. And my Ma? She died soon after that and it wasn't long before my old fella followed her, due to the Guinness poisoning. I mean, eight pints of that black stinking stuff isn't meant to fit inside one human being, at least not every day. I suppose it was bound to happen in the end.

Having weighed things up, worked on my courage and decided that we'll let the punter from The Swan Hotel have it, I look at her and say, "All right we'll do it."

She seems uncertain. "Are you sure? I mean it is a hard one to get away from if things go wrong."

I pat her leg in a reassuring way.

"I'll let you worry about the selling; you let me worry about the recovering," while all the time thinking just how much I need to get a grip of her.

Jesus she's so luscious, just about edible; when on God's good earth is she going to realise what's sitting right next to her? She's having an awful effect on me, I'm turning into an overblown big-headed brainless teenager. It's like I'm going to nick it back from somewhere very dangerous just to impress her. I've even starting to talk with a deeper voice and I'm posing almost as badly as Clive the key man.

Old Man of The Sea

Sixty-year old Peter Nancy left his wife to live aboard a boat and sometimes referred himself Captain Nancy. There had been several boats in his life and he was well-liked on Spike Island in Widness where his sailing career began twenty years earlier. The boat owners on the island gave everyone a nickname and his was "Peter the Liar". Though a stranger to the truth, Peter was harmless and his lies often involved boats, devastating gales and the biggest blue waves the oceans had ever produced. His first boat was a Carter, a plastic Bermuda sloop, thirty-three feet long and very wide in the beam; it was an excellent sea boat. He spent the first year with the boat propped up on the hard for essential repairs. He changed the anodes, the propeller and gearbox and fitted new rigging, before finally painting the hull and deciding it was ready for the high seas. Then, just before re-launching the vessel, he placed an advert and sold it for a loss. Of course he told everyone that he'd made a massive profit on the venture, but he was broken-hearted to see the vessel go.

His next boat was a fifty-foot ex-royal naval pinnace with a rotten keel, which he owned for two years, during which time the vessel remained propped up on the hard while he performed massive repairs; a new stem post new keel, several planks and a complete engine rebuild. Then, when it was ready, he placed an advert and took the first offer, losing another substantial sum. Of course, as was his way, he cried into his beer about the loss of such a lovely vessel but told everyone he was consoled by the healthy profit he'd made on the boat. Then he bought the old steel Dutch motorboat, which he described as a gentleman's motor yacht. As usual, straight after the purchase he hired a crane and had it lifted on to the hard. That was about the time his wife threw him out saying she was sick of all the lies and all the losses. She had quite taken to the idea of sailing the Med in the beginning but, after suffering chronic financial hardship and being let down so often, she said, "Either that boat goes, or I do." Unfortunately for Peter, he was drunk at the time so he declared proudly that he'd decided to live aboard. Had he been sober, things might have turned out differently but he was often drunk and, being a stubborn man, would never go back on his word when he sobered up. His drunken times were when he conjured up his best lies. He would lean across the table in the Doctors pub with that shock of white hair hanging over one eye and tell stories of the time he barely survived a mistral and the time a large blue wave deposited his vessel so hard on a sandy beach that she broke her back.

Sometimes, when he was completely wrecked, he would become tearful about the time he had to leave the wonderful island of Tuvalu where he'd fallen in love with the most beautiful native girl he had ever set eyes upon. The truth was that he'd found the Island of Tuvalu marked on an old chart aboard the Bermuda sloop, and the closest he'd ever come to setting eyes upon a beautiful island girl was when the spotty Filipino served him in the local takeaway. It was the morning after one such tearful exhibition in the Doctors pub, that he learned his nickname and became so ashamed that he acquired new moorings straight away. He hired a crane and had the gentleman's motor yacht loaded on to a lorry to be driven to the new berth on Lake Windermere. All the other boat owners had turned up to wave him off but he waited around the corner and followed the lorry, too ashamed and embarrassed to show his face.

Now, sitting alone aboard the mighty twin diesel vessel moored just a hundred yards from The Swan Hotel, he is finally afloat. Though he seldom unfastens his mooring lines and, when he does, only lets them go long enough to turn the boat around, he feels like a true master mariner but falls short of actually buying the cap. As is the way on summer mornings like this, a damp mist hangs over the lake's surface and all is quiet except for the few ripples lapping along the side of the boat, caused by ducks pecking at the waterline, tasting the green, fresh waterweed.

When Peter first arrived at the moorings, every one of his credit cards was maxed out. In fact, he was so strapped for cash that he took a job in The Swan's bar washing glasses but since then, his wife passed away and his finances improved massively when he inherited and quickly sold their family home. To avoid paying American Express, Barclays and the TSB, he quickly withdrew the cash and gained reassurance by keeping it with him. Now, sitting silently reading the Loot advert, he waits for Rebecca to arrive with the new Mercedes, half remembering the rum-fuelled telephone conversation during which he thinks he might have said he owned The Swan Hotel. He wonders what this Miss Williams looks like, wonders if a successful businesswoman might be attracted to an old sea dog.

Tony

Following the Mercedes along the lakeside, I flashed my headlights, letting her know I was stopping and parked close to the wishing well as she disappeared along the lane to The Swan Hotel. A hotel owner is bound to have a secure place to park his vehicles and there's always someone awake in a hotel. Most of them employ their own security staff so this really was the worst possible punter to hit and I knew it.

Peter Nancy wipes condensation from the wheelhouse window as he sees the Mercedes arriving in the car park.

"Yes that's definitely the car," he thinks, quickly sliding the wheelhouse door open to rush down the boarding plank. He must reach her before she goes into reception and asks for Mr Nancy, the hotel owner. He intercepts her just before she reaches the entrance.

"Ah Miss Williams, you've come to see me I believe, my name's Nancy, Peter Nancy." He's somewhat out of breath.

"Yes, hello Mr Nancy," she says smiling confidently then, turning back in the direction of the Mercedes, she offers him the key. "Well here's the car Mr Nancy, exactly as described in the advert, perhaps you'd like to take her for a spin?"

He takes the key from her outstretched hand smiling.

"It certainly looks perfect," he says opening the passenger door for her to get in.

As he gets into the driver's seat, she asks "It looks like a nice hotel Mr Nancy, how long have you owned it?"

"It's really Captain Nancy, Miss Williams, but you can call me Peter. No I didn't decide to buy it in the end. It was over-priced."

"Really; I had the impression that you already owned it."

"Just a misunderstanding. What I actually said was that I was thinking of buying the place but if I had bought it," he says, pointing at his boat, "I'd still live aboard the yacht."

Then, reversing to turn the car around, "Slow astern, ah that's it, what was visibility like down the lane? Any mist?"

Rebecca is struck by the oddness of his character but quickly gets into the spirit of it all.

"No Captain, no mist at all."

Tony doesn't react as the Mercedes drives past. If she succeeds in selling the car, she'll ask for a lift to Kendal and he'll pick her up from there. Back at the Swan Hotel car park, the Mercedes pulls up next to Peter's boat.

"Well, it really is exactly as you say in the advert isn't it? I like it. Why don't you come aboard and we'll talk money?"

She follows him up the gangplank on to the forty-foot boat.

"Nice boat Peter"

"Yes she's Dutch, a Bakdekkruiser, built in nineteen thirty-five. Not many of them still afloat. She's classed as a gentleman's yacht. So the Mercedes, you're asking fifteen thousand?

How about twelve?"

"I was thinking of something more like fourteen five. The car did originally cost our company thirty thousand and that was only three months ago. If we didn't have the cash-flow problem it wouldn't even be on the market."

He opens the cut glass door to the drinks cabinet and reaches in for the bottle of Lambs Navy rum.

"Would you like a drink?"

"No not for me, thank you Peter"

"Well Miss Williams," he says pouring himself a drink, "I've bought and sold enough boats to know that no one ever asks for what they really want."

He's definitely on the hook, Rebecca smiles. "I'm sure you have Peter but this isn't a boat, it's a nearly new Mercedes."

He sips the rum.

"But if I offered you fourteen thousand and had the cash to pay you right now, you'd take that wouldn't you?"

"No, I'm sorry Peter but I really wouldn't be able to let it go for any less."

He takes another sip, looking as though he's considering whether he should buy the car, then he places his glass on the chart table.

"Are you an honest woman Miss Williams?"

He's already decided he's having the car but what he's considering is, whether she'll be safe enough to impress. The truth is that he's incredibly lonely, she's already admitted a cash flow problem with her business and perhaps she might give him some kind of partnership if he was willing to make an investment in her business. She feels herself reddening as she replies.

"Well, I do think I'm honest Peter but, well, that is a strange question to ask."

He pours himself another large drink and downs it in one. Then lifts an old leather suitcase from the deck and places it on the chart table between them. Rebecca is intrigued.

"I hope that you are an honest woman Miss Williams, what's your first name?"

"Patricia."

"Well Patricia."

"Call me Trish."

"Well Trish, I will pay you the fourteen thousand five hundred pounds for the car but I must ask you to promise that you won't tell anyone else what I'm about to share with you."

"You've got my word on that, Peter."

"OK," he says, then pours himself another large drink, downs it and opens the case. Rebecca's mouth gapes at the sight of the cash inside.

"That's what a hundred and seventy-five thousand pounds looks like, Trish."

He pours another drink, swallows it and begins counting the bundles of cash until he reaches fourteen thousand five hundred, which he lays on the chart table.

"So, Trish if you give me the logbook and the keys, I'll drop you off wherever you need to go but before we leave, I did wonder what your particular line of business is and would there be any kind of partnership available for a quick cash injection?"

Rebecca takes the cash, passes him the logbook, the service papers and the key. Peter begins to look tearful as he pours himself another drink. Rebecca feels herself reddening even more.

"My business already has a few partners, Peter and, to be perfectly honest, you'd probably be really risking your money. That's a lot of cash to have hanging around. Don't you think you should bank it?"

"Yes I suppose I should really."

Then, as a tear rolls down his cheek and he continues, Rebecca begins to feel even more awful, guiltier than she has ever felt before.

"You must wonder how I came to have such a large sum of cash in a suitcase, so I'll tell you. I first met my wife twenty years ago when I sailed to the tiny isle of Tuvalu. She was a lot younger than me, ten years younger, and she was one of the chief's daughters." Now he begins to sob between sentences. "I blame myself really, no one else to blame. She never liked being in England, hated the cold, she belonged in the sunshine. When she died, I couldn't face being in the house alone without her so I sold it and moved on board." He breaks off for another fit of sobbing, pours another rum and continues, "And you must wonder about this old leather case. Well, it was hers. When we set sail for England she brought it aboard. Everything she owned was inside this; I'll never part with it."

When he breaks down completely, she puts her arm around his shoulders to comfort him and, as she does, she truly wishes she hadn't taken his money for the car.

"Listen Peter here's an idea; why don't I drive you to the bank right now. You could deposit your cash safely and I'll come back in a few days when you feel better. Then, if you still want to, you can have the car. You'd be helping me out at the same time because I could do with using the car for a few more days."

Peter takes a break from sobbing to look suddenly furious with an insane look in his eyes as he almost shouts at her.

"I said I'm having the car and I will. Put that cash back in your pocket. Don't think because you see a man crying that he's in some way sick and doesn't know what he's doing. That is what you think isn't it? That's how little you understand grief. Obviously I must be crazy because I'm sad. Didn't you ever feel lonely?"

Then he begins sobbing again on account of the fact that the world simply doesn't understand his rum generated grief. He looks up resentfully.

"I've had a little drink now so no doubt you'll imagine that I'm too drunk to drive, in which case you'll need to call yourself a taxi. Here, this should cover it," he says, almost throwing a fifty pound note at her. "What good's all of this cash when I've lost the only woman I ever loved?"

Rebecca gets up and moves towards the wheelhouse door.

"Are you going to be all right if I leave you now?"

"Don't pretend that you care, because you don't. Just take your money and go."

She falters at the door and tries to say something but he cuts her short screaming, "Just bloody well go will you. You're no longer welcome here."

Rebecca walks down the gangplank and out of The Swan Hotel car park without phoning a taxi. Instead she begins the half-mile walk to where she saw Tony parked. She only gets a few hundred yards before her burden of guilt is too heavy to bear and she bursts into tears.

I could see that she was crying before she even reached the car so I jumped out and rushed up to her, held her shoulders and looked straight into her eyes.

"What's happened, what's the bastard done to you?"

"Nothing; it's nothing he did, it's me."

You can expect a little unexplained emotion when you work with a woman but it was a shock to see her crying. I thought she was much too tough for that but, well, when all's said and done, she is a woman. I figure when a woman gets all weepy, what she needs is someone to listen; so, sitting next to her in the car, that's exactly what I did.

"Promise me something," she asks and of course I agree. Crazy as it is I'd promise her the world then die trying to get it. She's still sobbing, stops to blow her nose. "Promise me that, if I tell you where there's a whole lot of cash to steal, you won't do it."

Of course I promise instantly and she continues. "I just feel so awful, so completely worthless. I really wish I hadn't taken the money off this one. He's just a sad, lonely old man; he's got no one in the world who cares about him.

His wife died, he sold their house and now all he's got is a suitcase full of cash."

"How much cash?"

"You promised Tony, you gave your word."

"And I meant it but how much?"

"A hundred and seventy-five thousand pounds."

"Jesus that's a lot of cash to have lying around."

"He's in such a mess I really wish I hadn't let him have the car."

I feel all fatherly passing her another tissue. It's like anything that happens to her is all my fault; forget the fact that she started off by robbing me. It doesn't feel good seeing her cry.

"Why did you take his money for the car if it makes you feel like this? You should've just told him it wasn't for sale any more and left."

"I tried but it was too late, he'd already paid me. Are you angry with me?"

"You silly girl how could I ever be angry with you? Remember when I told you that conscience could get the better of you and when I said that there are sixty three million people in the UK and you're allowed to let one or two off if it doesn't feel right?"

"Yes."

"Well I wasn't joking; what's the point in stealing something if it makes you unhappy?"

Her eyes have gone red and puffed up when I pass her another tissue but, thank God, she's managed to stop crying. She was making me feel like bloody a pimp.

"Look," I say offering a solution, "it might be a little awkward but if you want, I'll go and give him the cash back."

"You'd really do that; give him his fourteen and a half back?"

"Jesus Christ Rebecca, it's not blood, it's just pieces of paper and plenty more where they came from. I could tell him you didn't have authority to sell the car, hand him his cash and we could go away."

She considers for a moment then says "No it wouldn't work; he's drunk. He'd probably refuse. If he wouldn't give you the paperwork back and went to the police or something. No it's too risky."

"Well it's up to you but at least if we let him keep his other hundred and sixty thousand. It's not like we took every penny he had is it?"

Brighton Pier - Autumn 96 - Fisher

That was something I never expected to hear from a career thief like Tony Hurley. It was quite a new concept to me; a thief with a conscience takes a few minutes to sink in.

Then I ask, "So you really let the drunken old man keep his hundred and sixty thousand pounds?"

I catch him looking at me as though I'm a complete idiot. "All black and white to you isn't it Fisher? Don't you know that thieving's just a game?"

"Still," I say, "must make things awkward being a thief with a conscience."

"Not really," he replies, "just meant I always had to work at it. Look at Nelson, he suffered with seasickness but he was still a great sailor. Anyway it doesn't matter either way now because I've retired. Jesus I could do with a drink."

I never would have imagined that I could feel empathy with any professional criminal, least of all Hurley but I was actually beginning to like him.

"No Tony you're not having a drink, not an alcoholic one anyway. What you need is a sandwich and another cup of hot tea."

He gives me a look of complete mistrust.

"Give me a fucking break; I had a probation officer like you when I was a kid."

As I turn to go into the café for the hot tea, he calls after me. "You did nick that briefcase full of money didn't you?"

Not bothering to reply, I just keep walking. Maybe he has changed, maybe I can help him, but first he needs to face up to what happened to Rebecca; then we'll see.

The Major

Patterson left Jameson with the MO at the Royal Welsh barracks. The good news for Jameson was that the rat poison on the nails that went through his hand and foot, only works when ingested and combines with digestive fluids to produce a lethal chemical. The bad news was that injured metatarsus bones are extremely painful and notoriously slow to heal.

Having been recruited straight from their old regiment, Mick Saddler, Jameson's replacement was equally well trained, reliable and discreet. The most important facet of the operation to remove Rutter is absolute discretion. If it hadn't been, Patterson would be able to solicit some media coverage and locate Rutter very easily. Having completely lost track of the target, he's left with few options. First he re-visits Liverpool Police Headquarters and collects all available intelligence on those present at the time of Rutter's beating and everything known about the McGregor brothers, including Marriott the fifty-five year old car dealer and car hire operator who provides their vehicles.

Marriott

Johnny Marriott was born in a caravan and his birth certificate described his father's occupation as 'horse trader'. He was proud of his Romany heritage and often bragged about his grandfather's arrest for being found drunk in charge of a horse and carriage. A long time since he actually lived in it, but the caravan in which he spent his childhood years is still parked under a tarpaulin in the corner of his yard on the Liverpool Dock Road.

In the late seventies, he ran a haulage operation with a fleet of articulated lorries. Half of his fleet comprised stolen vehicles; it was a simple but very profitable scam to steal lorries and duplicate their identities with other vehicles in the fleet. As long as he made certain that these doppelgangers never appeared together, he cut his tax and insurance bills by about half and, running on red diesel, his expenditure on fuel was about a quarter of what it should have been. With two identical fleets running out Brixton and Liverpool, the cash accumulated nicely for a few years and, even though he was sure that it could probably roll on undetected for a few more years, he gave himself a cut off point when he would chop the stolen trucks up for scrap and sell the genuine fleet.

With only about six months left before closing down, he decided to take a short break in Greece and that turned out to be the unluckiest decision of his life. Up until then, he saw himself as a sharp trader rather than a criminal. He only employed genuine heavy goods drivers with no criminal records and could guarantee his customers that all loads would be delivered complete, without loss by pilferage. It might have been better had he only employed ex-criminals and suffered a few losses here and there because, while he was away sunning himself on that well-earned break, one of his whiter than white drivers saw a lorry very similar the one he was driving. The make, model, year and livery were identical, the only notable difference being that the name 'Marriott' was spelt differently. Uncomfortable to be driving a goods vehicle fuelled by red diesel, he was already suspicious, so he followed the other lorry into the previously unknown Brixton yard, tucked away behind the prison down Lyham Road. Seeing that Volvo so similar to his parked in the yard, he got out and approached on foot, then had to do a double-take when he realised the number plate was exactly the same as his own.

When Johnny Marriott stepped off the plane at Gatwick, he was met by the North West Regional Crime Squad. The charges levelled at him were numerous and varied, from the more serious of taking and driving away nine heavy goods vehicles, to the mundane such as evasion of duty on his fuel, the falsification of tachograph records and obtaining duplicate road fund licenses by fraudulent means. He thought that several sentences totalling up to seven years for his first offences was a little harsh but soon came to accept that anyone who deliberately defrauded the

Chancellor would be stamped upon very hard. His barrister advised him against appeal since he would be in danger of having his sentence increased, so he settled in and began serving his sentence.

That's when he first met Rutter, the McGregor brothers and The Bumper. A minor part of his sentence had been the lifetime ban from obtaining a heavy goods vehicle operator's licence so, on his release, he started a car hire business and opened a car sales pitch in front of his yard. His fleet of affordable modern hire cars was complemented by several top end luxury vehicles and, somewhere on his sales pitch, he always kept an odd vehicle or two that weren't down to anyone and could be purchased safely for use on criminal ventures.

Marriott never shared details of anything shady that he was up to but he would happily gossip over other people's criminal enterprises. Initially, he was surprised to see Rutter getting out of a taxi and walking into his Portakabin office, but was more than pleased to supply him with a neat little BMW convertible with high mileage he'd sourced for cash from a private seller outside Queens Ferry motor auction.

He never really liked Rutter and found it difficult to disguise his joy at earning a quick fifteen hundred profit out of him. Over a cup of coffee, he proudly shared details of the McGregor brothers being turned over by The Bumper and how, with the aid of his latest toy, the tracking system, they'd been able to locate him down in Brighton.

"Tracking system?" says Rutter. "How does that work?"

"Simple." Marriott leans back on his reclining chair running the fingers of each hand through his mop of recently dyed curly black hair as he replies, "It works on the same system as mobile phones. All I do is call their number, give them the registration and they ping it. Within five minutes they can tell me where the car is now and everywhere it's been in the last five days."

"I hope the BMW hasn't got a tracker on it."

"No Jimmy, I only track the hire cars. Believe me, when trackers catch on properly, nicking cars will be a thing of the past."

"It's hard to believe the McGregor brothers let the little Irish bastard get away with that."

Marriott laughs a little as he replies. "They haven't, have they? He's out grafting, earning their money back; told them the police nicked it. Probably thinks, when he's earned enough, he'll do the disappearing act but then he doesn't know about the tracker, does he?"

Rutter thinks for a moment then asks, "Just how much cash does he owe them?"

"A hundred and fifty."

Rutter always resented the way Tony the Bumper considered himself a cut above the other prisoners, looked down on drug dealers and those locked up for violence but now, with a potential hundred and fifty thousand to tax from him, he has turned into a serious target. Before leaving he asks Marriott to keep him informed, gives him his mobile number and promises to make it worth his while. Marriott watches him go then sits checking his adverts in yesterday's Liverpool Echo. Sundays are always quiet in the office and, with no hire cars due to be returned, there might be one or two punters asking about cars on the pitch, other than that he doesn't expect any visitors.

If Patterson had been just an hour earlier arriving at Marriott's pitch, he would have caught up with Rutter and things would have turned out differently, but an hour in one person's life can so easily alter the fate of another's. Having left Saddler waiting in the Range Rover, he walks between the cars for sale and straight into Marriott's Portakabin without knocking. Marriott is instantly suspicious, definitely not a punter with his straight back, razor creased beige cavalry twill trousers and the somewhat dated but very smart sports jacket and tie. Too smart to be a copper, more like a country gentleman, definitely very odd. Uncomfortable as he is, Marriott manages to smile.

"Need to hire a car Sir, or is it a cheap little runaround for the wife?

Patterson flashes a warrant card and introduces himself as Detective Superintendent Roberts, then pockets it before Marriott has time to read it.

"Well then what can I do for you Sir?"

"Rutter, James Rutter, I wonder if you might have seen him lately?"

"Rutter?" replies Marriott, "Rutter, no doesn't ring a bell, to be honest I don't think I ever even heard the name before."

Patterson regards him for a moment then. "I find that rather odd since you shared a cell with him in Long Larton about eight years ago."

"Did I? Oh yes, Rutter, haven't heard that name in a while, Rutter, no I've never seen him since then."

Patterson tears a page out of his small notebook, writes a phone number down and passes it to him.

"Well Mr Marriott, if your memory suddenly improves or he does turn up, phone this number and there may be some reward in the form of a cash payment to collect."

Marriott pockets the number.

"I'm intrigued Superintendent; exactly how much money are we talking about?"

Of course Marriott has precisely no idea where Rutter might be at the moment but he will be able to find out and, if there's enough cash involved, why not collect it? He decides not to share the fact that he's just sold Rutter a BMW. If they knew what car he was driving, they'd be able to track him down and there would be no reward.

"If you were able to offer us information leading to his arrest, it would be worth something like, let's say, five thousand."

In Marriott's estimation, Rutter is no more than a brainless violent career criminal who accepts arrests and prison sentences as part of his life. It's only a matter of time before they catch up to him for whatever he might have been up to. Turning him in will be no major betrayal and will simply be altering the date of the inevitable.

"Leave it with me Superintendent I'll find your man for you. It will be cash in advance won't it?"

"Yes"

"Good as soon as I know I'll call you on this number. Do bring the cash with you when I call, won't you? I'd hate for you to have a wasted trip."

Tony

Recovering the Mercedes from our old sea captain took a little longer than we expected because every night he parked it on the grass right next to his boat and slept with the windows open. We had to wait about a week before he finally drove to Kendal and parked it in the supermarket. Kendal's right next to the motorway so I had it away while he was doing his shopping and we came off the M6 on that deserted highways department yard with the mountain of road salt just before Chorley, and changed the plates.

We discovered the truth about our sad captain in the form of bills, letters and receipts he left in the car. There was a note from his wife begging him to stop wasting their savings on boat repairs and come home. There were several threats and final demands he'd received from credit card companies and a letter confirming that his sister in law had agreed to vacate the family home straight after her sister's funeral, enabling him to take possession and sell it. Rebecca was far happier when she realised that his tragic tale about falling in love with an island princess was just a load of alcoholic bullshit and it was back to business as usual for us with her selling and me recovering our Mercedes.

As long as you formulate a plan and stick to it, accumulating money might sometimes involve a little work but it's never complicated. From then on, the final six deceptions were all as straightforward as a builder laying the last six bricks to complete a wall and went down without incident. In a way, I dreaded recovering it that final time because it meant that we would reach the moment when I fitted the original number plates back on to Marriott's Mercedes and she would decide whether to come with me on a trip to The Spice Islands, keeping the McGregor's cash, or to risk our lives by giving it back to them.

Who knows what makes a man go stupid over a woman? I certainly don't but I do know that when it happens, there's nothing you can do to change it; you're stuck with your feelings and you've got to learn to live with them. Following her along a country lane to the deserted farm track just outside Liverpool where I was about to finally solve our Mercedes' identity crisis, I thought back to when I was a kid and my father invited my uncle Liam Riley over to give me a quick talking to about the ways of the world. I was only fifteen and completely fucked up over Joan, a seventeen year old English girl who I'd been banging so often that there was hardly a spare minute left to do anything else. Never having enough time in my day to bother eating, I was losing weight and becoming very pale, very sick looking. My uncle Liam was about thirty-five then, a single man who'd been over in England for ten years driving a digger for Murphy's. When he wasn't working, he would always dress in a smart suit. My Ma used to refer to him as "that furiously hansom' cousin of mine". To be fair, he did have something of a reputation for being a rake and therefore they saw him as an expert in such matters.

He managed to get me to sit down for five minutes and listen to him. As far as I was concerned, I was in love and nothing was ever going to change that, but the fact was that Joan was quite insatiable and no one man or boy would ever be able to keep on top of her needs. He told me that I wasn't in love that I was only fuck-struck, that well-known syndrome which often affects young men. His actual words of advice were, "Women are just like apples hanging from a tree. Pick any one of them and take a bite, they all taste sweet. This girl you think you're in love with is no different than the rest of them. Pick any one you like son, they all do it and they're all just as good as each other."

I suppose he thought he understood what was going on between Joan and me, but he was miles away from the truth of it. The fact is that I was the last of my mates to have a go at her. All the lads called her the Bootle Bike since everyone had ridden her. All I was doing was trying to make her my own, attempting to swim up a waterfall, fighting a losing battle against nature. Having plucked a few tree loads of apples since I was fifteen, I'd have to disagree with old Uncle Liam as I never found two women the same.

So there I was, standing on that deserted farm track watching Rebecca getting out of the Ford with my number plates, in a worse mess than I'd ever been in with Joan or anyone like her but we hadn't even screwed each other. Rebecca was good at shifting cars and would probably make herself a reasonable living as a saleswoman. Our target had been a hundred and fifty grand but, due to her sharp negotiations, there was just over a hundred and sixty in the bag after expenses and we hadn't scrimped or gone short of anything.

Tightening those number plate screws for the last time, I was beginning to feel sad and it was hard not letting it show. It was like we were coming to the end of an era, the great partnership of a con man and the creeper who robbed him. I look up at her face from my position stooping in front of the Merc and, for just a moment, I think I can see a similar sadness in her eyes.

"Well." I say, tightening the last screw, "looks like we've managed it. Old Marriott gets his car back, we've got our hundred and sixty and that's the end of it."

"Not quite the end," she replies. "It's not finished until we've given those two animals their cash back, then we've got ten thousand to split."

"Yeah, well we'll talk about that later, why don't we book into my favourite Liverpool hotel?"

Now there's a mischievous girlish look to her that I almost remember. Perhaps that's the way she looked at me the first time we met.

"The Adelphi it is then," she says, pushing me over, then rushing back to her car to get a head start, "the last one there buys the drinks all night."

It doesn't take much of a push to topple you when you're stooping and, by the time I'm back on my feet, she's in the Ford, racing away down the lane. I could have caught her very easily driving the Mercedes but I was very willing to pay for her, so I almost caught up several times on the way to Liverpool but didn't quite mange it. By the time I walked up the Adelphi steps she'd already booked us in and was sitting waiting at the bar.

Over the few weeks that we had spent together, she never had more than two drinks, so I was quite surprised when she ordered the first bottle of champagne and drank it as quickly as she did. Perhaps since I'd known her, Rebecca's spirit had been crushed by the threat of the McGregor brothers hanging over her because now that we had their cash and a little more besides, she was smiling, giggling and flirting with me. It was as though a switch had been turned on somewhere, illuminating her soul. She still showed the same shyness when we were eating in the restaurant but she was on top of it and, even though she reddened occasionally, she ate the whole meal and consumed most of the second bottle of champagne.

The McGregor Brothers

Since receiving the BMK, the McGregor fortune had grown faster than anyone could have imagined. The addicted pharmacology student had been working hard fractionally distilling the BMK every day. The strong cats piss stink produced by the operation is a dead giveaway that every policeman is familiar with, but the house they were using as a factory had been cleverly chosen and adapted. It was a detached property behind a tall hedge at the end of a row of houses, backing on to farmland.

The room where the distillation equipment was set up had been fitted with heavy industrial ventilation fans that were ducted into an extra tall stench pipe which had been fitted on to the back corner of the house, the one closest to the fields. All the fumes were exhausted too high for the neighbours to smell and, if they did, it could be easily mistaken for the smell of silage, which sometimes wafted across the fields. The amphetamine crystals produced, had been affected somewhere in the process and were a pale pink rather than white. The pharmacology student blamed an impurity in the containers used for the chloroform. Initially Billy was furious, said the kid didn't know what he was doing and threatened to kill him but Joey quickly tested it and realised that he had the strongest amphetamine ever produced in the UK. They had a massive success and a new brand on their hands. British pink was magic, even cut by seventy percent; it kept its power and pinkness. In the first three weeks, they cooked and shifted four million pounds' worth and they weren't even an eighth of the way through their first barrel. Word spread quickly through the UK and into Europe. Joey joked with Billy saying that they should get a Queen's Award for Industry for supplying the Netherlands with drugs but Billy never got the joke.

A little after 9 p.m., having concluded the day's business and collected half a million from one of their Dutch contacts, they are driving back to Liverpool. Since failing to get the joke, Billy has been sitting in the passenger seat silently brooding over something and occasionally feeding his nose with cocaine. They stop at a red light and Joey asks, "What the fucks up Billy? Half a million in the boot and you're sitting there like we're on our way to a funeral."

"You know what's up; the fuckin' Bumper's what's up."

"You're not on about that again, I've told you just drop it. We're on to a fucking gold mine here. Don't get sidetracked over a few quid."

Billy begins to shake. "So that's it then, the prick fucks us over and just gets away with it?"

"It doesn't matter Billy it's just a few quid."

"A few quid?" screams Billy punching the windscreen, "He's fucked us over."

A crack runs across the screen and blood splashes off his knuckles.

"All right Billy, calm down, we'll get Marriott to ping his motor tomorrow and pay him a visit."

"And if he doesn't give us our money?"

"If he doesn't pay up, you can off him. I give you my word on that Billy; just don't break any more fucking windscreens."

Then, for the first time in the last three weeks, Billy smiles.

Tony

The change in Rebecca was extreme, wonderful and shocking in a very welcome way; we spent a couple of hours sitting close to each other in the bar, closer than ever before. The warmth from her smouldering thigh conducted like and electric charge through the material of our clothing into my body, speeding my heartbeat. The look of unashamed desire in her brown eyes was undeniably and irresistibly horny. She wasn't just hot, she was on fire.

Her lips touch mine with a gentle brush of a kiss that her hand terminates with a push, but she isn't just pushing me away or holding me off, she's caressing my chest, exploring the shape of my muscles, teasing my nipples which aren't the only things becoming erect. I'm in danger of losing control, of climbing on top of her right here in the bar, so it's just as well she's taking control.

"I think it's time you took me upstairs," she whispers, her warm breath on my ear, further fuelling my desire; she's got me as helpless as a kitten and, for the first time in years I've run out of smart remarks.

I try not to stutter as I reply, "OK let's go."

It can be really unnerving when a woman suddenly takes the lead and I find myself following her up the marble stairs, praying that I don't end up spooked and unable to live up to her expectations. She stops outside the door, fumbling the key into the lock as I kiss the back of her neck and my hands automatically find her hips to pull her close to press against her beautiful peach of a bottom. With the door open, she turns and, like a few minutes before, holds me off with a hand to my chest.

"Wait!" she says, moving her hand up to take hold of my tie, then leads me into the suite of rooms with a large and inviting double bed. So that's why she raced ahead and booked the room before I arrived. She wanted the second double bed we ever shared to be a surprise.

Suddenly feeling like the strongest man who ever lived, I snatch her up, carry her over to the bed and begin landing a barrage of kisses on her as I lay her down, but she wriggles free and stands.

"I told you to wait, I need a bath."

"I don't care I want you now," I whisper, pulling her back down, at this moment not caring if she smells like a donkey, which she doesn't. She smells like an angel and tastes like the best meal a starving man ever ate.

Her resistance is instantly replaced by passion as we tear at each other's clothes. Now naked, she's more beautiful than any woman I ever had, her wonderful upturned firm breasts shaking with every thrust, those two dimples in her back above that perfect bottom, her silky olive skin tastes of pure woman. Fifteen minutes, maybe even less than that, and I find myself unable to hold back for another second and five weeks of desire explodes in one unstoppable, massive orgasm. Laying still for a while, our hearts still beating fast, I'm behind her holding her close, our bodies damp, still shuddering. I draw her closer and taste the salty perspiration on her neck.

"You're not a lesbian then."

"Shut up Tony, don't ruin the moment."

"Sorry," I reply.

Over the next few hours, between more passionate lovemaking, we filled the giant marble bath several times. That's one of the best things about the Adelphi; those baths are almost big enough to swim in and never seem to run short of hot water. I figured that a bath together, sharing a bottle of champagne, is a great place to talk, so I began working on the idea of us running away to The Spice Islands and keeping the cash. I thought I'd just about convinced her when I painted the picture Moses had painted for me.

"We'll be like millionaires on Carriacou, Moses gets a living trapping lobster and selling them to posh American yacht owners. We can buy our own beach, half a mile long, for thirty thousand Grenada dollars, which are only worth about a third of the American dollar. Imagine that; we could build our own house and just get on with living the rest of our lives together. The McGregor brothers will get over it eventually. People like them always do and, if they don't, then it won't be long before they're back inside. You can't hope to shift millions of pounds' worth of drugs indefinitely, it's just a matter of time before it comes on top for them."

"And what if they do find their way to the island?"

"Hell, Rebecca, find their way to the island? They're lost as soon as they get five miles past Speke. Used to get me to deliver to London because they didn't like dealing with foreigners."

"It does sound like paradise Tony, if it wasn't for those two."

"Promise me you'll think about it?"

"Oh God Tony, I'll think of nothing else."

That's just the way we left it before becoming exhausted and falling asleep. Up until that night, sex for me had always been quite mechanical; ever since the first time when I did it because it was expected, because that's what you did if you wanted to be a man. I would find myself in bed with some beautiful woman, telling her I loved her and wishing that I knew what on earth love really is. I would always create fantasies to get me off, imagine myself with someone different, someone better, but that night with Rebecca changed everything for me. There were no fantasies, no wild imaginings, I was right there in the moment with her, doing without the need to pollute things by spicing them up with my own thoughts. In the moments before we drifted off to sleep, I realised that she was all I needed, all of those worthless liaisons of the past had been no more than a search and now I'd found her; the only woman I would ever want.

I woke at midday with the taste of her still on my lips. Reaching out, my hand searched for the warmth of her body but she wasn't in the bed so, still smiling, I decided to join her in the bath and got up. I almost cried when I saw the empty bathroom. She wasn't in the lounge either, she really had gone, just like that first time in Brighton, though this time she'd been decent enough to leave me with the cash and my trousers. I knew there could only be one reason this time, her fear of Billy McGregor, so I dressed quickly and went to reception to settle the bill but she'd already paid. I collected the car from the hotel garage and began my journey south to Brighton. That's where she'd be, no doubt about that, and all she needed was a little more convincing before we bought the airline tickets.

Marriott

Coincidentally, Joey McGregor telephoned Marriott about five minutes after Tony left the Adelphi, headed for Brighton. There was no way that Marriott could guess at Tony's final destination but, within another five minutes, he had his answer from the tracking company. Tony had been parked all night in Paradise Street Liverpool city centre. He had started the engine at 12.50 p.m. and was now moving out of Liverpool along the East Lancashire Road.

"I'll bet the Irish prick's on his way down to Brighton again with that bird," says Joey.

"I hope you're going to pay for this report," replies Marriott. "It costs me fifty quid every time I ping the car."

"Shut up you whingeing prick. The amount of cash we pay you for our fucking motors."

"Alright, point taken," says Marriott. "I'll ping him every half hour until you catch up to him."

"I should think so," replies Joey, then ends the call.

Marriott never liked the McGregor brothers and they didn't think much of him either, but a trustable car rental man is priceless when you're a criminal behind the wheel. The last thing you want is your name on the registration, informing any copper who reads the number plate exactly who is driving the vehicle. Marriott had been paid well for his services over the years he'd been supplying their cars, but their payments hardly compensated for the intimidation he received.

As soon as Joey hangs up, he calls Rutter. "Remember when I said I'd keep you informed about the McGregors and the Bumper?"

"Yeah."

"Well they're on their way to collect their hundred and fifty off him. What's it worth if I mark your card?"

"Twenty."

"Twenty-five sounds a bit more like it?"

"All right twenty-five it is then."

"Where are you now?"

"Southport."

"Good, head towards the East Lancs Road, it looks as though he's going to the south coast. I'll call you in half an hour."

He postpones calling Patterson until he's more certain of the final destination.

By the time Tony reached the M25 it was four thirty and, tired from having had very little sleep the night before, he pulled into Clackett Lane for an hour's kip before continuing on to Brighton. He had no idea they were about a mile behind him and it was only fate that Marriott pinged the Merc, just before he drove down the slip road into the services. In the next half hour, the McGregor brothers went straight past Clackett Lane and were half way down the M23 by the time they discovered that he had been at the services for half an hour. They turned around immediately and arrived at Clackett Lane five minutes after he'd left. If they had only arrived five minutes earlier, he would have parted with their cash very easily and this whole sorry mess wouldn't have unfolded. It was 6 p.m. when Tony parked the car on Madeira Drive and walked into Marine Square. The McGregors were just ten minutes behind him and Patterson was hovering over Handcross Hill in the chopper, waiting for Marriott to call him with the final position. As he hovers he scans the hundreds of cars passing on the road beneath, hoping to catch sight of Rutter's silver BMW M3 coupe.

Tony

I remember smelling the freshly cut grass when I parked the Mercedes in Marine Square and that I was feeling really good, as though my life was blossoming into something wonderful. My head was full of imaginings about swimming with her in the warm Caribbean and lying on the white coral sand together. I walked up the sandstone steps of Number 17 with the carrier bag of cash in my hand and pressed the doorbell for flat five, wondering if any coconuts would be low on trees that sloped gently enough to make climbing and harvesting them easy. There was no intercom so she pressed the release button and, as I pushed the door open, she called down from the fifth floor landing.

"Hello."

"It's only me," I called back.

"Come on up love."

As I began climbing the steep Victorian stairs, I knew that all I had to do was finish selling her the idea then, first thing in the morning, we'd go and buy the tickets. I was slightly out of breath by the time I reached the fifth floor and she came straight into my arms. We held each other for a moment before she pulled away and looked at the carrier bag.

"So you didn't give them their cash back."

"No love we need to talk about that."

Just then the doorbell rings and I get a real feeling of dread, almost a premonition that something awful is about to happen.

"Don't open it," I insist, rushing to the window and see their car double parked in the square. They're bound to realise I had no intention of letting them have their money back and Billy won't be able to stop himself hurting someone and I don't want it to be Rebecca.

"Quickly," I say dragging her through the flat to the kitchen window.

"But..."

"But nothing. That Billy's a crazy bastard, he can have the cash but he's not hurting you."

The sash window next to the fire escape is stiff but I manage to get it open just as we hear the front door crash in. I boost her over the sink on to the fire escape but, instead of running for her life, she stops and holds her hand out to me. We can hear their footsteps rushing up the stairs towards us. I tell her, "Run and I'll meet you at the Penny Lift. Don't come back unless you see their car leave."

She disappears into the darkness down the fire escape. I hold the carrier bag full of cash out in front of me and brace myself expecting pain from the Mcgregors, who are now inside. Joey's first into the kitchen, the steep stairs have taken their toll. He's out of condition, struggling to catch his breath.

"That's our cash? Good." Then, taking it, "I told you he wouldn't dare fuck us over again didn't I Billy?"

Billy's eyes are small dots of hatred as the wheels in his Neanderthal brain crunch slowly, working it out. Gripped in his right fist is the ugly boning knife. Then

Rutter appears in the doorway his automatic levelled at Joey's chest. "The cash is mine now, McGregor."

Billy's head turns slowly in Rutter's direction, then he dives with a downward stabbing motion aiming at Rutter's head but misses, only managing to plunge the knife into the top of Rutter's shoulder. Rutter's gun goes off twice. The cash falls on to the kitchen floor and, as the brothers fly at him, I'm over the draining board and on to the fire escape, landing on every third tread as I race down towards the ground. Assuming that Rebecca has done as I asked because she's nowhere to be seen, I run along the pavement at the back of the houses and turn right on to Portland Street. Another two shots go off but they're a long way behind me. I don't care who's shooting who, the only thing I do care about is that Rebecca is safe. Quickly across Madeira Drive, then along the pavement to the Penny Lift where I slow, it's cool, there's no one behind me. I find her cowering and trembling with fear in the shadows on the seaward side of the shelter.

"Come on, quickly," I say, grabbing her wrist and dragging her along behind me, determined to put as much distance as possible between us and danger. But we've hardly got a few yards from the Penny Lift, when I hear Rutter's voice bellowing from somewhere behind.

"Hurley you fucking Irish bastard!"

There's a loud crack and a bullet sparks as it ricochets off the railings next to us. Then a Range Rover bounces on to the pavement in front and a man springs out. His arms stretched in front of him both hands aiming the pistol. I see his sharp, alert eyes and hear more shots go off behind us as he speaks in a calm, flat military tone and his gun barrel flashes.

"Do not look at my face. Down on the ground and stay there. Do not look at my face."

We both hit the ground together and I lay on top of Rebecca shielding her. From my position on the pavement I see that Rutter is down and watch his body twitch with each of the two shots the man delivers from point blank range to his head. A second later, the Range Rover pulls up next to him, he steps in and they speed away. Seeing the banknotes from the carrier bag next to Rutter's body peeling off into the breeze, I realise that we're safe. It must be over, Rutter has definitely sorted the McGregor brothers or he wouldn't have the cash.

"It's over love; it's all over we're alright now."

But she doesn't reply and she doesn't move.

"Rebecca love, Rebecca." I feel her warm breath on my cheek. She's alive but there's a slow trickle of clear liquid coming from her ear.

"Jesus Christ, Rebecca. Get an ambulance, will someone please get an ambulance."

She's silent and doesn't move as people come rushing to help and I begin to cry.

The Arrest

The promenade is flooded with pulsing blue light as uniformed police pour out of police cars and two ambulances arrive at the scene. Two of the officers lift Tony to his feet, keeping a firm grip on his arms as they pull him away from Rebecca. He is still sobbing as one of them ratchets a pair of handcuffs tightly to his wrists and a paramedic kneels on the pavement to examine Rebecca. The paramedic is quickly joined by one of his colleagues who comes over, having finished examining Rutter, and sees the clear fluid leaking from her left ear.

"Might be an epidural hematoma, we'll have to be careful how we move this one."

"What about the other one?"

"Finished. Brains are all over the pavement."

Despite Tony's protestations of innocence, he is quickly searched and bundled into the back of a police van.

"I've done nothing wrong here. I'm a victim. You should be taking me to hospital with Rebecca," he shouts from the back of the van but the driver ignores him and continues to the yard at the rear of Brighton police station.

After the nurse has finished carefully bathing and shaving her head, Rebecca is still unconscious, being wheeled into the scanning room and lifted on to the conveyor. Her only visible injury is a bullet graze along the left hand side of her scalp but the clear liquid leaking from her left ear is an indication of increased ICP, inter-cranial pressure, and neurologist Mr Jay Patel has already decided that, since the patient has suffered a TBI or traumatic brain injury, after the scan, he will take her into theatre and insert a catheter with transducer in order to monitor her and, if necessary, relieve the pressure by draining the cerebrospinal fluid. She's a young, healthy woman and there is absolutely no reason why she shouldn't make a full recovery, as long as the ICP is kept down to an acceptable level.

Brighton Pier - Autumn 96

"I knew when I walked into that interview room and saw you sitting there that you were a victim. That was the first time I ever saw you look beaten like that but I could hardly let you go. Think about it Tony, the last time I saw you, she'd stolen a briefcase full of cash from you then she was unconscious on the prom, a hundred yards from a dead man with over a hundred grand in cash right next to him, and in her flat there were two more dead men."

He takes a cigarette out, offers one to Tony, which he lights, then lights his own. Tony takes a long draw on the cigarette and replies.

"All the same, it was awful sitting waiting in that cell wondering if she was going to live or die."

"I suppose it must've been and I'm sorry I had to put you through it, but it wasn't until Superintendent Commerford came in the morning after and tried to get me to ignore things I should've been paying attention to, that I realised something was going on."

"Things like what?"

"Like the fact that, when I took Rutter's fingerprints and ran them against the database, I came up with his name and date of birth but no criminal record."

Having served time in the same prison as Rutter, Tony was certain that Rutter did have a criminal record.

"No record? He'd definitely done a five and a three."

"Correct. It had obviously been wiped but, when everyone on the case except me was in the funny handshake brigade and they were closing ranks saying that they'd never heard of Rutter, there wasn't a lot I could do but I did draw the line when it came to fitting you up."

Appalled by what Fisher said, Tony gets up from the bench and shakes his head as he flicks his cigarette over the handrail into the sea, then turns to face him.

"Fit me up, how could you have done that?"

Fisher smiles weakly.

"I know what you're thinking Tony, that someone needs to be at least partially guilty to be successfully fitted up and that we reserve the practice to use on professional criminals who we think have been getting away with too much. It works on anyone you want it to and you might have provided Commerford with the perfect solution, if I'd have gone along with it."

He lights another cigarette but Tony doesn't want one, then he continues. "The scenario Commerford wanted to push was that you killed the two in her flat and stole the cash, Rutter was on their firm and came straight after you. When he caught up to you on the prom, you shot him once in the chest and twice in the head and Rebecca took an accidental hit in the crossfire. The only complication was that Rutter had been hit with an unknown 9mm weapon and the others with Rutter's smaller calibre gun, which had been found. Commerford's big mistake was when he offered to 'find' the missing weapon in the drains we'd already searched and said that he could be certain that it would be a perfect ballistic match for the bullets taken from Rutter's body. I could never live with that. Commerford obviously knew who killed Rutter and had probably organised it. Since you were the only person to actually witness Rutter's murder and you would be the accused, your evidence would be instantly discredited."

"So what did you do?"

"I went to the IPCC and told them everything I knew and said that I thought the men in the Range Rover were probably MI5 agents and that they'd been called in to remove Rutter."

"What happened then?"

"Well, so much for the impartiality of the Independent Police Complaints Commission. I was called into the Chief Constable's office where it was decided that the only safe course of action for me would be to take early retirement and agree to keep my mouth shut. I think it was quite literally the only decision I could live with."

"You really think they would have killed you?"

"I never doubted it; I think all of them are in the funny handshake brigade, the IPCC included. That was the day I signed out of my last duty. I'd had enough anyway. Like I said earlier, I joined the force because I believed in justice. That's also when they released you without any charges."

"Christ, I do owe you one don't I Fisher?"

"Not really Tony, I was just doing what I believed the right thing to do."

Six Weeks Earlier

Tony walked through grey drizzle down the slight hill from Brighton police station and turned left on to Edward Street. Since there had been no charges, the police returned his four and a half thousand pounds cash without protest. At any other time, on being released from police custody, there would have been a spring in his step and the feeling of joy that freedom usually delivered, but that day was different. The previous three days in custody had been spent being ignored, every time he asked about Rebecca. The only person who told him anything, was his old adversary Ted Fisher. At least he was good enough to let him know that Rebecca had been taken to the Royal Sussex and still hadn't regained consciousness.

Tony knew that hospitals are reluctant to give information about patients to anyone other than a relative, so he decided to introduce himself as her brother. By the time he had almost completed the half-mile walk through clouds of drizzle he was soaked; he stopped at the phone booth on the corner of the last side road before the Royal Hospital main entrance and felt ashamed looking at his own reflection in the mirror. His eyes were sagging and grey, his white shirt badly soiled and he had three days' growth of black whiskers on his face, way past anything that might be termed designer stubble.

Tony

She looked like a broken doll lying there, so pale, her head all shaved, with the tubes and wires hanging out, taped to the side of her face. Close to her bed in the intensive care room, the monitor bleeped steady pulses, the only indication that she was alive.

I sat next to her and whispered, "I'm here love, you're going to be alright now and all you need to do is wake up and we can both get on with living our lives together."

But there was no sound other than that constant bleep bleeping. I thought of sleeping beauty and leaned over the wires and tubes to kiss her cheek but she remained perfectly still. We'd all like to believe in fairytales but life seldom plays out to a happy ending. Then a young nurse came into the room, she might have been attractive on any other day.

"Hello Mister Moseley, you're Rebecca's brother then?"

She said with some doubt in her eastern European accent. Maybe she saw something more than brotherly devotion in my attitude towards Rebecca; perhaps she'd been listening to what I was saying.

"She is going to be all right isn't she? I mean, she is going to recover?" I asked and she looked up from then monitor where she was copying the readings on to the case sheet.

"It would be better if you asked her neurologist for a more exact prognosis. He will be along shortly on his rounds but yes, I do believe that she will recover."

Not wishing to let the doctor see me in such a tramp-like state, I whispered goodbye to Rebecca and went looking for somewhere to stay. First, I walked down to Marine Square and rang the doorbell to Flat 2 but when Rebecca's neighbour Peggy came out and told me that Rebecca's flat was still an official crime scene and still sealed off, I gave up on that idea and made my way down to Rock Gardens, where I paid a month up front on a cheap room. The following morning I got cleaned up, bought a couple of shirts and went into a florist on St James Street where I bought a miniature rose in a plant pot. Rebecca once told me that she liked miniature roses, so I sat next to her bed talking to her describing it.

"It's a beautiful little rose Rebecca; nowhere near as beautiful as you though. Yeah and the lady in the florist said that if we water it every day it will last for years and years."

But she never replied or reacted, not so much as a flicker of her eyelids, to let me know that she could hear anything at all.

Over the next two weeks, I went to the hospital every day, watered that rose and sat whispering to her, occasionally kissing her cheek, until I arrived one morning to find and empty bed. She'd been taken to the operating theatre. A blood vessel between her skull and brain had ruptured, leading to a dramatic change in the prognosis. The neurologist informed me, sadly, that the outcome for Rebecca was far less certain then before and that she may suffer seizures, nerve damage, cognitive disabilities and personality changes, changes in sensory perception, post-concussion syndrome and coma. So I kept visiting every day but every night, I sat alone drinking myself to sleep.

Another few weeks passed before I walked into the room and noticed that Rebecca's hair had grown back and that the miniature rose had wilted and died. The same young nurse caught on to my sadness at seeing the dead bloom and brought me a cup of tea. She was a caring kind of person and sat down with me for a while.

"It looks as though your rose is finished. Do you want me to throw it away?" she asked.

"If you want," I replied. "Good, I will then," she said, adding "That's what we should do when things are finished."

A few minutes passed, then she asked me if I believed in God.

"That's an odd question," I replied and asked her if she did.

"Not really," she replied, which would have been my honest answer because what kind of God would let a beautiful soul like Rebecca get mixed up with a worthless idiot like me.

That night I sat alone in my room at the Hamilton. I never expected to be staying in the worst bed and breakfast in Brighton again but funds were tight and I just didn't feel like going out hunting for cash. It was a depressing place, smelling of wet rot and filthy carpets and I remember thinking what a dump it was, when there was a knock at the door. The manager was a skinny south Londoner of about forty who smelled as bad as the carpet and saw himself as some kind of big time property developer. I was holding a glass of whisky when I opened the door to him.

"Your rent's due again tomorrow. I'll be out all day. You can pay now if you like," he said through the wet, yellow part of his tobacco stained beard.

There was something about that skinny little man I really disliked. I finished my whisky, wondering how those two months could have passed so quickly.

"I'll pay when it's due and not before," I replied, shutting the door in his face.

Then he shouted, "Well make sure you do or I'll have you out of here."

I think that was the moment I decided to go. I'd already given him sixteen hundred pounds for the first two months; I only had twelve hundred left and didn't see the point in wasting any more of my cash.

Drunken men aren't ever welcome in hospitals, even as visitors, so I'd already decided to end the daily visits. Instead I would spend my days sitting on a bench in the Penny Lift, the perfect vantage point from which to see her arrive at Number 17, Marine Square if she ever gets discharged from hospital. It was an ideal place to live rent free. I could sleep a few hours every day and watch the windows at night for a light letting me know that she's home and safe and, if she doesn't come home, then nothing matters anyway.

I'd been in my new residence for about a week, sitting in the public shelter laughing at the passers-by, estimating the futility of their existence, their pointless aspirations, even their dress sense. Didn't they know anything about life? Basically I was lying in the gutter looking down on the rest of humanity. Nights could be quite uncomfortable, so I always made sure I kept drunk.

Drunk and still drinking is the best way to beat the cold but the few times I fell asleep just before dawn and woke up soon after, were the worst times I ever had to live through. When your eyes open to blinding daylight and you're freezing cold, too sick to swallow another mouthful of whisky, you try to escape back into sleep. I used to lie rolled up on my side and force my hands down between my thighs so that at least they were warm.

It was on such a morning, with my teeth chattering against the sound of waves breaking on the beach that the two shoplifters arrived. I can't remember their names but I nicknamed one of them 'Jaws'. They were both skinny, pale-faced Glaswegian heroin addicts. They must have been in their twenties though the pair looked older, down to the smack I suppose, and Jaws had a gap where his front teeth should have been. The one who still had a full set shook my shoulder.

"You'll catch your death of cold in a windy place like this," he said, unrolling his sleeping bag and covering me up.

They were the first people who'd spoken to me since I'd been living in the Penny Lift, so I resisted the urge to tell them to go to hell and sat listening to the glory of their shoplifting stories and three month prison sentences. I didn't tell them anything about my adventures because I didn't want to upstage a couple of bewildered people who were kind enough to help me. Eventually I warmed up and their conversation was so boring that I fell asleep again. When I woke up they were gone, along with my holdall full of clothes and my last bottle of Jameson's. I threw the stinking sleeping bag off and kicked it. Maybe they thought that such a rag was a fair exchange for everything I owned. More likely they left the sleeping bag because taking it might have woken me and then they wouldn't have been able to steal my few possessions.

Above me half a dozen seagulls hovered, gliding on the wind just out of reach. Their squawks sounded like laughter. Even the fucking seagulls were laughing at me. I grabbed an empty whisky bottle and hurled it at them, but missed.

"That was yesterday when I came past, I thought you'd lost your mind altogether."

"Maybe I had."

"Perhaps, but you're alright now aren't you? Yes, of course you are. Listen to me Tony, I'm no shrink but I do know that you need to deal what happened to Rebecca or you'll end up just fading away."

"And how exactly do you think I should do that?"

"It might sound tough but first you need to go up to the hospital and find out whether she's alive or dead. If she's alive but never likely to recover, you need to let go of her and start living again."

"Jesus Christ, let go of her, I never had her. We slept together once and the day after she was shot in the fucking head. I should've just left her alone. She was running away from me, she fucking hated me. If I hadn't gone after her, none of this would ever have happened and she'd be getting on with her life. I'm the most selfish bastard the world has ever known."

Fisher takes a crumpled letter out of his pocket and hands it to Tony saying, "You're wrong mate, she did love you. I found this when I was searching her flat. It's addressed to you, care of your mate Kenny in North Wales."

Tony gives Fisher a filthy look.

"You've read this then?"

"I had to Tony, it was my job. I should have followed it up and bagged it with the rest of the evidence. I don't know why I didn't. I just pocketed it. She did care about you, Tony. Read it!"

Dear Tony,

By the time you get this letter, I'll be hundreds of miles away from you and I'll be sad. I enjoyed the time we spent together and, yes, you were right when you kept saying that I wanted you because I did, and will always miss you. The fact is that I never was any good at lying and being dishonest to you made me feel so awkward when we were together, I suppose because I cared too much. That's why I always avoided your beautiful eyes. I feel that, out of all the people in the world, I owe you the truth and, if knowing that truth makes you hate me, then that's the way it will have to be. You were a great teacher Tony. The best and most important lesson was when you made me believe that, if it doesn't feel right, then just once in a while I should not be afraid to let someone off. Well that's what I've decided to do my sweet lover; I've decided to let you off. It wasn't DI Fisher who stole the cash and got you into such a mess. It was me. I'm sorry and I've regretted doing it, ever since that McGregor gorilla beat you up. If I had owned up to the truth there and then, they would have just taken their cash and you would've gone away when I really wanted to be with you. So if you haven't given those two animals their cash back yet, there's no reason why you shouldn't. I'd hate it if anything bad happened to someone as special as you. So here's the deal; you go to my grandmother's in Brixton, the address is on the back; she'll give you a parcel. Your cash is inside. Then, if you still want me, you know where I am and, if you don't, I'll understand. Love Rebecca x

Tony's eyes are wet when he finishes reading the letter.

"So you really didn't steal the money. I can't believe you kept this for me."

"Well I did keep it and you're going to need to face up to reality."

Tony sighs and nods solemnly.

"I'll drive you to the hospital first, then when you've been there, I'll drive you to her grandmother's if you like. Perhaps then you might be able to pull yourself together. You might even want to visit AA."

"Do me a favour?"

"I'm doing you one Tony. About time you did one for yourself."

The two men walk off the pier to Fisher's car and drive along Madeira Drive and up Portland Street to The Royal Sussex. Fisher stops on the main road opposite the entrance. Tony gets out and turns back to him.

"Aren't you coming in with me?"

"No this is your demon Tony. You need to face up to it; I'll be here for you when you come out. And if you get all upset, don't be ashamed, I've seen it all before. Just come back to the car."

Tony walks up the sloping corridor, enters the lift and selects the floor he used to visit every day. He always hated the smell of hospitals but he hates it more than ever now. The rubber soles of his shoes squeak against the blue floor covering as he approaches her room. He is about to enter when he has to step back to allow a cleaner to push her bed out. The bed has been stripped. He feels tears welling up and struggles to contain them. Stepping into the room, he sees the kind eastern European nurse unplugging the monitor from the wall. It's all too much for him to handle. He breaks down and the tears stream down his face. The nurse rushes over to him and takes his shoulders. He averts his eyes from her face, ashamed.

"Tony what's wrong? We can't have this; this is no good at all. You've been drinking again. Look at yourself, your clothes you're in a mess and you stink."

"What do you think's wrong? Rebecca's what's bloody wrong."

She grips his shoulders more firmly.

"Look at me Tony. You need to stop this."

His blank red eyes stare straight into hers as she speaks.

"When we discharged her yesterday, we didn't expect that she would be coming home to a drunken man. Now, please pull yourself together, acting this way won't help her recovery in the least."

The beaten look on his face is replaced with joy as her words sink in.

"She's alive?"

"Alive and almost fully recovered. Didn't you know?"

Tony breaks free from her grip and rushes for the staircase, no time for the lift. The kind nurse hears his "thank you" echoing along the corridor. He races straight past Fisher's car. Fisher sees him running and starts up to go in pursuit. He overtakes him on Portland Place and steps out of the car blocking his way.

Tony stops for a second or two, his chest heaving, and screams joyfully, "She's alive. She's at home."

Fisher's eyes show a moment of disbelief then he smiles. Tony remains still with his hair blowing in the wind just long enough to return the smile, then continues running towards her flat. Fisher follows but he's no longer in pursuit, he just wants to see what happens when Tony reaches the front door of 17 Marine Square.

Fisher

Everyone's got their own beliefs and I don't know what yours are, whether you believe in God, luck, fate or just getting even. One thing I do know is that, whatever gives you strength, you would have been blessed with joy watching her open the door and seeing them together. To tell the truth, I was kind of emotional watching that, like when you find a sweet surprise at the end of a sad film but you keep a lid on it in case the lights come on. Then, just before they went inside, they both glanced in my direction smiling and, though I knew it wasn't the end of their film, I'd seen all I needed and just walked back to my car

I don't know if Tony and Rebecca went back to their criminal lifestyle or if they changed, and I don't care either way whether they went to the Spice Islands or just moved away from Brighton. All I do know is that it was a wonderful feeling being able to let them off, to help a little and that, every time I pass Marine Square, it brings a smile to my face. I've been able to sleep easier since that day.

*****

Printed in Great Britain
by Amazon